Among the
Dead

ALSO BY MICHAEL TOLKIN

The Player

Among the
Dead

Michael Tolkin

William Morrow and Company,Inc.
New York

It is the policy of William Morrow and Company, Inc., and its imprints and
affiliates, recognizing the importance of preserving what has been written, to print
the books we publish on acid-free paper, and we exert our best efforts to that end.

Library of Congress Cataloging-in-Publication Data
Tolkin, Michael.
    Among the dead / Michael Tolkin.
      p.   cm.
    ISBN 0-688-12083-0
    I. Title.
    PS3570.O4278A48   1993
    813'.54—dc20   92-18503
                                CIP

Printed in the United States of America

2   3   4   5   6   7   8   9   10

BOOK DESIGN BY CLAIRE NAYLON VACCARO

For W. L. M., S. T. T., E. C. T.

Minutes nearer midnight. On which stroke
Powers at the heart of matter, powers
We shall have hacked through thorns to kiss awake,
Will open baleful, sweeping eyes, draw breath
And speak new formulae of megadeath.
NO SOULS CAME FROM HIROSHIMA U KNOW
EARTH WORE A STRANGE NEW ZONE OF ENERGY
Caused by? SMASHED ATOMS OF THE DEAD MY DEARS
News that brought into play our deepest fears.

James Merrill, *The Book of Ephraim*

All their plans and hopes burst like a bubble!
Infants by the score dashed on the rocks by the
enraged Atlantic Ocean! No, no!

Thoreau, *Cape Cod*

Among the Dead

1. A Long Lunch

The night before everything changed, Frank Gale wrote a letter to his wife. She was asleep in the bedroom, upstairs. There were so many things he wanted to tell her, but in a certain way, the right way.

Before he thought of saying it all in a letter, he had thought of taking her to an expensive restaurant and telling her at dinner. Was there ever, he thought, a plan with more drama or elegance? The attention to the details of the evening would require from him such concentration that he would have entered a state of pure meditation, without fear, without stage fright, in which nothing he

said would be awkward or out of place, and by the example of his
grace in this terrible situation, his wife could only forgive him. They
would hire a baby-sitter for Madeleine, and he would reserve a quiet
table, or a booth. They would drive to the restaurant, and he would
gently ask Anna questions about her day. He would be nice to her.
How else but through the right performance of mundane actions
could he hide how uncomfortable the pressure of his feelings made
him, when Anna, so sensitive, would know something was wrong?
Unless he solicited her feelings, she would ask him what the trouble
was. If he were to let Anna see his unhappiness, this would provoke
from her a flow of understanding and compassion, and then he would
be tricking her away from the right to be angry without constraint.

But there were problems with setting the confession in a restaurant. What if his trance broke, and he hesitated in the middle
of a sentence? Anna would wake up and suddenly realize what he
was saying, and what if she screamed at him? How much farther
away from her mercy would he have pushed her? He wanted to be
fair to Anna. If she needed to be angry, and he knew she would,
he wanted to help her. She needed to be someplace where she could
expel her grief and her rage without hurting herself, or anyone else,
where the humiliation would have no audience. When he had the
brilliant idea of taking her to Mexico, he had at first pictured telling
her while they were walking on the beach, where the sand would
slow her down if she wanted to run from him, or even on a late
afternoon swim in the ocean. Madeleine would be with a Mexican
baby-sitter, one of the maids working for a few extra dollars, a
grandmother. Frank would take Anna for the swim, and then, bodies
attending to the business of floating, their minds and their emotions
at a gentle null, Frank would say what was finally impossible not
to say. But the water would hardly give Anna the advantage. Why
force her to swim and listen to him at the same time? What if she
choked on her unhappiness, what if she drowned while he was telling
her? And what was that advantage? And why did Frank want to
concede the advantage? Because he wanted to be fair. And justice
demanded of him that he concede to Anna her right to leave him,

to never see him again. And when it came to him that he should write a letter, he had the answer to his problems.

For a few days he composed it in his head, and it made him think of Mozart working out a symphony before taking up a pen, and he felt great peace, the relief of someone who has given up fighting for a bad idea. For how long had he been so sick of himself? When he considered how close he had come to confessing in a restaurant, he could have fainted from the shame of what he had almost done, as if he *had* done it, as if the impulse to make this piece of theater for himself and Anna so demonstrated his basic moral weakness that acting on it or not made no difference, since someone heroic would never have such stupid thoughts flitting across the mind. How can you hope for a reconsecration of your marriage if it begins with your wife's public humiliation? The restaurant confession would force Anna to behave in a well-mannered way; she couldn't scream or cry if she felt the wound deeply. The meditative grace that he had planned for himself would have been a weapon. And while swimming? No, the water is another kind of manacle. And so the letter. And nothing could be more dignified, nothing could better protect her dignity, or his, than an elegantly composed letter, handwritten, not typed. Out of the decision to write the letter it came to him that there was only one way to deliver the letter. He would let Anna read the letter while he took their three-year-old daughter for a walk on the beach, or into the town to buy her something. When Anna read his letter, she would be alone in a hotel room, she could react however she wanted. She could leave, she could stay, the choice was hers. She could break every window in the room, she could tear the sheets with her fingernails, she could throw his clothing into the hall, she could smash the mirrors and she could burn the carpet, and then, because he would make no protest, she could see that he loved her, and she could forgive him.

After he knew he had to write a letter, he knew that if the letter was true, they would need time to recover from its effect, which would push her away from him. Mexico would heal them. There would be a moment, a few days after the letter, when she would look at him and say, "I love you," and she would mean it, and he would say, "I love you," and it would be all over.

He had alarmed Anna with his frantic enthusiasm for this trip. There had been vague talk about going away, and then, with three days' warning, Frank showed Anna the tickets.

For six months Anna had told him that she felt an empty space in the house whenever he came home, and that he was becoming mechanical in all of his attentions and responsibilities. She would wake him up and tell him about her bad dreams in which she saw him with other women, or with another family, and he would help her analyze the dreams in a carefully thoughtful way. For some time Frank had been unhappy at work, and with his wife's encouragement he had pursued an early ambition, to produce records. He told Anna her dreams of other women showed her ambivalence about this pursuit, since success in the music industry would probably lead to temptations he never had to confront running the business he shared with his brother.

"You have to tell me the truth," she would say. "It isn't fair to me if you don't."

Then he would lie to her. "The dreams about other women are symbolic," Frank told her. "You're worried I'll be married to the music business."

This would keep her calm for two or three days, and then she would say to him, "I think I'm going crazy. I feel paranoid about everything and everybody." He recommended therapy. He told her that he loved her.

It hurt him every time he denied her intuition, and he wanted to throw the whole problem at her feet and beg her to help him with this demon that made him cheat and lie, but he didn't want to take from Anna the right to be the one who was hurt. He could so easily say, "Help me, Anna, help me get over this disease which makes me do nothing but tell lies." Against the impulse to degrade himself, he felt sucked down by a terrifying weakness, which he took to be the first tremors of the muscular dystrophy that waited for him if he continued to steal the attention from his wife's right to hate him. Unless he could tell her the truth in the right way, so Anna could

hate him, so there would be no other issue than his lies, and not
his feelings about his lies, he would rather keep on lying. How
could he confess without pride? How could he make amends? Each
lie gave Anna more reasons to punish him, but what punishment
could erase the memory of the fun he and Mary Sifka had ripped
from each other's bodies? Unless she left him, he wondered what
she could do to him that would finally make him feel the pain he
had caused his wife.

He sat at his desk and took out his diary. This was not a journal
of events, but each day he tried to write down a few words that
summed up whatever the day had meant to him. He hoped, someday,
to go back through the diary and fill in the spaces between the
words, but as time passed, he usually forgot whatever it was that
had inspired him to write down whatever words he had written down.
Yesterday he had written HOPE—BRIGHTER—LETTER. Now it was
time to write the letter itself. He would compose it in the notebook,
and then, when it was ready, he would copy it onto a notecard he
had bought at the County Museum's gift shop. It was a Mexican
painting, of a woman carrying a basket of flowers. He began:

> *Dear Anna,*
> *This is difficult.*

Or is that already begging for mercy?

> *I'm on the beach now. I know you'll be*
> *upset when you read this.*

Still not direct. Don't presume to know her feelings. Maybe
she'll be relieved. Maybe she's been having an affair and can at
least leave me, now that the masquerade is over. Do I believe she
is seeing someone else? She would have to be a better actor than I
am, and I don't think she is.

> *I love you. You asked me why I was so*
> *desperate to take this vacation and I said*

that I needed to get away from the office
for a while, and that's true, but there's
more. For a few months

No, this was a denial, a few is not enough, he had to tell the truth.

For six months you've noticed that I've
been distant, and I have been. I had an
affair. It's over now. Completely. I
wanted to take this trip so that we could
find a way to heal ourselves. I don't know
how you'll take this, and all I can say is
that I beg you to forgive me, but if you
don't want to, I will understand.

He crossed out the last sentence. Somehow he thought the letter was stronger if he didn't ask Anna for anything. Saying that he didn't know how she would take the news implied that he had already anticipated a set of possible responses. If she studied the sentence, and the letter with the intensity in which it was written, how could she miss the strategies that lay behind each measured word? He wanted her to think that the letter came out of his heart, quickly, a confession for his heart alone, not for hers. If he left off the last sentence and ended with the two words "heal ourselves," how could she feel anything for him but pity? In the "heal ourselves" was a plea for his wife to join him in work they both needed to do. The subtle gravity of that phrase pulled his wife, her behavior, her attitude to him, into the reasons for the affair. So he was that much more sure that he should drop the plea for her understanding. In "heal ourselves" he forced her to be his equal. The sacrifice of those two words granted her a position superior to him. Would she appreciate the gift? Perhaps someday, he thought, I can show her the early drafts of this letter. No.

He knew that Anna's first question was going to be "Who was she?" or more likely, "Who *is* she?" He couldn't say, "That doesn't matter, it's over now," because of course it did matter. Unless he gave her the answer to the question without her provocation, how could he defend himself against the charge that he was protecting the other woman, and if he was protecting her, how could he say the affair was over? He went back to the letter and copied it over one more time, keeping the sentence that ended with *I will under-stand . . .* Now the letter read:

> *I love you. You asked me a few weeks*
> *ago why I was so desperate to take this*
> *vacation and I said that I needed to get*
> *away from the office for a while, and*
> *that's true, but there's more. For six*
> *months you've noticed that I've been dis-*
> *tant, and I have been. You asked me if*
> *there was another woman, and I said no,*
> *but I was lying. I had an affair with*
> *Mary Sifka. It's over now. Completely. I*
> *wanted to take this trip so that we could*
> *find a way to heal ourselves. I don't*
> *know how you'll take this, and all I can*
> *say is that I beg you to forgive me, but if*
> *you don't want to, I will understand. I*
> *love you.*

He reread the letter and cut out the word "Completely" because the emphasis, the word as a sentence by itself, called attention to his style; it was a useless rhetorical flourish. If he'd already said that the affair was over, how could the word "Completely" help him? Either it was over or it wasn't, and if it was over, then it was over completely. Satisfied with the letter, he took the notecard out of its envelope. The card opened sideways, like a book. The other card he had considered, of a Rothko, two large fields, one black, one muddy red above a smaller field, dark green, had opened from the bottom, to rest like a tent on whatever mantel where it found a home, and now he wished he had bought that card, since it would have been easier to write from the top of the card to the bottom, instead of on the two sides of this card. And the choice of the Mexican art now seemed sentimental and predictable, although at the time the Rothko, with its brooding sense of something final, seemed to him also pretentiously serious. Wasn't he giving Anna flowers? And a woman. She would think about the woman, and her burden. But he didn't want to write across the two sides. If he wrote carefully, and slowly, and if he didn't dedicate the letter to her, "Dear Anna," but just began at the top of the card, with small margins, then the letter could fit on one side.

Something in the letter made him happy as he copied it. He was pleased with the choices he had made, and if the care he took meant that he hoped to tilt Anna's attention away from his adultery toward something general, something about the two of them, he was sure that she would know that he was, finally, sincere. It was important that Anna not stumble over a single word trying to make sense of his writing. Usually he wrote in a scrawl, but now each letter was separately crafted.

When he finished copying the letter, he took the card upstairs.

He went to the bedroom and undressed. Anna always slept deeply. He was not afraid of waking her up. The luggage for tomorrow's trip was open on the floor. He took his letter to her and slipped it into a pocket inside his suitcase.

He was thirsty and went back down to the kitchen. He drank from a bottle of grape juice, leaving enough for Madeleine. He wanted more and drank it, with the excuse that in the morning she could have milk or water, and her mother could buy her juice at the airport.

Then he regretted this theft, and he went upstairs, to see her sleeping. She was on top of the sheets, and her hair was damp. What made her sweat? he wondered. Dreams of exercise, or just the heat of growth?

Perhaps he should have written "heal the family." Certainly he needed time not just with his wife, but with his daughter. He was afraid that she hated him. She was three now, but how long did they have before her character was so formed that part of it would always be made of contempt for her father? If it wasn't contempt, it was something close to it, not all the time, but when he talked too much, say, if he drove through an area he didn't know and stopped to look at the map, and he told her everything he was doing, she would tell him, from the baby seat in the back, to stop talking. Whenever she told him to stop talking, he could suddenly hear himself, and what he heard was the tiring drone of a bore. And if I sound like this to a child? he asked himself. No wonder I have so few friends. He talked so much to her because he thought she would like the comforting sound of his voice, and that she would grow up to be a better person if he paid her the respect of explaining what he was doing. He thought he was being helpful, a good father. She had no interest in his explanations of things.

He would look at her in the rearview mirror, and he would see her distance from him, and he would tell himself that the little bit of detachment of hers in which he saw himself was a reflection of his detachment from this marriage. He blamed himself for what he thought would be the foundation of his daughter's general misery when she was older, estranged from the world, unsure of love. She would finally understand, probably through a long and expensive analysis, how it was her father's example, and the forces driving that example, that molded her character.

Now she was asleep, and smiling, her favorite white teddy bear under her arm. Those seeds of future misery were tucked deep inside. What would he change in her if he could? A few times they had been to the mountains, and when they walked in the forest, she screamed to be carried. She was happy only indoors, or on the beach. She was afraid of trees. It was a small fear, and he told himself all the obvious reasons why a child who loves to run through airports would hate the terror of trees, shadows, trails. She was born into a world of right angles.

So was that all he despised in this daughter who despised him, her fear of trees? He was willing to say that he loved her hatred of him, a feeling so precocious that she might escape a family trait to hang on to people rather than to know when to leave, that she would become a woman who demanded respect. The trip to Mexico was as much to help him find a way to win her love as it was to win his wife's.

He showered and then got into bed beside Anna. He rolled a leg over her hips, and when she didn't move, not that he expected her to, he rolled away. But it's the honorable thing, he told himself, to leave a space between us until she allows me into her embrace.

In all the months of the affair, he had never spent the night with Mary Sifka. She was the assistant to the insurance agent who handled the business that Frank shared with his younger brother, Lowell. Together they owned twenty music and video stores in California. Lowell was homosexual and had never been married, and because Frank had a family, and wanted to stay in Los Angeles, Lowell was in charge of the stores outside of the city. Although he kept a condominium in Santa Monica, now he was living in San Diego, where they had three stores. It was part of the family mythology that Lowell always went to the city with the newest stores because he was homosexual, and could more easily travel than Frank, but it was easier for everyone to agree on that story than the truth, which had nothing to do with Lowell's homosexuality. Lowell watched over the business's expansion because he was the better businessman. Everyone knew this, but no one ever said it, because to admit this might allow everyone to reflect on Frank's incompetence in business. It was possible that the family had accepted Lowell's homosexuality because of this convenient excuse it gave for Lowell's position. In a bad moment one night, when Frank came home after Lowell had yelled at him for some kind of mistake in the way he had managed an inventory, Frank wondered if he would have been a better businessman if he had also become homosexual, or whether Lowell would have been so good if he had been straight. But there are plenty of good businessmen who are straight, Frank cried to himself that night. And there must be incompetent homosexuals.

Lowell always took care of insurance, but on a day when Lowell could not fly back to Los Angeles and something had to be signed by one of them, Mary Sifka came to the office with the papers. She was married too. Her husband was a lawyer. She had no children. She didn't want them.

Frank was in love with Mary's bitterness. Had he ever kissed a woman with so clear a philosophy of the world? Anna was a casual optimist, like everyone he knew, and if she thought the world might end in her lifetime, she buried the idea quickly. Mary was different. He was ready to grant that her sense of global doom might not be the sum of an equation whose every clause represented logic and reason, and the world wore the colors of her own dark spirit because the world had been brutal to her, but he didn't want to diminish the achievement of her unhappiness by finding the location for her view of things in psychology, because he needed her to be smart and strong. He liked her because she had a dull job that she took seriously. She worked hard because she was afraid of falling quickly into a state of decay. She worked harder than he did, and they both knew it, and he paid himself in three months what she made in a year.

Now it was time to not love her. He would miss her, but the woman beside him was more important to him, and so was the little girl down the hall.

He went to sleep with the feeling that he had prayed, and in that meditation had made a true offering of his heart; there was nothing left. He had been generous.

The flight was at three in the afternoon. He was going to meet Anna and Madeleine at the airport. Anna asked him to take the day off, but he told her that since he was taking off a week and a half, he had to go to the office. He would take a limousine from the restaurant where he was meeting Mary Sifka.

At breakfast Madeleine asked to sit in his lap while he fed her cereal from his bowl. He thought about the breakfast the next morning, in Mexico, a big buffet with fruit, cheese, and pitchers with fresh juices on a long table in the dining room of the hotel, one wall open to the ocean beyond. Madeleine would ask for jams and jellies, and he would let her have them, even though he tried to keep her from eating sugar at home. These treats would come in little stain-less-steel bowls, three or four on a rotating trivet, with little spoons. There would be other families at breakfast, and Madeleine would find, as she always did, a boy or girl three or four years older, and force this child to be her friend. The parents would talk, the usual chat about children's ages, schools, habits good and bad, and Anna would make a date with them for dinner that night, both families together. After she read the letter, there would be no other families at the table, but he would give her a day and a night before he gave her the surprise, before she knew about Mary Sifka. They would be in Mexico for a week and a half. He owed her one day of peace.

If she didn't leave immediately, and he expected her to forgive him, there would still be two or three days of terrible sensitivity. Yes, and there was something even to be happily anticipated in the prospect of suffering, an exhaustion, a bath in strong feelings that would leave both of them raw, open, and then, with a little help of a few more good days, they might even be tender with each other. If Anna demanded proof of his love, he would tell her that it was time to have the second child he had always refused her. What more could he offer her? And when she asked him, when she told him to look her in the eye and promise fidelity, would he mean it, in his heart, what he promised? Or would he say, "I hope so"? And if he equivocated, no matter how much hope was carried on his sincerity, would that be too clever a way out of the pledge? If he wanted her forgiveness, if he wanted the marriage to last, he would have to swear his faith, and he knew that he would have to make this oath in the court of eternity.

Besides, he was tired of seeing his family through gauze. He wanted to be a man, and if being a man is doing more than what is expected, he would tell the truth. He would tell his wife the truth all the time, otherwise how could it be the truth? Something in the threatening power of this vow made him drunk; he saw himself standing on the mountain of truth, hands joined with the righteous. And then he felt the tug of a wonderfully happy thought, that the reward for this perpetual exposure, this unveiling would even lead to an increase in their passion. Was that selfish? No.

He said good-bye to Anna and Madeleine after breakfast.

"Where are we going today?" he asked his daughter.

"Where are we going?" she said. They had shown her pictures of Mexico, and she had chosen the bathing suits she wanted to take.

"We're going to Mexico," he told her.

"We're going to Mexico," she said. Was she repeating what he said because she was learning to talk, or was she making fun of his condescension? He patted her on the head and then bent down to kiss her nose. He kissed Anna good-bye.

"I'll see you at the airport," he said, and he was out the door.

It was such a dreadfully mechanical moment, three robots brushing their electrodes for a data exchange. Everything will be different in a few days, he thought. We will be alive.

At work in the morning he spoke to his brother about their store in La Jolla, and whether the manager might be stealing. He looked at the plans for an expansion of their Palm Springs store. He spoke to a friend at a record company. These are the things I do during the day, he thought.

On the way to lunch he worried about what he would tell Mary. The affair had a boundary: Mary knew that he wasn't going to leave his family for her, and he knew she wasn't going to leave her husband. Why were they together like this? It continued for the excitement, he supposed. It was fun to be naked with a new person, but he pursued this affair with the same flat affect that he felt with his family. He was going through the motions of lust. He would have to tell her the truth just as he had to tell Anna the truth. If he lied to Mary, then whatever he told Anna would also be tainted by that lie.

Mary was already at the table in the restaurant. He thought that she looked ordinary and tired before she saw him. She was drinking a glass of grapefruit juice, or orange juice from yellow fruit, and he wondered if, knowing that she was going to hear him say what was inevitable, Mary had ordered something with vodka in it. She was staring at the table, and her skin looked loose on her face, but when she saw him, she smiled, and it bothered him to know that he made her happy. Her feelings for him made her beautiful. Of course, she

was probably scared to be in public with him, even though this was
not a restaurant where anyone from their lives usually went. They
had never run into friends here. Once they had kissed at the table,
but neither was happy when the kiss ended. Their fear of attention
reminded them of their guilt. Had she thought of her husband at
that moment? During the kiss he imagined his wife and daughter
coming into the restaurant and seeing him with Mary Sifka. He
probably did love her. But what could they do with that love? If he
left Anna for Mary, and Mary left her husband for him, would they
get married and stay together until they died? Or would they leave
each other, and then end their lives with a third, or a fourth,
marriage, or no marriage, end their lives single, alone? And could
he leave his daughter?

He kissed her on the cheek, and she didn't seem to expect more.
They ordered their food.

"When is your flight?" she asked.

"At three."

"You're cutting it close."

"I'll make it."

"It should be nice there."

"Yes." It was dangerous territory under any circumstances: They
didn't talk to each other about their families; neither complained
that home was insufficient. He didn't really know anything about
her husband.

He wanted the opening line to be right, but the impulse to say,
"This is going to be difficult," was almost impossible to resist. Maybe
it was the right thing to say, and it was the truth.

"This is going to be difficult."

"Oh dear." She knew immediately what he wanted to tell her.

"I think . . ." he stopped. Already he was proposing the breakup
in terms of a debate. If he *thought* they should break up, she could
say that she *thought* they shouldn't, and they could argue about it,
and perhaps she could persuade him. There was no other way to
say this quickly, and be done with it. He checked his watch, a
gesture she observed, and now he was ruined for her, he had revealed
to her his new attitude toward her, that she was an expedient,

something in the way. Of what? His wife, or a new mistress, the woman who could be perfect, the woman he had not yet met.

"I'm going to Mexico so that I can connect with my family again. I've been feeling all wrong for the last few months. I love you, but I didn't know how hard it is to split the heart between two women. Three if you include my daughter, and I do." Writing the letter to Anna had given him a new sense of the pleasure in words, and it was easy to talk, it was a pleasure to talk. He could have gone on, but it was only fair to give her a chance.

"So it's over? Is that what you're telling me?"

"Yes."

"I guess it's for the best."

"There's no good way to end something that's probably wrong to begin with."

"I probably love you too, you know." She said this defiantly, as though it was something he might have overlooked, her feelings, that he could hurt them, that she would miss him, that she needed him.

"What are we supposed to do?"

She smiled. She was letting go of him. "We're supposed to say that it couldn't have lasted forever, we had fun, whatever it was that we needed we got, and now it's time to eat, and not talk about it anymore."

The food was at the table. He asked for a saké; it didn't matter if he got a little drunk, since he was taking the limousine to the airport. It was time for the vacation to begin.

They were so comfortable with each other that he thought they might now be able to continue as friends, but he knew that Anna would never permit this. Why not, though? No, the temptation would always be there. Would it, really? Yes. Was it there now? Yes.

It was time to say good-bye. The conversation drifted along. The relief he felt when she let him break it off—and what had he expected, what scene, what tears?—had followed its own course, and now he looked at Mary and knew that he could leave her and not miss her. So perhaps he had not loved her either. The letter he had written to his wife, for all that he meant it as he put it in his suitcase, had been composed in a spirit of some fraudulence, since he had not yet told Mary Sifka that he was ending the affair. He should have broken with Mary first, because the letter, as he wrote it, said that the affair was over.

What if he had died of a heart attack in his sleep, last night, before he had been able to say good-bye to Mary, and Anna had found the letter? She would have assumed that he had said his good-byes to Mary, but Mary would not have known about his change of heart unless Anna showed her the letter, and would Anna think of doing that, something so cruel, while she was grieving? Or would she show Mary the letter so she could understand just who it was she had married, who it was she had shared a child with? But when would she have discovered the letter? It was in a pocket in *his* suitcase, not hers. If his heart had stopped that day, she would have unpacked the case, or someone else would have done the job, maybe his mother, and would they have found the card slipped into a pocket with nothing else? It might have stayed hidden for months, or longer, or ever. Perhaps on a vacation years later, perhaps with her new husband. Perhaps she would remarry, and her new husband would pack the suitcase she had never thrown away, and at the hotel, when they got there, she would have unpacked both her suitcase and his, and found the letter. This was an interesting scenario, thought Frank. Anna reads the letter two years after I am dead, but does not realize the note is from me and thinks that her second husband is making this confession. She confronts him, she screams at him, and he says he doesn't know what she is talking about. She shows him the letter. But I didn't write this. Then who did? she says. Look at the handwriting. She looks. Frank, she says. Frank? he asks.

Perhaps she remembers a woman at his funeral who stood in the back, and lingered at the grave as the family walked away. And that was Mary Sifka. Does she remember when he had packed the suitcase?

Does she remember the trip to Mexico canceled by my death?

But if she found it, he trusted Mary to behave well, not to embarrass him, even if he was dead. After all, this was why he had loved her. And his wife, when she found out about the other woman after he was dead? How could any woman, reading the letter he had written, not love him even more? He was happy that the letter was so careful and transparent. In a way, he thought, I should die now, tonight. Then I would fulfill my obligation to her, to make things right.

He said good-bye to Mary on the sidewalk. He wished now that he had, not now, but earlier in the affair, bought her something precious, a necklace or earrings. But a gift on parting would have been vulgar, a kind of severance pay. Yes, it was part of her attraction that she wanted nothing from him—and anyway how could she explain an extravagance to her husband—but now he regretted never having given her a relic, even something small and insignificant, for her to treasure secretly. So they had their memories. So be it.

She gave him a shy, patient smile, and when he saw that the moment saddened her, he hugged her and kissed her on the lips. His tongue left his mouth and flicked her teeth. So she was opening herself to him too. They stopped. He knew he was cheating a little, already bending his resolve to be pure for Anna forever, but he decided to forgive himself. He would even tell Anna about this good-bye if she asked him; it was here that his problem, his weaknesses, could be brought into their life; after they had repaired the marriage, why couldn't he tell her about his temptations and his struggles? He couldn't expect himself, or he couldn't imagine Anna expecting him, never again to look at another woman, or even meet a woman and fall a little bit in love, and have her fall a little bit in love with him. What was to be expected was self-discipline, and an eventual cessation of uncontrollable desire. Why that? Because as the years passed, and there would be years, the attention to only one person, the devotion to the other, would focus the heart, and in the end, become an obsession. This would be love, he told himself, the great project of his life. Now that he was rich, what other work was more important? Charity? Yes. I will give to good causes, thought Frank. And not only the popular charities. I will give money to the library. I will give to the poor.

It was two o'clock when he left the restaurant, and the traffic was slow. He hated himself for taking so long to say good-bye to Mary. And he could still taste her, still smell her. Well, if I get there just in time, Anna will be angry with me for almost screwing up, and she won't want to kiss me, not on the mouth. She won't taste Mary. She might smell her. He thought of asking the limousine driver to smoke, to cover Mary Sifka's scent, but he would have had to leave the backseat and sit next to him, and how could he ask for that?

Frank asked the driver for a cigarette. The driver gave him one, and Frank lit it. He had once smoked for a few years, in college, and he took a few puffs, and let the cigarette burn near him, for the smoke, or the ash, to settle on his jacket and in his hair. He didn't want the cigarette on his breath, but Anna, in the frenzy of getting ready for the flight, would not likely feel romantic. He was sure she suspected something; the rush to take the trip had betrayed a necessity greater than the need for relaxation.

He took another puff of the cigarette, and the little charge of the nicotine, a pleasant dizziness, brought him a moment's happiness. This is a drug, he thought. No wonder people still use it. He took a few more drags and put the cigarette out. Will I smoke again? It was impossible to say.

The traffic was slow, and the plane was leaving at three o'clock. At two-thirty he knew he would never get to the airport in time. At 2:45 he was still a mile away. He would never make it. This was going to be a mess, since Anna had his ticket and his passport. He would have to ask her to find someone at the airport to hold them for him, and who knew if that kind of request could be honored? There was a phone in the backseat of the limousine, and he called Information for the phone number of the airline. There was no number for the terminal, but the reservations clerk gave him another number. He asked to have his wife paged, and explained why, although he wasn't asked for a reason.

Anna was on the phone quickly, in less than a minute.

"I have your ticket and passport, and you're going to miss the plane," she said, without any introduction. It bothered him that she

didn't even ask how he had found her. How had she known it was
him? Who else could it be? People knew they were going away, but
nobody knew which airline they were flying.

"It's the traffic."

"Where were you, why couldn't you leave earlier?" She was
angry and suspicious.

It was still time to lie. "I tried. I couldn't get away. It was
important."

"Nothing you do is important, Frank."

"Anna, please, what are you saying?" Something awful was about
to happen. She was saying something to him in a voice she had
never used with him before, but it was the voice she used with
people when she has lost all patience, when she stopped trying to
see things their way.

"Oh, Frank, now what are we going to do?" Was she backing
off from this frightening rage? And what was he scared of? That she
would drown Frank in a flood of insights into his failings, that she
would finally tell him who he really was?

"You take this flight now, and I'll take the next flight. Can you
find out when the next flight is leaving?"

She was gone a moment. "There's a flight to Acapulco at six.
What if it's sold out?"

"It won't be. If I can't fly coach, I'll fly first class. There's always
an empty seat in first. And if I can't come today, then I'll come
tomorrow."

"Are we going to lose money on your ticket?"

"A little, yes." He had bought the ticket at a discount, but it
couldn't be exchanged. Though they had enough money for first
class, they always flew coach, no matter how much they spent on
a room. Although they never said this to anyone else, there was
something about this frugality that they thought of as charity, that
the money for first class was a silly waste and better spent on other
things, or given away to people who needed it. They would have a
suite in Mexico with a private swimming pool for six hundred dollars
a day, and still they looked for the cheapest seats. Paying the extra
money for the first-class ticket was a tax on today's bad behavior,

he knew, a tax for licking Mary Sifka's teeth. It was turning into an expensive lunch.

"Do I need a reservations number when I get to the hotel?"

"No."

"I'll give your passport to the gate agent."

"And the ticket," said Frank.

"And the ticket," she said, with a note of something in her voice, what was it, impatience, annoyance.

He heard Madeleine in the background. She wanted to speak to him. "Is that Madeleine?" Why did he ask if he knew? "Put her on."

She wouldn't come to the phone.

"They're calling us to board now."

"Have a good flight."

"Fuck you."

"I told you I was sorry." Why was she swearing at him? He could feel something awful was about to happen.

"No you didn't."

"I'm saying it now." He said this in a way to calm her down, as though he was rational and she were insane, and he hated his tone of voice, it sounded rehearsed and out of scale with Anna's rising anger.

"There wasn't enough room in my suitcase for all of Madeleine's clothes, so I had to put some in yours."

Something in the universe was tearing. He couldn't think quickly enough to sew it back up.

"Oh?" he asked, but he knew what was coming.

"I read the letter."

He could only say, "So you know I love you." He was disturbed with how quickly this came to him. Here he was, taking from her the right to be angry. He wasn't being fair.

"I don't know anything anymore."

"You were supposed to read it tomorrow. I was going to give it to you while I took Madeleine for a walk. The beach or something. Maybe to town."

This is good, thought Frank, I am acting like someone bewildered by his sins.

"Why are you late? Were you with her?"

"If you read the letter, then you know I love you." He said this slowly, talking her down from the window ledge.

"We'll talk about it in Mexico." There was a hopeful sound to this; she wasn't ready to leave him. It seemed to him that she was also puzzled by the affair, that she wanted to understand it, clinically.

"I'll see you tonight." His relief might have been premature, but he said this in a way that assumed the amnesty she would grant him.

"Frank, you're an asshole."

"I want to have another baby. Let's have the baby." Why did I say this now? he asked himself. How much uglier can I make myself?

"You don't want another baby, Frank."

"Yes, I do." I have to say this.

"No, Frank, you don't want another baby, you just want me to think you love me now, that's all."

"But I do love you."

"No you don't."

She hung up. The flight was leaving in five minutes, but he was at a red light half a mile from the airport. He could never catch the plane.

2. The Gate

Frank was twelve minutes late when he ran to the ticket counter. There was a long line, but he pushed ahead to the closest ticket agent, and told her who he was and what had happened. "I was supposed to be on flight two-twenty-one. My wife and daughter made the flight, and she said she was going to leave the ticket and passport here for me."

A couple in the line behind him complained loudly that he had run ahead of everyone.

"I'm sorry," he said to them, "but I think I just missed my flight."

The woman at the counter was black. Her name tag said, "DONNA" on it, in quotes. Did the quotes mean that Donna was her nickname?

"Two-twenty-one just left the gate."

"My wife said there was a flight at six."

He leaned against the counter, and he thought that he might be fainting. The agent asked him if he was all right.

"To Acapulco? Let me check."

"And my ticket and passport. She probably left them at the gate."

"Let me check," she said.

Donna made a call and told the story, and then said, "Someone will be right down with them."

"And is there room on the six o'clock flight?"

"Let me check."

Frank watched the agent type something on a keyboard and then wait for an answer on the computer screen. The agent smiled, as though she had actually done something to be proud of. "Yes, we have seats available."

"And can I exchange my ticket?"

"Let me check."

Some more typing.

"You had a restricted ticket, but let me check." The agent made another call, and while she did, another woman in a blue jacket arrived with an envelope. While the ticket agent explained the situation to someone on the phone, she opened the envelope and took out the passport and ticket. She looked at the passport picture and mouthed, "It's you," while listening to the person on the other end of the line.

"Thank you," said Frank. The agent held on to his ticket.

She hung up the phone and told Frank that the surcharge was a hundred dollars. She apologized.

Frank gave her his credit card, and the new ticket was printed up.

She asked if he had any luggage.

"My wife had it."

"Have a nice flight."

"At least I won't be late for this one," said Frank, trying to make her smile.

"Flights aren't announced, you know, so you have to be at gate forty-seven at least half an hour prior to departure."

"I'll be there," said Frank.

He left the counter and walked up a flight of stairs to the terminal.

If he had not kissed Mary, or if he had not had the saké, Frank would have been on the plane. But now that Anna knew about Mary Sifka, now that she had read the letter, wasn't it actually better that he was coming into Mexico three hours later? Given the disaster of Anna's discovery of the letter, flying separately was a blessing. How could he have had the talk he wanted if they were on the plane? If she was going to find the letter, if that's what Fate wanted for him, then Fate had also protected them both by clogging the roads with so many cars, slowing him down, making him late. This way, there would be no painful silences, no tug-of-war for Madeleine's attention.

But has Fate really made things better for us? he wondered. He had planned the vacation and the timing of the letter to shrink all of the emotional battles into one act, but the strategy had failed. He had made a mess of things.

He passed the magazine and gift shop, walked beyond it, and then, without thinking, drifted back into it, and studied a few of the magazines, but decided to wait until just before the flight to buy anything, because if he bought them now, he would read them in the three hours he had before takeoff, and then he'd have nothing to read on the plane. He looked at the paperbacks, but he didn't have the energy to read a book.

He went to the bar and ordered a beer. He never drank during the day, but he told himself to relax, he was on vacation now. He had to enjoy himself. He thought about wanting a cigarette, not that he wanted one, but that he understood that the taste of the cigarette in the limousine, which was fading now, had awakened an old addiction. That would be something, he thought, to show up in Mexico, smoking again. What would that look like, to Anna? That I smoked with Mary Sifka, that my sins were unremitting.

The beer came, and he took a long first sip and then put it back
onto the counter. He smiled at the bartender, a black woman, and
she smiled back. He thought she would have liked to chat, but he
lowered his eyes and took another sip of the beer, and thought about
the horrible moment when Anna would open the door to the hotel
room in Mexico.

I check in at the desk. The manager knows what happened, not
about the letter, but about the missed flight. Señor Gale, the traffic
in Los Angeles, it's worse than ever, no? But you should see Mexico
City now. Terrible. We're glad you could find an empty seat on the
next plane, this is a busy time for us. You have room three-forty-
five, do you need a bellboy to show you the way? There's nothing
for you to sign, you're all checked in. Three-forty-five.

What's going to happen when I get there? First I'll shower, and
then get into fresh clothes, from my suitcase, and right away I'll
have to think about the letter, and where it was hidden. Not hidden,
tucked way. No, hidden. I owe her the truth.

The wrong turn in the hall, and then doubling back, and then
the room. A deep breath outside the door, for the audience of his
own attention. He knocks. Madeleine, excited by the trip and missing her father, might still be awake, and if she is, Anna tells him
to get something to eat.

"I'm sure you didn't eat on the plane. You must be hungry. Why
don't you go to the dining room? Or you can get something to eat
in the bar." This would be her way of asking him to leave, so she
could save all of her feelings until they were alone, so she wouldn't
have to pretend to an emotion in front of their little girl. He wouldn't
be hungry, but he would put on a cool shirt and then wander through
the resort and find a bar with a few women who would smile once
at him, see his wedding ring, and go back to their drinks and
cigarettes.

Outside the terminal there was nothing but planes and the gray
sky and the gray buildings of the airport. Foreign planes, Alitalia,
Iberia, Korean Air, passed by, and with them he thought of changing
his resolutions and just finally walking out on his family. I have the
money, he thought. I could be ugly, I go to Italy for a few weeks,

and come home, and accept the divorce. Or Korea, I could go to
an industrial city a hundred miles from Seoul, someplace where the
only Americans who visit are on business, and I could be a tourist,
I could walk in this strange city and think about my life.

He finished the beer, and he looked forward to the next drink
he'd have that day, in the bar in Acapulco. The next drink on land.
He'd have a drink on the plane, Bloody Mary for the spices, which
would keep him focused on sensation, keep him from thinking about
emotion. In the hotel bar he would have a margarita, on the rocks,
no salt. Or maybe with salt, why not, and he'd finish the complimentary basket of tortilla chips, and go through two little ceramic
bowls of salsa. The chips in Mexico always come stuck together—
something about the oil they use; it's heavy. The Mexican food in
America is better, but he wouldn't care, because after his second
margarita he'd flirt with a team of sunburned women sitting at the
bar. There are always teams of women from the States, and at the
more expensive resorts, some of them are even of my class, he
thought, college graduates, good-looking, maybe divorcées down
from Brentwood; some of them were pretty enough to have landed
rich first husbands, who leave them with a little money, and their
jewelry. Frank liked the type. Mary Sifka wasn't that type, but he
liked hard women who drank too much and liked to fuck, loose
enough on vacation to fuck a stranger and not waste time feeling
degraded. He had never done this, but he had seen these women.
He ordered another beer. No, he couldn't drink while he was downstairs at the bar in the resort. A drink would violate his resolve to
follow the path of honor. When his beer came, he paid for it and
then left without drinking it. If he drank a second beer, he would
get sloppy inside. Anna didn't drink, not even wine at dinner parties.
She used to, when they met, but she stopped after the baby was
born, and she was nursing. She liked being sober, she said, and
she kept to it. He could say to her, if he met an irresistible inclination
to be pitiless, that he missed the drinker. He could say that to her
when she asked him why he had this affair. Maybe he would. Maybe
it would be good for her to hear this. And then maybe in Mexico
she'd order a margarita. Or two. Or three. He thought it might be

good for both of them, good for their marriage, if they got sick drunk together, if they woke up with hangovers together, if they got too drunk to screw. Would it be so terrible if they purged something together, if they held each other's hands while she vomited five Bloody Marys into the toilet? Or did he need to see her at her worst, to make her his moral equal?

He looked around the terminal. He could tell Anna that he'd been punished enough, to sit around the terminal for three hours.

She would ask him, when he came to the hotel room, if he had seen his mistress at lunch. He would have to tell the truth. He rehearsed his lines.

"Yes, we had lunch." He would say this quietly, get it over with.

"Did you fuck her?"

"No." He would shake his head and try to resist turning his eyes away from her. Could he make her feel sorry for him if she thought that to demand more of him after the confession was torture?

"Not today, you mean." She would continue to attack, telling him that his attempt to play the honest little boy was transparent. She would torture him, because she would know that he was trying to avoid it.

"No, not today." He would show her that he was dying. That she had wrung from him the last piece of his affair, the part that he wanted to hold on to in his memory, unknown to her and unjudged. When he gave up that part, she would have, so he hoped, the feeling that he could no longer reflect on his times with Mary and not think of the pain he had caused his wife. But would Anna see through this, would she try to destroy that place in his memory where he could have Mary to himself? Would she try to kill the little pleasures he would always take remembering how he had fucked her, how she had come to him, how they had laughed together?

Or he could continue to lie, and deny that he had left Mary at a restaurant. I can confess the affair, and still keep the lunch secret. Cake and eat it. Although there was something alluring about telling the truth, apart from morality. The truth could lead anywhere, even if it destroyed the marriage.

How many different truths were there? There was the first truth, that he had made love to a woman other than his wife. Unless Anna pressed him to admit more, they would stay at this level, but there were other truths, the truths that, once announced, would not so nicely be excused by tearful pledges of repentance. If Anna asked him why he had committed adultery, he could tell her one truth, that he was weak, or lonely, or worried that he was going to get old without ever having once done something like a bad boy. This last truth would come out late, as though this were the real truth, and all the other excuses were a screen. They could talk for a long time about trust, and she could give him a lecture that he could just as easily write, the point of which was the obvious truth, that as ye sow, so shall ye reap. That old lecture: Trust breeds trust.

But what, in any of these truths, was more hurtful than the first confession of having fucked another woman while his wife was making dinner for their daughter?

Following the commandments of his new god of truth, though, he could think of a few truths that would never be forgiven. Mary was younger, and her skin was smooth. Those were the truths he could tell if he was drunk. He could tell these truths, which made his letter to her seem like a lie, even though it was true, but he avoided, in his letter, any truths that, once stated, could not be recanted. So his letter was a lie, that restrained and strategically designed confession was a shield. Anna could scarcely argue with a letter that seemed to invite all the rage she might have for him, and any action, including divorce, but if he told Anna everything, he would drive her away; she would leave him without a lingering affection, a garden for the little flowers of doubt, whose plaintive beauty would remind her that perhaps she should have forgiven him, and saved the marriage. So long as he muted himself, he could hold Anna in thrall for as long as he needed her. If he told her something hateful and sincere, then she could leave him, and he didn't want to give her that freedom. So I am a monster, he thought.

His notebook was in his carry-on bag. He took it out and wrote down two words: *Freedom—Monster*, but now meaning that freedom was a monster. He wasn't sure how he would emend this thought when he came back to the page in a few weeks or a few years, but he liked the idea. He would write about the connection between freedom and responsibility, and the frightening burden that with confession came the obligation not to commit the sin again. If he didn't publish these thoughts, at least he would have something to show to his daughter when she grew up. Or not even when she was grown, but in her teens, when she would need guidance, his wisdom. Or is this really wisdom? he asked himself, turning back at looking at all the random words he had written down.

But why tear myself apart now, for trying however clumsily to make peace with the truth, to love the truth? He saw truth as something to which he could surrender, the higher power that would write a new life for him. He wanted the truth to save his marriage, but if the truth wrecked it, well? His vague fantasies of the consequence of this conversion bounced from the happy pictures of his life becoming an adventure to bleak pictures of himself in a boardinghouse somewhere in the Southwest, drinking alone, muttering to a few sun-baked rummies, "I should have gone to Korea." And none of them would care, or even ask him what he meant. That would be the way they would torture him at this bar near the Yuma gravel pits, to let him rant without relieving him of an explanation.

No, he would stay with her; as he told the truth, he would acquire power, and this magnetism would grow as it fed on the admiration of those who sought him out, since his advice, an emanation of the pure light, would be flawless. I can become perfect, thought Frank, or almost perfect, like a Buddhist.

So many people in the airport, waiting for planes to leave or friends to arrive. All of them alone with their thoughts. Are my troubles so special? No, and that should be a comfort. All of us have our own troubles. What was the story? A man walks into a church, or maybe heaven, maybe the man has died? And he meets Jesus in this huge cathedral, and the man says, Oh, Jesus, my cross is heavy, and Jesus shows him an immense room filled with crosses, huge crosses, and in a corner is the man's little cross, and Jesus says, These are the crosses other people have to bear. This is a stupid, obvious story, thought Frank, why am I thinking about it?

I'm not even Christian. But it works on me, in spite of myself. He felt a stupid rush to ask everyone to hug, to hold hands, and to sing an old Negro spiritual, a song of such uplifting love and hope that from this congregation of tourists there would grow a political movement as each of them spread the Word on their travels.

How could he ask Anna to face reality? When he came back to the business after he quit his attempt to produce records, after that failure, reality made two clear statements to him. The first piece of reality was that he would never produce a successful record, and that real musicians, the artists he admired and envied, had no special interest in him. If he told himself the truth, if he made truth the rule, then he had to admit how ashamed of himself he was when he realized that the only parties he ever went to with musicians were those paid for by record companies. Had he ever been to a party at a musician's house in the Hollywood Hills, an old Spanish mansion with high ceilings, where tall women with long hair talked to him for an hour, and people smoked marijuana, and women danced with each other, and everywhere you looked, there was someone of great achievement, relaxing? And even if Frank hated their achievement, because their songs were insipid, they had still done something of consequence in the world. He had never been to that party. After a recording session, the band never invited him out for a drink. At first he thought this was a sign of respect, the crew's separation from the officers, but then he saw other producers, successful producers, getting drunk and stoned with their musicians, and his musicians too.

The night he told himself to give up music, he had finished hearing the song he had worked on all day. Frank asked the singer if he wanted a drink, and the singer begged off. An hour later Frank passed a Thai restaurant down the block from the studio, where musicians often went, and the singer was there at a table with another producer and another band. The other producer saw Frank pass by, and nodded at him, with a brief smile, at once sincere and defensive; there was the spontaneous response to recognition that brought the corners of his mouth up, but it dropped as quickly as his mind could win control over his autonomic system, and then as the momentum

from the sudden release of the unrehearsed smile pulled his eyes
down, Frank saw that the record producer felt himself ashamed of
his own dismissal of this man standing outside the restaurant who
wanted nothing more from him than to be included at the table and
numbered among his colleagues. And for the feeling of shame he
felt, he had no one to blame except Frank, for putting him in the
position of having to see his own awful nature, and so he now hated
Frank, and made a joke to the others at the table. One of them
looked over his shoulder and saw Frank, who turned his eyes
quickly, to avoid contact. A series of small tics shuddered across
the record producer's face, as though his body could find no other
way to expel the bitter toxins of the shame, provoked or felt, that
circulated among all of them.

Frank stumbled into the parking lot and ran his hand against a
stucco wall, trying to make himself bleed. He would never be friends
with a real musician. All that Frank had was the business, and a
wife for whom he no longer felt great love, if he had ever felt it.

There was something in his character that artists avoided. He
was a salesman. And what was the crime in that? That the connection
to the thing he sold was so small, because unlike a musician, whose
life was his music, his dedication, he could just as easily sell one
thing in place of another, and wasn't that why he wanted to produce
records, to have his life be about this one thing? But then Lowell
was also a salesman, and musicians seemed to like him. Did they
like him because Lowell didn't seem to need their company, except
as he needed to bring them to the stores, to sign autographs and
sell their work? Or did the musicians forgive Lowell his job, selling
things, because he was homosexual? Or did they not forgive him
because there was nothing to forgive, since in their eyes he was an
ally, a friend, the owner of the record stores, while Frank was just
someone who worked there, someone whose eyes should be avoided,
because they asked for a friendship that Lowell, not seeking, won?
Frank knew that he was uncomfortable with himself, and nervous
around musicians, the very people he wanted to share his life with.
What was wrong with him, what did they see in him? He wanted
to please them. He had no faith in his ideas, he talked just to hear

his voice. He wasn't flawless. The great producers were flawless. If he had sold the record stores and devoted himself full time to creating music, maybe then he would have been accepted, but he couldn't let go of the company. He had considered giving it up, but he was scared of failing as a producer, and then having no business to which he could return. Lowell made it easy for him to come back, and for the first year, when he was miserable, Lowell did not press him for extra devotion to the stores. What kind of man would he have to be so that drummers would ask him to stay out late at night and visit clubs and flirt with beautiful women? Or more than flirt. Until Mary Sifka he had been faithful, but not because he wanted to be. The women he desired, the tall women with long hair, paid him no attention. There was something in him, some bit of self-loathing, that repelled the beauties. Yet Anna stayed with him, and Anna loved him. But had he ever appreciated her beauty? In how many songs had he heard about the love of a good woman, and the troubles that beset the man who gave up that selfless love for someone new?

Now he regretted the letter. What stupid demon had convinced him to write it? Already he had caused more pain than he intended. He wanted Anna to read the letter when she had been with him for a day at the hotel, when they had already made love, when she could see him with their daughter, loving her, reading to her, helping her swim, a demonstration to his wife to show her how much the family meant to him. Anna's discovery of the letter had ruined his careful plans. He was back to smearing his elbows in the bourbon stains on the counter of that shitty bar somewhere south of Yuma.

Could anything good ever happen to him now? He tried to find something hopeful. If he wanted to be fair, if he had wanted to give his wife the advantage, then the accident of her discovery, being more abrupt than his intention, was better than his intention. Yes, they would miss the day of peace he had wanted before giving her the letter, but since he wanted to allow his wife her pride, by this premature discovery she was taking from him his last portion of control. Now she had the power. And hadn't she gone to the airport? That was a hopeful gesture, wasn't it? She could have created any little drama she wanted, but she didn't. Anna loves me, and she wants to make the marriage continue. He felt terribly sad for her. There she was on the plane, with Madeleine, thinking about him, picturing him in bed with another woman. He had wrecked her trust, and there she was, devoted to repairing the damage. He wanted to tell her that he loved her too. No one forced her to go to Mexico. She could have played a terrible trick on him, she could have left his ticket and passport for him and then returned to the house, she could have sent him alone to Acapulco. So she wanted to fix things too.

Frank took a seat facing gate 47, the airline's "Gateway to Mexico," decorated with a picture of the Mayan Sundial, and a few colorful blankets. It was the kind of silly but effective decorating that Frank and Lowell appreciated. They usually tried out new design schemes in their Santa Monica store, where, over the jazz bins, when Lowell hung cutout photographs of saxophones, they sold more jazz. Frank knew it was sometimes hard for people, especially in the family, to know exactly what he did for the company—he was sure that a lot of people thought that Lowell was carrying him—but he knew that he made a real contribution to the business, and that Lowell appreciated him. Their parents tended to dismiss Frank's efforts, but when they did Lowell always defended him. And Frank thought that Lowell was careful never to complain about him.

Do I want another beer? he asked himself, regretting the beer he had left untouched. No, here he despised the drinkers, the fat people, the cigarette smokers in the airport bar. Soldiers and women with gray skin. Tomorrow he would be doing the breaststroke in the hotel's swimming pool, with his daughter hugging his shoulders, and he could pull himself up to a submerged stool in the shade of a thatched roof, and charge to his room a rum mixed with pineapple juice, served in a coconut. Madeleine would sit on his lap and eat the cherry. She would be perfectly happy. Everyone, all of the Mexicans working at the hotel, would be perfectly nice to her. And the guests, those not threatened by his fecundity, would also be sweet to the pretty little girl.

He watched the crowd gather for the arrival of a flight from Hawaii. The plane arrived, and the gate attendants opened the door to the ramp. What were the emotions of the people waiting? Envy for the travelers? When he came back from Mexico, would he be transfigured, if only for a few days? What is so terrible about tourism? he asked himself, or asked his friends who made fun of him because he always took his family to resorts instead of taking them closer to where the real people were. But who were the real people except the maids who worked at the resorts? Frank loved resorts, he loved everything about them. He loved how safe they were. He loved how they shut out the world. He particularly loved the resorts after the sun went down, when the harsh lines of the hotels disappeared into the night sky, and you could walk through the gardens and over the bridges that crossed the huge swimming pools and think about honeymooning lawyers from provincial capitals falling in love all over again as they stared at the gold and blue lights surrounding the bases of palm trees. And the bars of the resorts. He liked resorts with three bars, one of them wood-paneled, with a pianist playing classical music, and the thatched bar with the native band, and the disco that opened late, where the tennis players went to dance, and after dancing, to fuck each other. Frank never saw anyone in a resort who looked like a musician, who had beautiful eyes and long hair, men who were skinny, and wore jewelry and had tattoos, and were straight. Or even who were not straight.

One of the women working at gate 47 was on the phone, and she was crying. Another gate attendant came to her and put her arms around her, and they hugged, and they were both crying.

The woman on the phone did not give it up; she held on even while attendants from other gates came over to her. The abandoned passengers herded together, trading indignations, but the gate attendants seemed oblivious to them. More than oblivious: In their concern for the crying woman, they fluttered with shock. Had she been fired? Was this a strike? Why were the men and women working all of the gates gathering around her? And as they ignored the passengers waiting on the lines, where they had been servants, they were now superior, their indifference to the passengers, and their attention to the crying woman, gave them power, and on the fringes of this cluster there was disdain for the passengers who pleaded with the departed agents to help get them onto their flights. There were now twenty gate attendants, all of them in the airline's regulation blue jackets, hugging the woman who still held on to the phone, and if they couldn't wrap their arms around her, they touched her shoulders, or even hugged those who had just had the full embrace, passing along the hug from the center of the group. This is so obvious, someone has died, thought Frank. He was delighted with his perception. He could have strolled with a certain insolence through the nodes of now-frustrated travelers, offering them his observation and letting the truth sink in, so they would regret their tantrums, and instead offer condolence to the woman just touched by death.

He kept this to himself though, and enjoyed the show. Passengers were yelling at the gate attendants. Someone, hidden by a column, shouted at an agent, "What the fuck is going on? I have a connection in San Francisco!" And then, with a surprising speed, the swarm of irate travelers around the gate agents was quiet; something had been said to them. There was an apology.

The quiet whine of an electric cart, which was usually in service when crippled passengers needed help getting to the plane, passed Frank. A black driver and his passenger, a woman in a suit. Frank assumed that she was a corporate officer. Her hair was better cut than the gate attendants', looser. The cart stopped at gate 47. The woman in the suit got out and took the crying woman in her arms, but where the gate attendants all tried to burrow into the crying woman's misery and share it, her hug showed discipline. She spoke quietly to these passive mutineers, and she seemed to be giving them what Frank would have said was the obvious talk, that they would be better people for containing their sorrow, for remembering that they had important jobs, that an airline depended on them, that an airport needed the planes out of the gates at the right times, and that nothing could move without these attendants, that they had real power. "Guys," Frank heard the woman say, "you have the real power here." She took the crying woman with her, and the electric cart disappeared around a bend in the terminal. The hard rubber tires, on the clean pavement of the terminal floor, an imitation marble, sounded as if they were going through a thin layer of water. This was supposed to be the sound of the future, thought Frank, when the whole world was going to be electric; this was the world promised him when he was ten. A quiet city with no pollution, and everyone driving little electric carts, greeting each other with good manners.

The gate attendants stood about for another minute, and then they returned to their posts. Frank invented this story to explain what he had just seen: The crying woman had just heard that someone close to her had died. Her friends, her co-workers, out of sympathy, had rushed to her. Someone had called upstairs, although upstairs in this case probably meant a room somewhere below them, and management had quickly sent the woman in the jitney to restore peace. He might describe the scene to Anna, although he didn't think she would care. She might ask him why he wasted his time telling her about something that bored her, and he would tell her that if something unusual happens, it's nice to talk about it. In the spirit of his rededicated marriage he would rather talk about too many things than to contain himself.

There was a flight ready to leave for San Francisco from gate 51. A woman who had received her boarding pass before the breakdown at gate 47 was yelling at the attendant. Everyone could hear her.

"I'm not getting on that plane. I want my money back! I'm not getting on the plane."

The attendant spoke quietly to her. Frank couldn't hear him. He couldn't imagine her problem, unless she'd just had a psychic vision of her plane going down in flames.

A blond guy in a T-shirt with a surfing logo sat down next to Frank. He was so typical that Frank could hardly see him. How old, thirty-five? He had a job he liked, just a job, somewhere in the city, it wasn't his life. He made enough money. Was the shirt for a trip to Hawaii, or just his shirt?

"I don't blame her," he said.

"For what?" asked Frank.

"Well, they're not saying exactly, but it seems like the plane that left that gate at three"—and he pointed to gate 47—"just went down." He seemed to like the way he said "just went down." It gave him a measure of participation in the event; he said it with the sober experience of a flight-deck commander on an aircraft carrier.

"The plane to Acapulco?" asked Frank.

"*Adiós, amigos.*" He held his hand parallel to the ground, and then, making the sound of a falling bomb, tilted his fingers toward the floor, over the falls, and the hand went down.

"You're sure?" asked Frank.

"That's what I hear. *Adiós, amigos.*"

Of course he didn't know that Frank had family on the plane, so Frank thought it would be unfair of him to strangle the man right there, to kick him in the face, to bite off his ears.

Frank wasn't sure what to do. He thought of Anna and Madeleine, thought of a plane crashing, and his wife and daughter pitching forward, facing the nose as the plane pointed to the ground three miles down. Five miles. He said good-bye to the man in the Hawaiian shirt and walked to gate 51.

The gate attendant, a thin man with the damaged eyes of someone who lost his last two good jobs for drinking, was getting a flight ready for Salt Lake City. He seemed to be homosexual, and Frank wondered how he guessed. What was it? So many small signs. Frank went to the front of the line.

"Excuse me, I have to ask you something."

The man didn't look up.

"What happened to the flight to Mexico? The one that left at three?"

The attendant said nothing for a moment but looked at Frank, and now Frank felt himself liking the man. He wanted to tell him the truth, which he already knew, but he'd been ordered not to say anything, and he didn't want to lose this job. "If you have any questions, sir, would you please wait. Someone will be here in a few minutes."

"My wife and my daughter were on the plane."

Frank could see that the attendant wondered why Frank was still there if his family had left an hour ago. He held a finger in the air, to hold himself up, Frank supposed, the effort let him forget his feelings. "Just a second." But he looked sad. He got on the phone. "Hi, Betsy, there's a gentleman here who says that his wife—whose wife and child were on flight two-twenty-one." He studied Frank with suppressed awe. "What's your name?"

"Frank Gale. And my wife's name is Anna Klauber, and my daughter is Madeleine." He wanted to say "was," but something held him back. He knew the plane was down, there was no mistake, and he knew his family was dead, but the moment demanded a certain form, and the time for the past tense had not arrived.

"Frank Gale, wife Anna Klauber, daughter Madeleine." The woman working beside the gate attendant was young, with bad skin under a thin crust of makeup. She had listened to the conversation, and she came around the desk. There was still some word necessary from the person on the other end of the line. Was it the woman in the suit? The gate attendant said a few noncommittal "okays" and then put the receiver down. "Amy, why don't you sit down with Mr. Gale? Someone will be here in a few minutes."

Amy put a hand on his shoulder. "Come over here with me." She might have been enjoying the moment.

Frank asked her if the plane had really gone down. He felt something bubbling inside his heart, something giddy within the fire. He was starting to make a new relationship with time, which continued at its old beat while he was speeding up, separate from time. He probably had a temperature already, but there was no headache or pain. Amy took him to a seat and held his hand.

"I was almost on the plane," he told her. "I was late. That's why I'm here. I'm waiting for the six o'clock flight."

"I'm sorry."

"Do they know what happened?"

"Right now I can't even say for sure that there was a crash."

"You mean you can't because you've been told not to talk about it?"

"Mr. Gale, I'm a Christian. I don't want to lie to you and tell you that there wasn't a crash if I knew there was, but until the official word comes from upstairs, you know, it would be awful to tell you that there was a crash if there wasn't." She didn't mean upstairs literally. "The best thing to do is to pray."

"I'm not really religious."

"The Lord can be a tremendous comfort. He has been for me."

"Maybe someday."

"You have to be patient." He watched her, and she seemed now to be on television; she was a projection of herself into this space in front of him. *What would I say to her if the situation was reversed? From whom did I inherit the obligation to be cordial? If this is true, what will I say to my mother and father? To my brother? To everyone? To Mary Sifka? If this is true, does that mean I will never again swim with my daughter in a hotel pool, never again give up the maraschino cherry?*

He could hear the electric cart's erratic whine again. This time it was driven by a white man in a suit. They were coming for him; something big was about to start. The corporate woman sat next to him. The gate attendant nodded in Frank's direction.

Frank knew that by tomorrow he would be in the news, the husband who missed the flight of death. *And they will suspect me,* he thought. He hoped that the plane had hit another plane, anything but a bomb or an implosion from an indeterminate cause, so that no one's doubts about him would linger. *I have an alibi. I was here, waiting for the next flight. Or is that too perfect? And am I capable of such a demonic strategy?*

The electric cart stopped about ten feet away. The man got out and walked to Frank.

"Mr. Gale?"

"Yes."

"My name is Ed Dockery. I'm a vice president of operations with the airline. This is Bettina Welch, my assistant." Now the woman in the suit had a name. Dockery looked like so many Americans, a persistent dumb guy promoted to a job with a little authority. Was he a lost man, a big baby with his big baby's beer belly, or was he a man comfortable with his job, comfortable with his pleasures, who liked to eat and watch his belly grow? And Bettina Welch—there was something slightly diminished about Bettina

Welch now that she was up so close. She wore a thin gold chain around her left ankle, and her suit was cheap, a light purple that matched her lipstick. Like Dockery, she seemed to be someone who would forever stay in the middle of the corporate bureaucracy. But why? Another one of those collections of indications, unsophistications, but what did that mean? He was right, he knew he was right, but how did he know? Because she looked dumb? What does that mean, dumb? Because her fabric was stiff? Because the color was ugly? But why ugly? And how did senior management look at her? Frank imagined that if she ever went on weekend retreats with management, where the president and the senior staff would present the company's goals to the airline's regional managers, Frank was sure that in the competition for sex, she would go to the best-looking highest-ranking executive, unless there was a band at the Saturday night cocktail party, in which case she would sleep with the bass player.

"What happened to the plane?"

"We don't know yet. But the N.T.S.B. boys are terrific, and when they're done with the investigation, they'll know the whole story. You'll just have to be patient."

"N.T.S.B.?" asked Frank.

"National Transportation Safety Board," said Bettina, in a way that convinced Frank she voted Republican, something in her pride in knowing acronyms, and her superiority over those who don't.

Frank took a seat in the cart, and Dockery drove them through the terminal. By now word had spread about the crash, people coming into the terminal had heard about it on their radios, and the gate attendants knew about Frank. People watched him, cooking up faces that tried to show their sympathy.

Dockery took them to an elevator for which he had the key. Frank recognized in himself the rush of grandiose anticipation he felt when he went backstage at concerts, when the girls who did anything to sleep with musicians looked at him, trying to gauge, by his clothes and his hair, what role he had in the concert. But no one ever offered him a blow-job to get backstage.

"Where are we going?" asked Frank. It occurred to him that

they had no hold over him; he could leave now if he wanted. What
if he made a joke; what would they do if he told them that he
wouldn't talk without his lawyer present, and that before he went
anywhere else with them, they had to advise him of his rights? They
would not laugh. He supposed that until the truth were known, he
should conform to ACCEPTABLE STANDARDS OF GRIEF. The
woman at the gate, the attendant, her tears, the way she held back
only her screams. Will I cry like that? he wondered. Not now.

They went up one floor and then walked down a hallway. He
was taken to a heavy wood-paneled door, with a discreet button
beside it on the wall. There was a small brass plate with the airline's
emblem on the door.

The woman who opened the door was about fifty, with carefully
styled gray hair. Frank guessed she had been a flight attendant,
because she had dry, lined skin on a youthful expression, and she
was trim; there were so many women about her age who looked
young, thought Frank. Did fifty-year-old women always look so
young? Diet and exercise and a positive attitude. She was introduced
to him. Mary Aberg. Another Mary. He was going to have to remember a lot of names.

They brought him through the lounge to another door, to a
conference room with couches and telephones. Mary Aberg offered
him a drink. He said no.

Ed Dockery and Bettina Welch nodded to Aberg, and she re-
treated. Now it was time to make the news official. It was Dockery's
job.

"Mr. Gale."

"Call me Frank."

"Frank, flight two-twenty-one crashed about an hour ago. It
exploded in midair just south of San Diego, and crashed into a
crowded neighborhood. Everyone in the plane was killed, and we
don't know how many people on the ground were killed, possibly
fifty or sixty more, possibly many more. The plane was at twenty-
eight-thousand feet when it went down. I'm sure they never knew
what happened." He stopped. Frank could see that this kind of
speech had been rehearsed, and research must have proven that

the best way to handle the survivors was to tell the truth quickly, and to let the questions come. Frank could have asked Dockery how he knew that no one suffered, but what would have been the point? Unless they were killed in the explosion, if that's what it was, they fell with the plane. One one thousand, two one thousand, three one thousand, four one thousand, five one thousand. Even if the plane hit the ground five seconds after the event, there was time to have a few dreadful thoughts. Five seconds is a tennis ball from an office building. This is twenty-eight-thousand feet. Five miles? Almost. Thirty seconds? The plane flying. Seat belts already unfastened. People walking. Madeleine standing on the seat. The flight attendants with the drink carts in the aisles. Free-fall. And then what? A wing tank explodes, an engine falls off.

What is the rate of a falling object? Thirty-two feet per second per second.

What does that mean? Faster and faster.

"Do they know what happened?"

"Not yet."

Bettina Welch sat beside him and took his hand. "We all lost people on that plane, Frank. The airline is a family too. I knew the co-pilot, and one of the girls, I was her bridesmaid last year." One of the girls—that meant one of the flight attendants. At that moment he could have fucked Miss Welch on the carpet; he had an erection and the feeling that at this moment, if he gave in to all of his impulses, he could taste immortality, no one would punish him for anything, he had the king's right to take whomever he wanted, because he was superior in ways only dimly imaginable to someone as common as this cheap groupie in a dead-end job. He could have fucked her, and she would have let him. He forced himself to hold a steady gaze until her eyes brushed his, and she felt it, because he'd seen that look before, it was Mary Sifka's when they'd first met. But Welch wasn't as smart as Mary Sifka, so she couldn't elaborate the sexual moment, and Frank let the hurricane of possibilities pass away. Did Miss Welch know that this had been a flicker of rape? She relaxed; her shoulders had been tense, and now they fell. He tried once more to see himself pulling down her panty hose and twisting her pubic hair, but there was no pressure behind the fantasy; the image seemed borrowed.

"I want to make a phone call." He said this without knowing whose voice he wanted to hear, but he didn't want to deal with Miss Welch anymore. Has she felt anything of what I've been thinking?

She gave him a phone. "Just dial nine to get an outside line." He dialed 9, and then Lowell's number in San Diego. The phone wouldn't let him complete the call; a recording told him that he couldn't dial that area code.

"I can't dial that area code," he said.

Ed Dockery took the phone. He tried a number. "Shit," he said. "There's a block on this phone. It's to keep anyone from calling long distance without paying for it. You're supposed to use this only for local calls."

"This modern age," said Frank.

Dockery dialed another number. He spoke to someone and then asked Frank what number he was calling. Frank told him, and then Dockery hung up. "They'll get it for us," said Dockery.

The three of them looked at the phone for the minute it took to complete the call. Dockery answered and then gave the phone to Frank.

"Hello?" Frank wasn't sure who he'd be speaking to.

"Yes?" said the woman on the other end.

"Is this Lowell Gale's office?"

"You have the wrong number."

Frank hung up. "It was a wrong number. Let me call collect."

"Maybe that would be better," said Dockery. "And then submit the bill to us, we'll reimburse you."

In the other room, the main lounge, Frank could hear a woman screaming. Welch got up to see what the problem was while Frank pushed the 9 and then the Operator button.

Lowell's secretary accepted the call.

"Is Lowell there?" Frank asked.

"He's in La Jolla."

"Could you connect me?"

"I think he's in his car."

"Then you can definitely connect me."

"Just hold on. What number are you at if there's a break?"

There was no number on the phone, just an extension number, 3. "I don't think you can get through to this line. If it doesn't work, I'll have to call you back."

She put him on hold, but it didn't take long.

"Why aren't you in Mexico?" asked Lowell. Frank heard the sounds of traffic in the background; his brother's voice was surrounded by a wall of noisy air.

"I was late for the plane, Lowell. I missed the flight. And it crashed, they say it crashed in San Diego."

"Wow," said Lowell. "Talk about luck." So Lowell thought that Anna and Madeleine missed the flight, too.

"I said that *I* missed the plane," said Frank. "I was late to the airport, I was meeting Anna and Madeleine, but they made it."

"What?" asked Lowell. He understood.

"They were on the plane, Lowell. They're dead."

"Anna, Madeleine?"

"They're dead, Lowell."

"It was that crash south of the city."

"How close to the border?"

"I don't know."

"I was just wondering."

"Frank. My God, Frank."

"I'm at the airport now. Maybe you could come up. I think I'm going to need some help."

Lowell was crying. Frank had seen people crying in their cars, usually women; he always imagined that they had just left their boyfriends, or that their boyfriends had told them to leave, or that they had been fired for incompetence from jobs that weren't so demanding. He had never seen a forty-year-old man in a car crying while he was talking on the car phone. Lowell drove a Ford Explorer.

"I'll be there in three hours. Should I come to the airport?"

Ed Dockery and Bettina Welch had walked across the room, to the door that was now open to the lounge. There were three groups of people in the lounge: airline officials, a few first-class travelers, and another ten or so people who only an hour and a half ago had said good-bye to their families and friends who had just died in San Diego.

He heard someone say that she had heard about the crash on the radio. Someone else said the same thing.

His privilege as the first of the next of kin to show up would soon be over, and he would be ushered into the crowd. He called to Ed Dockery, who came to him immediately.

"What do you need?"

"How long will I have to be here?"

"You don't have to be here at all if you don't want, but the airport chaplain is on his way over and also some grief counselors. And personally I don't think you should leave on your own; is there anyone who can meet you here?"

Frank nodded and returned to Lowell on the phone. "I'm not going anywhere for a while."

"She was so beautiful, Madeleine. She was just so beautiful."

Frank said, "Yes," and then he put the phone down. Bettina Welch was standing next to him. She had something to say, and he guessed she wanted him to join the others in the lounge.

"Mr. Gale, the chaplain is here now, and so is Mr. Dahlgren, who'll be acting as liaison with the airline. Would you come into the lounge?"

Someone had moved the first-class passengers out of the room. How many people were canceling their travel plans because of the crash? Or would they say to themselves, like gamblers playing a roulette number because it hadn't come up in a long time, that they were safe now, because the odds were against two crashes on the same airline leaving the same airport in one three-hour period?

A television crew was trying to get into the lounge. The chaplain was a Catholic priest, a Filipino with a little charisma. As he began a benediction, another airline official opened the door for the cameras. Frank supposed that part of the airline's strategy now was to show the world that THE AIRLINE'S FIRST RESPONSIBILITY IS TO THE MOURNERS. The language of the catastrophe would be managed by the airline. He had seen this before, disasters on the

news, and now he was a part of it. How many crashes are the direct
fault of the airlines? They said this was an explosion. Terrorism?
Arab? Or some other group. A plane to Mexico. It could be anyone.
Mexican politics. What a stupid way to die, worse than just slamming
into a mountaintop because of bad weather and bad radar. They
probably know more than they're saying. All that crying at the gate:
Was there a feeling of some extra shock, an added horror? Why
had the crying woman been so fiercely miserable? A friend of hers
died, and she was feeling her grief. What other explanation? Lam-
entations. The keening of women. Not so self-conscious—they are
not like me.

The priest blessed the living and the dead. Did he believe what
he was saying, or was it only by rote? People around him were
crying. It had been a day of different kinds of tears. In the morning
Madeleine had asked him to carry her from the den to the kitchen,
and he told her he would hold her hand. He didn't like carrying
her in the house, he wanted her to walk by herself, to tolerate being
alone in a room, he wanted to build her character, make her less
dependent. He didn't know if this was a stage from which she'd
grow, in which case carrying her would not sap her moral fiber, or
if she was testing him, in which case it was essential that she learn
to walk by herself. He offered to hold her hand, and she had taken
it, lightly, and kept crossing his path with her arms wide, blocking
and imploring him. He had refused to carry her, and so she had
cried, but the tears were not from a deep well, and by the time he
half pulled her by the hand into the kitchen, she was already asking
him to let her feed the goldfish. He had to lift her up to the counter,
and she got the hug she had wanted. Later he had seen a tear in
Mary Sifka's eyes. He had brushed it aside with his finger, a gesture
he regretted in the limousine on the way to the airport. He should
have let her cry, alone. Just as he should have let Madeleine walk,
alone. But was it fair to compare those tears, since Madeleine's
were strategic, and Mary Sifka's, although they rode on the surface
of a grief that was complicated, for an impossible love that had run
its course, told him that she mourned the death of a passion, of a
friendship? Mary was going to miss him; she was going to miss the

friendship. Why had he given this up? Why did I construct this stupid drama? If I had left things alone, I could have kept Mary Sifka, and my family would still be alive. Don't some people manage with a mistress and a wife? Lowell has his share of lovers, thought Frank. Before the plague, he had a boyfriend, and other friends. And he never caught it. Lowell had the flu once, and everyone was scared; no one wanted to say what they were afraid of, that he was going to get sicker and sicker, with sores, and pain, and that Frank would have to take over the business, and would run it into the ground. And when Lowell had that flu, and before he recovered, Frank almost welcomed his death, because he thought, If Lowell dies, I can show them all, I can run the business too. I just need to have it to myself. And then Lowell got better. Frank's mother called him with the news when Lowell's fever dropped, and he hated her at that moment, because he knew she would never have called Lowell with such relief, such gratitude to God, if Frank had been through the same thing. His mother's tears that day came from an abundance of emotion. They were different from Madeleine's and also from those of Mary Sifka, who cried from self-pity, but who else was there to give her the sympathy she needed?

The gate attendant's tears were the deepest he had seen today. Some of the tears around him in the lounge were unconvincing, exaggerated, theatrical. A woman in front of him, screaming out loud and looking at the cameras, was she a bad version of herself, or was she connected to the people who had blown the plane up, and therefore acting the part of the mourner, or was she secretly, even from her unsophisticated self, relieved about the death, and already counting the money from the insurance settlement? But I cannot cry, thought Frank. This hurt him, that he couldn't find a grief large enough to extinguish the world, that the mundane distractions of life were still so close, so much a part of the moment.

How much money would this be worth? he wondered. Frank was insured for $2 million, Anna for $1 million. Because he was worth more to the marriage. What will the airline pay? How quickly will the money come? They'll want to settle, of course, avoid the lawyers, that has to happen soon. Someone will approach me and say something about how difficult it is to think about insurance at a time like this, but lawsuits can take years, and the lawyers claim a third, and this is what we've settled for in the past, and this is what this kind of crash has traditionally brought, and wouldn't you rather get over the tragedy and get on with your life, knowing that you'll never have to go to court and face the story all over again?

And it all depends on fault.

If the wing fell apart because of bad maintenance, how much? Ten million? A wife and a child. A wife and a child. Think about that.

And will there be a funeral? Will I have to go to a funeral with all these strangers? People I don't know?

And how do I claim the bodies? Will there be bodies? An explosion. They could have been launched into the air as the plane broke up in the sky, and when they hit the ground, or a roof, or a tree, what happened? Does the body keep its shape?

And if they stayed in the plane, strapped to their seats, and there was a fire when they hit, what would remain? Drop a melon from a few feet, a mess of seeds, flesh, and rind. A body from four miles? Does the body maintain its integrity falling from twenty-eight-thousand feet? Thirty-two feet per second per second. Thirty-five pounds, and 122 pounds. The body is made of mostly water. Water balloons filled with blood and bone. And the fire on the ground. And houses. Someone had told him, he'd forgotten who said it, that sixty people died on the ground. I am a part of the news.

There was a television, and people were watching it. A squad of airline executives was in the room now, taking down names, making phone calls to relatives, arranging for rooms at a nearby hotel for anyone who wanted them.

A man with a large belly came to ask him questions. He looked like a drinker and a fisherman, something about his confidence, he knew he wasn't ever going to be rich, or running the company, and he knew he had as much sense as any executive, but it didn't gall him. Frank wondered if he had ever been twenty-seven and unhappy.

His unhappiness would have come only from immediate dramas in the family; he wasn't a man to change jobs or even think of anything like a career.

"Mr. Gale?"

"Yes."

"Bill Modell." He said it Moh-*dell,* the way he would before he told people over the phone how to spell it. "I'm with Customer Service. I've been asked to pitch in and help out with this, and they'd like me to ask a few questions, if you don't mind."

He smiled at the end of each sentence. This annoyed Frank, but he didn't want to say anything, although he thought that the event had given him sanction to say anything to anyone today.

How can I use it? he wondered. So much money. A rich widower in Los Angeles.

"How can I help you?" asked Frank.

Modell sighed. Frank thought that this was a man with genuine emotions. "It's important, as we put this all together, to know as much as we can about every aspect of the crash."

"What do you want to ask me?" Frank was losing patience; he had hoped that Modell would have presented a way to manage grief, but he was floundering.

"Do you know what your wife and daughter were wearing?"

"I came from work, from lunch, a business lunch, sort of, a friend, an old friend, but it was business." There was no reason to say this, but he felt a compulsion to explain why he missed the flight, why he was something of a ghost. "I don't know if Anna changed for the flight. She was probably wearing something black, probably expensive exercise clothing, you know, sweatpants and a sweatshirt—she liked to be comfortable when she traveled. Maybe she wore a skirt, I don't know, I doubt it. This was a vacation. And Madeleine, I don't know. I'm sure Anna changed her outfit. She was wearing these green overalls in the morning, but I doubt she had it on for the flight. I can go home and look in her closet for what's missing, but I don't know her clothing that well. I'm sorry I can't be of any help."

"The reason we ask is that clothing, even pieces of it, can be tested for traces of chemicals, explosives, if it was a bomb, and by tracing back to a particular seat, we can figure out what kind of device was used, how big it was."

"Was it a bomb?"

"We don't know. These questions have to be asked, Mr. Gale."

"How many people were on the plane?"

"A crew of ten, and a hundred and thirty-nine passengers."

"How many children?"

"Six or seven. There may have been an unregistered infant."

"And on the ground? How many were killed in San Diego? Sixty?"

"We don't know yet." He paused. For a moment he stared at the floor, and then his shoulders relaxed. He looked back at Frank. "Mr. Gale, I want you to know how sorry I am about this." There was a tone of personal responsibility in his voice, he emphasized the first *I*, as though others might not want Frank to know about their sorrow, as though by expressing himself, he was already violating the company's orders. If Modell had bitter children, and they saw him now, trying to be honest, would they regret their contempt for him? He asked if Frank wanted to stay at a hotel.

"Where is it?"

"The Sheraton. Two minutes by car. We think it might be a good idea—it gives all of you a chance to help each other through the first hard days." And keep us from the press, thought Frank, but he liked the idea of a hotel room. He could tell the desk not to let through any phone calls. He could watch a movie on television. He could order room service. Lowell would be here soon, and they could stay up late and talk and get drunk. If Modell was around the hotel, Frank supposed that he could be invited in for a drink, but he thought that Modell would be interesting only in the loose way that all people are sort of interesting if you ask the right questions and find out about their obsessions, even if all that keeps their minds going are a few old insults and family squabbles elevated to the central facts of their lives. But if he started to talk to Modell about music or movies, he knew that the fat man would disappoint him, and with his stupid opinions try to hog the conversation at the same time. So he wouldn't talk to him once this little interview was over.

Modell asked him what kind of luggage Anna had taken, and what she had packed. Frank described it as best as he could. He thought that these interviews were a clever device; he was talking about the crash in a way that was strictly controlled, and even if this was just the expression of a sinister corporate protocol for disaster management, something developed by psychologists as a good way to get the person with the potential lawsuit to think of the airline as a friend, there was comfort in the process.

No one had yet introduced any of the survivors to each other, and there were now about fifty in the room. Frank thought that he was the only one who was alone, since everyone else had brought someone for support.

Ed Dockery got up and called for everyone to listen to him. For those who wanted to go, it was time to move to the Sheraton. They were to board a bus and would be settled in at the hotel in twenty minutes. Frank stopped Dockery after the announcement and told him that his brother was coming, and Dockery told Frank not to worry, they'd tell him where to go.

3. Buffet

Lowell called from the lobby, and Frank gave him the room number. He had a few minutes to think about things while his brother found the elevator. He worried about his brother, how his brother would try to take over the situation and tell him how to suffer and tell others how to treat him, how to give them both respect.

There was a knock. Frank opened the door, and Lowell was there. The expected hug. Frank patted Lowell's shoulder, as though Lowell needed the comfort more than he did.

In the family's mythology Frank had one respected attribute, his role as peacemaker. Lowell, for all of his brilliance in business, brought his attack to the dinner table, and what had been, in childhood, to his mother, a lawyerlike precocity, was now sometimes exhausting. The only time their mother was ever really impatient with Lowell was at dinner, when Frank was the least indignant. But Frank knew, and he told himself, too often, as a kind of punishment, that to face the truth, any truth, he had to first admit to himself that Lowell really was his superior, emotionally, morally, intellectually. Let their parents pretend they were equal, because they owned equal shares in the business, but Lowell had the better ideas. Did their parents always know that Lowell was better? Or did they believe that the business started as a true partnership? He imagined better parents had the courage to see the differences between their sons, and then act on this knowledge, help them, help the one who needed help. And is this why I was so reluctant to have two children? Fear of the pain of their competition? Fear of having to distinguish between them?

And did their parents ever admit to themselves what they so obviously thought of the partnership? Or did they pretend that it was a kind of unspecific soup of ideas, no separate areas of expertise?

What did they tell their friends? Lowell is the businessman, but Frank is the one closer to the artists. And did the friends think, How odd, since Lowell is the homosexual, and by rights should be closer to the artists than dull Frank? Or did their parents avoid the topic?

It was Lowell who found the locations for the stores, and moved near them as they opened. He kept a condominium in Santa Monica and came to the city for a few days every two or three weeks.

Frank worked with the record companies and distributors, keeping up-to-date on the schedule of new releases, because he was supposed to be the more musical of the two, but that was a convenient lie the brothers told themselves, an accommodation to this: If Lowell died, the business died; if Frank died, the business continued. The business was not about music, but about making a profit selling records.

"My God, Frank. My God."

"Yes," said Frank. He felt a wave of shame for having called
his brother to his side. If his brother had a family, and the family
had been killed, and his brother called for his help, Frank thought
that he would have been annoyed at the interruption of his
daydreams.

"Fuck God, Frank," said Lowell.

Frank wanted to leave God out of this. Frank felt that it was
important to protect God right now and not blame Him for the crash.
He might need God soon and didn't want to give Him an excuse to
bargain with his prayers.

"This is a terrible question," said Lowell, "but I don't know
how else to ask this. How do you feel?"

"I guess I'm in shock. It's hard to feel anything."

"Of course, of course. It's Nature's way, I guess. It protects
you."

"I'd like to feel more."

"Have you cried?"

"Not really."

"If you want to cry, go ahead."

"Thanks, Lowell. But if I don't cry, don't think I'm not unhappy."

"Have you called Mom and Dad?"

"Not yet. I was hoping that you would make the call."

"I thought about it, but I decided to wait. I wanted to see you
first."

"Do you want to call them now?" Frank asked.

"You don't want to speak to them, do you?" Lowell, with this
question, had just left the deaths and entered the arena of gossip
about their parents, which was, more than business, the real event
that united them, and that had brought Lowell close to his now-
dead sister-in-law. What he meant was: Frank would have to use
whatever energy he had to keep his parents from falling apart and
devouring him with their own drama.

"Tell them I can't. Tell them I'm too broken up." Later he would
recognize this as the moment when he began to create his grief for
public consumption.

"They'll want to speak to you."

"Lowell, call them." He insisted, coldly, relieved for a moment of his grief, happy for the right to tell his brother what to do, and Lowell went to the phone.

Lowell started to dial, then stopped. He took a breath and dialed again. "Mom, it's Lowell."

She was used to Lowell calling, probably more often than Frank. Lowell said he was fine and then asked for his father. He asked so abruptly that when he said, "No, I'm fine," Frank could tell that his mother was wounded, she must have had something to say, and here he was, on the phone to talk business. Perhaps she had called him early in the day about something, and when she heard his voice, she thought he was returning the call. And where was Lowell's courtesy, to ask something personal of her, ask after her health?

Lowell covered the receiver with his hand and said to Frank, "She has to get him. I want to tell him and let him tell her."

Then their father came to the phone. Frank watched his brother give him an inappropriate wink. What did it mean? That everything was in control? "Hi, Dad. I'm fine. I don't know how to say this. . . ." He started to cry.

Frank felt betrayed by his brother. The tears were real, but his brother was showing weakness. Why couldn't he just say, calmly, that Anna and Madeleine were on a plane that crashed and they were dead? He wanted to take the phone from Lowell, but then he would have had to speak to his parents. He didn't want to have to offer support to them; he wanted their support.

Lowell tried once more to tell his father what had happened. More tears bubbled from him, and his face broke into a dozen shaking pieces. Frank walked over to him and put a hand on his back, which seemed to be what he needed, a touch.

"I'm sorry, Dad. There was a plane crash. Frank missed the plane, but Madeleine and Anna were killed. Yes, the crash in San Diego. I'm with Frank now, in his hotel room. The airline is putting him up."

Frank took the phone. He wondered if Lowell would have cried had he not told him to tell his parents that he was too upset to talk. He had given his brother the burden of a lie, which ignored his brother's right to grieve.

"Hi, Dad."

"This is real?"

"Yes."

"I don't know how to tell your mother."

"Could you try?"

"Let me call you back. What hotel?"

"The Sheraton. Room ten thirty-five."

"Near the airport?"

"Yes."

"Do you want to stay here?"

"Not now. The airline is putting me up, there's a lot of us here, people who had family on the plane."

"She was so beautiful." Who did he mean, daughter or wife? Daughter.

"I know."

"I'll call you back."

Frank knew this would be hard on his father. He wasn't sure if his father had ever really liked Anna, but his father had loved Madeleine, his first grandchild, and her shining armada of promises. And his mother, what had she thought of his wife?

Did his mother love Anna for loving the son no other woman had ever loved? It was true, Frank had never really said "I love you" to anyone who said "I love you" to him until Anna. Did his mother love his wife for being the daughter she never had, finally to have a woman in the family who would keep her best jewelry after she died? And then to have a granddaughter! So his mother loved Anna for what she brought to the family, although he wasn't sure if his mother loved Anna for herself. And perhaps his mother was, at least before the wedding, suspicious of Anna for loving this awkward, unlovable boy, although Anna's love for Frank may have taught his mother something about him, that he was capable of love. Or did his mother love Anna simply because she married a twenty-eight-year-old who had never lived with a woman and whose brother was homosexual? Yes, it was possible that his mother would have loved any woman he had married, because the woman who married Frank rescued Ethel and Leon from having two homosexual sons. So his mother could say that Lowell's homosexuality was nature, not nurture.

Lowell asked Frank if he wanted a drink.

"I don't know," said Frank.

"Why not?"

"You can have one if you want," said Frank.

"But why don't you want one?"

"I'd like to know what my feelings are."

"There's no shame in wanting to give yourself a little warmth," said Lowell. "You're not some kind of Mormon. You can have a drink."

Frank wanted to ask his brother how he could be so sure of Mormon grieving rituals, but checked himself.

"I want to stay sharp," said Lowell, "in case you need help."

"What do you need to be sharp for?"

"If your wife and daughter had been killed in a car crash . . . it would be different, but this, this is . . ."

"What are you trying to say?" Frank cut into Lowell's meandering thoughts quickly, even with a suggestion of impatience and cruelty, telling his brother that to be anything but precise and honest, right now, was morally without defense.

"If they died with no one else, if it was their fault . . ."

"What are you trying to say?" Frank felt himself rising toward hysteria, and this flight into a vicious rage at his brother's pauses felt to him like the first good thing that had happened since he heard that his family was dead.

"The airline is keeping you here because they know that this is going to cost them millions of dollars, if it's their fault. And I need to be sharp, to make sure that someone doesn't get you alone and try to put your signature on a settlement."

"So why couldn't you just say that?" Frank heard himself scream at his brother.

Lowell stopped crying. "Because I'm thinking about money, and I wish I weren't."

The phone rang again. Frank picked it up.

"Mr. Gale?"

"Yes."

"This is Bettina Welch. I met you this afternoon."

"Yes."

"I'm here in the command center, in the ballroom. It's extension two-oh-one-five. Or you can just ask the operator to connect you. We're down here on the mezzanine level if you want to come—we're available for all the survivors. Or you can stay in the room, and you can order room service if you're hungry, of course, or you can join us down here. The buffet will be open all night."

"Thank you," said Frank, aware of his automatically good manners. Frank thought there was something dishonest in calling him a survivor, an inflation. The survivors were the people who were on the plane but didn't die. But everyone on the plane was dead. So the survivors were people on the ground whose houses were destroyed, and who were in the houses but were not killed.

"How are you feeling?"

"Not well."

"Is there anyone with you? Do you want someone to come up to your room and be with you? Would you like to talk to a minister or a rabbi?"

"My brother is here."

"That's good. Because you need to be with someone now. Our psychologists are telling us that it's important that all the survivors have someone for support right now. We have grief counselors with us now, and we'll assign one to you as soon as we can. We don't want you to be alone. And you're not alone."

"No. I have my brother."

"You can bring your brother down here too, of course. Whatever he needs, whatever you need, we're here for you."

"Thank you."

Lowell looked up at Frank and made a face to say, What are they asking you? Why are you saying so little? Who is it?

"And please feel free to take advantage of the hotel, use the room service, it's available twenty-four hours, or make all the phone calls you want."

"Thank you."

"If you need any clothing, let me know your sizes, and I can get you what you need, underwear, a shirt, socks."

"Not now."

"And toiletries, toothbrushes, toothpaste, shampoo."

"I think there's shampoo in the bathroom."

"Well, if you need more."

"Right."

"We all lost people we loved, Mr. Gale. All of us."

"Yes."

"Whole families were killed."

"Unh." It was all he could say, a grunt.

"When will you be coming down?"

"I don't know."

"The buffet. It looks very good."

"I don't know how hungry I am."

"Of course. Maybe you'll just have some soup."

"That sounds good."

"Soup is very comforting."

"I'll see you down there."

Lowell turned on the television. It was a few minutes after seven o'clock, and the crash was the hour's lead story.

A woman who lived across the street was describing what she had seen. The plane had rolled across the street, breaking into three pieces, tearing up the block. She was asked if she had known people across the street. Of course she had. "This is a neighborhood. Of course I know my neighbors."

At least fifty people were known to have died on the ground. The count was expected to rise. Someone expected as many as another hundred dead from the neighborhood.

The reporter on the scene was replaced by the anchorwoman in Los Angeles. She then introduced an interview with a crash expert, William Hoyt. The interview had probably taken twenty minutes, but only one sentence of the interview was shown, Hoyt saying, "We don't know yet what caused the crash."

Before the anchorwoman returned, and then introduced a commercial, the last shot of the crash scene was of a dog running down the street with a child's shoe in its mouth. "Jesus, how can they show that?" asked Lowell. "That could be Madeleine's shoe." He was screaming at the television.

"Lowell, that's not her shoe."

"How can they do that?" asked Lowell. Frank could see he was getting ready for a fight.

"Do what?"

"Show the dog with the shoe. That's so exploitive. Can't they leave anything alone?" Lowell screamed at the television, "You sentimental assholes!"

Frank had to put his arms around Lowell, and he turned off the set. He repeated, "It's okay."

Lowell guided Frank's hand away and then slumped forward, staring at the floor for a long moment. He was ashamed of himself.

"Come on, Lowell, let's get something to eat."

In the hall they passed a room with someone inside, another mourner, crying, "No. No." Unless it was someone making love, and they weren't hearing "No," they were hearing a sound, the usual pleasure of pain, release delayed.

Lowell walked a little ahead of Frank. It was always this way, Lowell thinking about something and Frank thinking about Lowell's better thoughts.

When the elevator opened to the lobby, Frank saw a crush of news people, photographers, camera crews, reporters with microphones. They will find me, he thought. It's only a matter of hours before they find the man who missed Death Flight 221.

They walked across the lobby to an escalator that brought them back up to the mezzanine. Bettina Welch was at the door to the ballroom.

In what must have been the quick setup of the room, the hotel mixed the symbols of different occasions. The buffet, beginning in salads, with the irrefutable peaks of a ham and a turkey in the center, and then falling away again to a flat zone of cookies and cakes and packages of yogurt, was too lavish, and the three chefs, in their toques, were more appropriate for a brunch. Mustard-yellow tablecloths were on the fifty or so round tables, without the rest of the service, no napkins or silverware, so the room looked as if it were about to be cleared. Not set? No, the tables were dirty, a lot of people smoked, and there were ashtrays everywhere. There were a hundred or so people—as many as the dead on the ground in San Diego?—in the room, at the tables, and airline officials were with them. Someone had placed a few television sets around the room, tuned to the news. And the crash was the news.

Frank closed his eyes. He tried to construct from the sounds in the room a feeling of unhappiness, but there was something else that he couldn't yet define for himself, something that made the room unpleasant, a feeling of privilege. If he blocked out the occasional sobbing he could have been in a nightclub before the headliner came onstage. What was it? Cigarettes, alcohol, air-conditioning, the disinfectant that adhered to the carpet. He opened his eyes. There were a few tables of Mexicans, little children tended by older children, and Frank, who usually felt envious of these large families, now hated them for their resignation. They sat quietly, waiting for direction. Two Mexicans wearing blue jackets and brass name tags were with them. They were reservations clerks pulled in for the assignment, to translate. Frank supposed they were hoping that their good work here would lead to promotions.

"No!" a woman cried. Frank looked for her.

She cried again, "No!"

She was a tired woman in her fifties, with copper-colored hair and skin healed badly over acne. She sat in the middle of the room, at a table with (her husband?), thin, quiet, chewing gum, and a friend (her sister?), the same generation, the same look of defeat. There was a feeling coming from the table of people choking on their own gall, that the deaths of whoever had brought them to this ballroom were just more cards in the bad hand that life was always dealing.

"My baby!" she screamed. "They killed my baby!" She stood up. She screamed again, without a clear word.

"Sit down," said her husband.

*"My baby is dead!" she screamed again. The shriek brought others in the room to tears, reminded of their own dead.

Her voice rose and fell on surges of emotion and complicated streams of memories that shifted with all the feelings of a bad relationship that will never be reconciled. Her desperate shrieks might have been unbearable for everyone in the room, but there crept into this extended solo of pure feeling a cheap ornament, a self-consciousness that announced her indignation, her lawsuit. If she had not admitted the deposition into her grief, then everyone in the room might have been sanctified, if only for a few hours, by the presence of so strong and real a thing as these cries. Instead, she was embarrassing, and reminded everyone of the fortunes waiting for them.

Bettina Welch rushed to her table. The woman was standing and screaming, "They killed my baby. They killed my baby," and Bettina forced the woman into her arms, to give her a hug. The woman didn't want to accept or return the embrace; she was hysterical and pushed Bettina back, but the executive held on, as though she were the one who needed comfort, and in the effort it took the woman to give this hug to a stranger, in the awareness of the public spectacle of her reluctance, her misery was brought to scale. Tamed, she sat down, and Bettina stroked her hair. She sat down next to her.

Now the woman broke into silent crying, and Bettina hugged her again, pulled the woman into her chest. The sister reached a hand across the table, and the copper-haired woman held on to it while Bettina slowly rocked her from side to side. Everyone in the room was quiet, watching. There was only the sound of the news on the television sets, which had left the scene of the accident to return to local stories. One of the Mexican reservations clerks thought to turn the televisions off, and went around the room, like a butler blowing out the candles.

Bettina guided the sister to her side of the table, without breaking contact with the woman's hands, and then gave her control of the hug. The husband put a hand on his wife's shoulder, and if he seemed ashamed of her, Frank thought perhaps he was too lost in his own unhappiness and could not find the way to ask for help. Or else he wanted a hug.

"Jesus," said Lowell, to no particular end. It was just a thing to say, to finish the ceremony for himself.

Then Bettina Welch came over to Frank and gave him his own hug.

"I think you need one too," she said.

It was stronger than their brief intimacy would have deserved under other circumstances, but the hug she had just finished now granted her the franchise on mercy for the room. There was something unfairly demanding in the hug; Frank could not hate the airline as much as he wanted to now that this woman from the airline was telling him that they shared something so powerful each would forever recognize the wounds of this day in the other, that they were now both initiates in the same clan. We are not, he wanted to tell her. We are not the same. We do not suffer the same disaster.

Against his will, he returned the hug with force. She set the rhythm, forcing him to sway with her. The belligerent sweetness of the hug, the unrequested familiarity of it, gave way, and he could feel her spine, her breasts, her belly, and he began to judge them, to think about how firm or soft she was, whether her stomach was flat or a little round, and what her breasts would look like. So there was sex, finally, the moment of awareness of difference, and the hug ended.

He introduced her to his brother.

Lowell said, "Did you lose someone on the plane?"

"I knew two of the girls real well." Bettina's friendship implied something at least equal to the loss of Frank's wife and young daughter.

"Do they know what happened yet?" Lowell asked.

"We probably won't know for a few days," said Bettina.

Lowell persisted. "Do they have any ideas?" Frank could see

that his brother wanted to be angry with Bettina, since she represented the airline. Lowell's secretary once told Frank that he wasn't
an easy man to work for. Frank had then said to her, pointlessly,
as though her intimacy breached something significant. "We're equal
partners, you know." And she looked at him, and he saw she thought
he was a fool. Did everyone in all the stores think of him in the
same way? Yes. And now his boss was trying to find Bettina Welch's
breaking point, so he could make her cry.

"It's too soon to know," said Bettina, "and it's dark now, so the
crews can't search for clues."

"They have voice recorders on these planes, don't they? And
wasn't the plane in contact with the ground? What were the pilot's
last words?"

"I don't know."

"Somebody does."

"Sir, I'm here to help the survivors, I'm not here as a spokes-
person for the airline."

"You can help the survivors by telling them what the airline
knows. Otherwise, the lawsuits are going to be even bigger."

"Mr. Gale, I can promise you the airline is doing everything in
its power to help the survivors."

"You're a fucking corporate whore, you're a fucking corporate
liar," said Lowell. Lowell was used to making those who worked for
him unhappy, but Bettina Welch worked for something else, not a
man but a company with thousands of people on the payroll. Bettina
Welch was not frightened of Lowell.

"Lowell," said Frank, "don't." Meaning: Don't be your usual
posturing, difficult self. Meaning: You have put this woman in an
impossible position, she can't tell you what you want to know, you
have to speak to someone higher up. Meaning: Apologize for your
language.

Frank had no real power; he was everyone's buddy. When he
was angry, when he yelled, there was a gracelessness to his rage;
his energy was not contained, and he threw his arms into the air,
awkwardly, and lost whatever little presence he had.

"Frank, she's not on your side, she's working for the airline. You can't trust her."

"I understand how you feel, Mr. Gale." Bettina Welch was in harmony with the gods of public relations now, and she read her line perfectly. The way she said *I*, weighted with a penny, just enough to register her own ego but not so much to compete with the corporation. And then *understand how*, a small break in the first word dropping as she spoke it, to say, I can't possibly feel all of your grief, of course, but I know that your grief is making you not responsible for your actions, and so I cannot take your actions personally, and so I cannot take your promised threats seriously, because no one cares to listen to a lunatic, which is how I am treating you now, and which is how you will see yourself when you think about the awful things you said to me. And then after *understand how*, she said *you feel*, telling Lowell that the crash was not a matter of metal, flame, and flesh, but opinions.

"No, you don't understand how I feel," he said, but he sounded nasal; the anger had drifted out of his belly into his head.

"Mr. Gale, both of us are under a lot of stress right now, and I have to talk to some other families. If you want, we have psychological counselors here in the ballroom. Would you like to speak to one of them?"

"Forget it," said Lowell, backing away from the fight as though he hadn't lost it. "I guess I am getting a little out of control here."

"Let's sit down," said Frank. Frank took Lowell by the arm and led him to a television set.

"I feel terrible," said Frank.

"I know."

"I hope they didn't suffer too much," said Frank.

"Well, if the plane blew up in the air, if there's any consolation, they probably passed out."

"If they weren't killed immediately," said Frank.

"It's probably a good idea to let yourself have all these feelings right now. Whatever images come to mind, I want you to talk about them with me."

"I wish I didn't feel so numb."

"Would you mind if I had a drink?" asked Lowell.

"Are you giving up the lawsuit?" asked Frank. He meant this to be taken lightly, and his brother smiled.

"What the hell," said Lowell, but Frank didn't know what he meant by this. Was he throwing the lawsuit away, or was he just taking a vacation from his anger, in which case, was he also taking a vacation from his grief?

"Go ahead," said Frank. "Get me one."

"What do you want?" Lowell looked relieved that Frank was joining him. Frank began to make a silent vow not to get drunk, but checked himself. He would try to have only one drink, without making any sacred promises. He asked for a beer, then changed his mind and said he wanted a scotch.

"You're sure?" said Lowell.

"No, give me a beer." He was worried about the headache he might get from scotch, since he hadn't tasted any in months.

When Lowell went to the bar, Frank regretted asking for beer; beer was not a drink for comfort but celebration. Nothing here had been achieved except an accidental massacre. And what of the beer he drank in the airport bar, before the news broke? He had been celebrating two things, his thirst and the inevitable fight he would have with his wife, now that she had read the letter.

Lowell came back with the beer in a glass in one hand and a scotch in the other. Lowell gave him the beer, and he took a sip. It was all wrong, the way he had expected it to taste; it was like having a beer in the morning when he didn't want a drink at all. Even the pleasant kick of the alcohol annoyed him, an inspiration to relax that made him hate himself, but he finished the glass.

"That guy over there, at the bar"—Lowell pointed to a man in a T-shirt and running shorts—"his next-door neighbor lost her parents on the flight. She was screaming when he heard her, she was on the phone, and he drove her down here."

"Her parents," said Frank, dumbly.

"He heard someone say that it was a bomb on the plane."

"Terrorists?"

"Not necessarily. Maybe someone who worked for the airline."

"Does it really make any difference?" Frank snapped. It was the beer; he was feeling gloomy when he should have been miserable, and the gloom led him to sulk.

"Why are we here?" asked Lowell. Meaning: We are sitting in this awful hotel conference room like students detained by the vice principal who caught them running in the halls. We don't have to be here. And more: We are better than these others in the room, we have more money. Even more: We can get better lawyers, lawyers as good as the airline will hire.

"Where would we go?"

"Home."

"I don't want to go home. I don't want to see the house." He thought this was sloppy of him, cowardly not to face his daughter's dolls, books, blocks, and his wife's French shoes, her makeup, their bed.

Ed Dockery was crossing the room, and Frank knew he was going to have to talk some more about what couldn't be changed. Frank Gale was Ed Dockery's assignment. There were other men in the room with the same sober respect, who moved among a few tables, sitting for ten or so minutes, talking, making notes on legal pads, and Frank guessed that each had been assigned to only a few families, not to spread the airline's attention so thinly that in the inevitable lawsuits the surviving relatives could add corporate indifference to the list of complaints. "We lost our family, but as if that weren't enough, the airline couldn't find time to talk to us for three hours, because they only had two people in charge." Like not enough waitresses in a crowded coffee shop.

Dockery introduced himself to Lowell. Of course Bettina Welch had warned him that Lowell was difficult.

"I'm his brother," said Lowell.

"There's been a new development here, and we wanted you to know before it goes out on the ten o'clock news."

Frank's heart began to pound, unreasonably, he thought, as if he were guilty, and about to be caught for the thing he had done. Or was it just the fear that he would learn something dreadful, and the foundations of his control would erode in the space of a few seconds, however long it took to hear Dockery's revelation?

"What happened?" said Lowell. It was a challenge to Dockery: He should stop playing the part of the saddened messenger; he should tell the story and not act as if there was anything eternal in Lowell's disdain for him.

"We think that the plane went down because one of our employees, I should say one of our former employees, sneaked a gun onto the plane and killed the pilot."

He told his story quickly, and directly.

"Thank you," said Lowell.

"For what?" asked Dockery.

"For telling us the truth."

Frank wanted to say, Yes, that was kind of you. Something between the two men went unspoken; it had to do with integrity, and Frank didn't understand it. Instead, he asked, "Why?" although he didn't really care. So they died for nothing. If a Palestinian had blown the plane out of the sky, Frank could always warm himself on the fires of history, he could tell the world that his life had been touched by the terrible events of this awful century, that he was now a part of history. Their deaths, however tragic, would have been given some meaning. He would have had an enemy too, a movement, an ideology. He saw himself, letting the fantasy roll ahead to its conclusion, as someone who could even RELUC-TANTLY ACCEPT a role as the public spokesman for the victims of terrorism, as the great champion of innocence. Of the innocent victim. But a FORMER EMPLOYEE? Where was the glamour in the fatal radiation from the decaying misery of a DISGRUNTLED EMPLOYEE? Was there anything to gain from the death of his wife and his daughter if a nut case had killed them? What if their murderer had been released from a mental hospital, or had been denied entry to one because the state had no money to take care of him? All the boring editorials! How they would add the name of the nut case to the list of victims of his unhealed rage! Surely he was as much a victim, blah blah blah. And until we solve the problems of the blah blah blah . . . And all the predictable anger at the government, at the social workers who will defend themselves for not having seen the DANGER LURKING in this unhappy man! I will be forgotten in all of this, thought Frank. I will be abandoned. Emptiness surrounded him.

"We don't know why, not yet," said Dockery.

"Did you know him?" asked Lowell. Of course it was a man.

"Just to say hello."

"What did he do?" asked Frank. "What was his job?"

"He was in the freight office."

"Why was he fired?" asked Lowell. Frank was glad his brother was asking all the obvious questions. He didn't want to seem too curious; what would they think if they saw how this interesting development submerged his grief? Lowell could ask any questions, because Lowell had charm; he could make a person happy to answer a rude question. People liked to talk to him. And these questions weren't rude, they were just obvious. Anyone would want to know. Frank thought he should have been able to ask them. I have a RIGHT TO KNOW! Now he wanted another drink.

Dockery was uncomfortable with the question. "All of this was very recent."

"Why did he take down the plane?" asked Lowell. Implied in the way he stressed the word "plane" was the thought that something was out of scale, that the man's murderous anger and need for revenge, if justified, should have satisfied itself with the death of whomever he was angry at. Because it was routine news for people to get fired and go back to their offices and kill the person who fired them. There was no revelation in that kind of news. But a whole plane? And a neighborhood?

"Now look, I'm not supposed to be telling you this," said Dockery, and Frank thought that were the situation reversed, were he the one whose brother had suffered the loss, the airline executive would not confide in him, if Lowell was overcome by his sorrow and couldn't talk for himself. "The man who fired him was on the plane. And he had seven children." Three feathers on a delicate scale tipped the weight on the word "he" and then again on "seven." Is this, Frank wondered, a dig at me, a way of diminishing by comparison my grief for my one child, Dockery's retaliation for Lowell's tirade at Bettina Welch?

Lowell felt the same way but wouldn't keep it to himself. "That's a little tasteless, isn't it, Ed?" He said the name as though only dumb people were called Ed, as though a man with the dignity of a full name, Edward, would be higher up in the company, wouldn't have to take the public's abuse. They teased him as a child. Mr. Ed! Frank loved his brother for defending him like this, but he also heard the insinuated diminishment of his own loss, and had not reacted so quickly.

Dockery said, "I don't know what you mean."

"I think you do," said Lowell.

"Lowell," said Frank. "Forget about it."

"You know what he's saying," said Lowell.

"What am I saying?" asked Dockery.

"The way you said that the man had seven children. You were telling Frank that the death of his wife and daughter was smaller."

"If I said anything that could cause you to feel like that's what I said, then let me apologize now. I had no intention of saying anything like that," said Dockery. He was lying, anyone could see that.

Frank put a hand on Lowell's arm. "Forget about it."

"You have to understand how it sounded to me," said Lowell. "It didn't sound right."

Dockery said nothing. It was an odd ploy, this unassailable quiet; now the executive was the center of their attention, he was the issue, his feelings and not the plane crash, and what could be done about something about which nothing could be done; the plane could not be pulled from the sky before the crash, but maybe he had meant it as it sounded; in his frustration with Lowell he tried to say the worst thing that was on his mind.

Frank thought about the man on the plane who died leaving seven children. Was his wife in the room? He looked for a table with a woman who looked like she might have had a large brood, but he couldn't tell. And he imagined that there were small children, so he looked for a woman in her late thirties, but there was no reason that a supervisor couldn't have been with the airline for a full career, and have seven grown children, with maybe one still in college. So he could be looking for a grandmother. Anna had wanted more than one child, but he had resisted. She wanted three. She wanted a son, a big boy who would bring all of his big friends over to the house after school, to stand in front of the refrigerator and drink milk from the jug. Well, not the jug anymore, although that was what she called it. The bottle. The container.

And what of the copper-haired woman? She was sitting with a rabbi (skullcap, forty, curly hair, eager and attentive posture), and she was shaking her head from side to side, saying no to him. If her daughter was the salvation of her life, was that equal to losing seven children?

And what of families that had been wiped out, mother, father, son, daughter, daughter? Or sisters on their way to visit uncles. Who goes to the funeral of a family killed at the same time? Who arranges the funeral? Who gets the record collections, the books? Someone would say, It's better in a way that they all died, no one had to suffer the loss of the others, or: Now they're all together in heaven. But what if one of them went to hell? Would the others in heaven miss him? And if they did, if they felt the pain of loss, would that be heaven? If he had been on the plane and had gone to hell for the sin of his adultery, and Anna had not read the letter and had gone to heaven and had found out, in heaven, that she was there with Madeleine and not with her husband, because she was saved while he was damned, what would she feel? If she felt a sudden hatred for him, would that slip (if it was a slip) consign her to hell? Would she feel sad? And for how long?

Maybe Dockery's line really was disgusting. After all, there was a woman with seven children mourning one husband, not one husband mourning the extinction of his family. The woman had seven anchors, at least!—and all I have, thought Frank, is my brother and my parents, and he wanted to say, they will need me, I will have to be their anchor, and I will have to beg for comfort.

Then he thought of Mary Sifka. He had never called her to cry

about the things that wounded him, because he felt—what?—that
if he told her he was upset about his failed music career, or that
he knew that his brother was more capable than he, she might see
him in a new light, in his light, and come to share his bad feelings
of himself. She sometimes talked about her childhood and alluded
to things she wanted to keep hidden, but when he pressed, she
always said she didn't like to talk about those things. Something
bad had happened to her, beatings or worse. He had believed,
listening to her when she said anything about her bad childhood,
that abuse was the beginning of her intelligence, and having been
set apart from her family by its cruelty, she was able to see into the
nature of Nature, which was cruel. This had been his theory of Mary
Sifka's special attraction, her bleak youth and the intelligence that
had come out of it.

But what if she wasn't intelligent, the proof of which was her
acceptance of Frank? What if she was a lonely woman, dulled by
this soul-destroying childhood, whose affair with Frank fit a pattern
set long ago, something she needed to maintain her bad opinion of
the world, by breaking the trust her husband gave her? What if she
chose Frank not for his sensitivity, his humor, his sincerity? What
if she liked him for qualities he despised in himself? In this case,
abuse had not yielded to her any special insights; it had made her,
not sardonic or cynical, but only distrustful, and what she might
have liked in Frank was his lack of power, and his acceptance of
the limits of his ambition, that he had made peace with himself.
But if she couldn't see his frustration, then she was lying to herself,
or else she saw it but didn't care, and her adultery with him fit into
the plan of her reprisal against her husband for things she never
talked about with Frank. Frank knew almost nothing about her
husband.

He thought of his own childhood, and the thing he wanted to
name as his own intelligence might not be so grand. He envied
Mary Sifka for the clarity of her father's crimes, since his parents
had muddied it all up, never beating, but almost, never raping, but
invading in other ways that had left him so confused. Lowell had
escaped with a little more confidence, but then, thought Frank,

don't they work together because they both feel too weird for the rest of the world, and doesn't that strained and peculiar character they both share leave them incapable of feeling right with anyone except each other? In that case, aren't we really a team? Doesn't Lowell really need me? Don't I make a real contribution to the business? If Lowell, to escape the family's pressures, had launched himself beyond their gravity with his homosexuality, was he too, in his own way, a kind of failure by still having to work with his brother? Frank had never considered this before, that if Lowell were free, he would be free of Frank. Unless Lowell didn't share Frank's hatred of his parents, who, after all, had long ago accepted his homosexuality. It was something that they had understood about him, from high school. Unless they accepted his homosexuality as something that was just his NATURE, to protect themselves against the inescapable judgment on their failings as mother and father, if they looked for an interpretation for his NATURE in psychoanalysis.

It was too late to call Mary Sifka now. She was home, and he only called her at the office, where no one would suspect them. She would hear the news of the crash, probably not pay it any special attention, until she heard the destination and matched it with the time he had left. And even then, would she immediately think of him? She hadn't known his airline or flight number, but she could have called the office to find out if he had been on that plane, and the office would have told her yes. So she would think he was dead. A lot of people would think he was dead. Unless she called after he had talked to Lowell.

"Lowell?" asked Frank.

"What?"

"Did you tell the office that I missed the plane?"

"Not yet. It's too late now."

"So they must think I'm dead."

"I'll call tomorrow."

Or not even something so defined as abuse, only a dulled tantrum for the sufferings of childhood injustices, smaller pieces of birthday cake, someone else's better bicycle. Or he didn't tell Mary his deepest troubles out of respect for Anna, that there was a limit to his infidelity. He thought that if Anna slept with someone else, she would not set up a boundary that would allow her the sin of adultery and then the sin of pride, for keeping her heart a little bit faithful. He thought Anna, if she had ever fucked someone else, would have given her lover everything, would have forgotten her husband.

Dockery apologized. "Whatever I said, however I said it, if it made you feel bad, I'm sorry." He said this in a tone that declared he would not back down from them again. If Lowell pressed Dockery again, he would say what he wanted to say, and there was much to say to a man who took advantage of his brother's anguish and found a way to bully people who were just doing a job that could only be difficult.

"Okay," said Lowell, not meaning to tell Dockery the event would be forever buried but to tell him that as long as Dockery was direct with Lowell, and did not embellish with his own foul thoughts what his job demanded he say, there would be no more little storms of rage. So there was a truce between them.

"What's next?" asked Frank. He was tired of Lowell's condescension. He wanted to take charge.

"Well, you're welcome to stay here at the hotel for as long as you need. There's a few psychologists here, and we'd like you to talk to one of them. They're experts at grief counseling. They do a real good job. Very compassionate people. Or if you'd prefer, a clergyman or rabbi is available too."

"And then?"

"Well, it's too dark in San Diego to really see what's on the ground. They have lights up, but the area of devastation is pretty big. Three blocks were pretty well taken out. Right now they've got the National Guard out to keep the looters away, and the sightseers. In the morning they'll go in and start cleaning it all up. I have to warn you, a lot of people think that in a crash, the bodies just disintegrate, but they don't. In all likelihood, every body will be accounted for."

"I thought there were fires," said Frank. He was surprised with himself; he was leading Dockery into an area of gruesome detail, ashes, pieces of charred bone.

"Well, the fires don't concentrate their heat in any one spot for a long enough time. What I'm trying to say is, even after a fire, there's a body. Those bodies will have to be identified. We do our best using dental charts and fingerprints, when we can get them, but sometimes we have to rely on visual identification. There's no other way. We've also found that photographs don't work; people get more upset sometimes looking at pictures of a body than at the body itself."

"I can do it," said Lowell. "Anyway, I live in San Diego." As though proximity made the gruesome job easier? Or would it be harder to look at his sister-in-law's body if he had to drive a long way to see it?

"They'll probably return the bodies to Los Angeles. That's the practice, going back to the point of origin."

"Whatever," said Lowell.

"I'm sorry to have to speak about these things so directly, but I figure you don't want me to pull the punches, and frankly, I appreciate that. A lot of people, and this isn't to say that they're not entitled to their feelings, but a lot of people in this room don't want you to say what has to be said. They want you to almost say it, they want you to give them a taste of what you really mean, and then they want you to back down and apologize for going even that far. But I say, if it happened in a certain way, you're obliged to say that's the way it happened." Frank saw Dockery win respect from Lowell for this, for separating Frank and Lowell from the others. And was this something he did with everyone, take them all into his confidence, show them all how much he trusted them?

While Dockery was talking, one of the men cruising the tables came to his side and put a hand on his shoulder. Dockery introduced him. "Mr. Gale, I'd like you to meet Dale Beltran. Dale is one of our grief counselors. If you don't mind, I think it would be good to talk to him."

"Frank Gale," said Frank. "And this is my brother, Lowell."

"Dale Beltran," he said.

"Are you a psychologist?" asked Lowell.

"Yes," said Beltran. Frank hated the way he looked. His hair was too long for his curls, and the effect of suspended youth with his soft face and body bothered Frank terribly. Why am I threatened by this guy? Frank asked himself, but he had no answer. "Do you mind if I chat a bit?"

"It'd be a good idea," said Dockery.

"Sure," said Frank.

Beltran sat down. "How do you feel?" he asked.

"Not great."

"Like you can't believe it's really happened."

"I believe it."

"Intellectually, yes, but emotionally?"

"I don't know."

"Well, Mr. Gale . . ." He paused, and Frank knew why; he wanted Frank's permission to use his first name.

"Frank."

"Frank. There are a few stages of grief, and I wanted to share them with you, to help you get through them, so you won't feel so alone. The first is denial, which is what you're going through now. And with that, you'll feel alone. That's the isolation stage. Then comes anger. And that's a hard one. After that, well, you'll feel pretty low. The experts like to call that the depression phase; I'd prefer to call it the period of sadness. And then, finally, after the storm, you'll make peace with it. And that's acceptance."

"And then what?" asked Frank.

"Hope."

"That's the one that seems so far away," said Ed Dockery. "And that's the one we have to live for."

"Good luck," said Dale Beltran. "I'll talk to you again." He left them with a round of handshakes, and then walked away and introduced himself to the copper-haired woman.

It was only eight-thirty, but Frank felt as tired and alive as he had the night he worked in the recording studio until five in the morning, all those hours working on one song. The singer wasn't sure if the song was best done slowly or quickly, and what kind of beat he needed. Frank began by suggesting variations that were too different, which confused everyone and wasted their time as they tried to please him, since he was paying them, since he was their boss. There were four musicians in the studio, the singer, the guitarist, a drummer, and a pianist with a keyboard connected to a computer. The pianist was a friend of the singer, and he was used to playing with stars. He was there as a favor. Frank had at first resented the deference paid to him, but around one in the morning, after they had started at seven, he realized that yielding to the pianist would be the first creative thing he had done in the control booth. He would let the artists create, and if the song came out well, Frank would get the credit. He felt, with that decision, a glimmer of what it might mean to be a professional, and with that, this node of understanding, this seepage from the great occult mysteries that only the boldest seekers could penetrate, he saw, clearly, the possibility that he could leave the record stores, leave his brother. What were the lessons of the great mysteries, really, but instruction on how to live? The pianist inspired the singer, and Frank found it easy to find the right levels for the balance of tone among the instruments and voices.

That morning he knew the sensual weariness of exhausting himself at work that was play. If they failed at creating a song that would live forever, at least they knew what it meant to give all of their effort together in the service of something like beauty. And of course they would fail, the song was awful, but it didn't matter. They were trying to find in something bad, this stupid song, the bit of divinity that hides in all things.

Frank thought about the pianist's confidence. Failure was never part of the pianist's view of things. He knew his worth. He had depended on certain processes, he had faith in practice leading to perfection. He was an adept, and his musicianship was just the manifestation of the progress of his soul. And my failure? thought Frank. Was I aware of failure because it lay before me, so obviously, because I was not a musician? Everything about the pianist's maddening hostile sweetness proclaimed his membership in an elite to which Frank had only a ten-hour pass.

Frank's attitude, his bearing, the way his private turmoil registered its battles in his sullen expression, the way he made small talk when he knew better and should have kept his mouth shut, would never improve. He would never, even with the death of his family, be anyone other than who he already was. If there had ever been the chance to break free of himself, to rename himself and become a new person, the time for that was ten years past. The whole point of the pianist's life, Frank knew, was to live correctly in the light of a truth that he found in his music, and in the whole world of music. The whole point of the pianist's life was to live correctly so that he would never make the kind of false step with his life that would, if seen in another form, mean death, like the false step on a mountain. To see his life as an allegory. The real mountain is a test for the metaphysical mountain. The pianist took his life seriously, thought Frank, and was appreciated by other serious people. I am not serious, thought Frank. I am a dabbler. The whole point was to be conscious of his actions, so that he could die in peace, without despair. The pianist would never regret a marriage.

Frank started to cry. He was crying also for his daughter, but until he remembered that long night in the recording studio, sitting behind the console, in a comfortable chair, reading the dials and fiddling with knobs, like an airplane pilot!—like the airplane pilot who had died with Anna and Madeleine—he had been far from tears. He knew no one would fault him for his misery so long as he didn't tell them that he cried now because he would never produce a record, never write a song that the world would sing, that he would always and only be a salesman. He brought a hand up to cover his eyes, and before he closed them, he could see that the people in the room were watching him, just as he had watched the other mourners in the room whose sadness had already erupted.

Lowell massaged his shoulders, and Dockery patted him, awkwardly, yes, but also, Frank thought, for a little luck. Now Dockery could anticipate courage in a bad situation. He would always know that he could touch someone who had been electrified by (tragedy?) this force, this angel of death in whose wake everyone close was given a measure of charisma. At last, thought Frank, I am fascinating.

4. Amtrak

"When the baby was born," said Frank, not looking at his brother, looking at the freeway, and the big Jewish cemetery against the hill that faced to the west and a little south, "everything felt different. I drove through the city, and everything felt charged up. The colors were alive everywhere, the city looked beautiful."

"This city can never look beautiful," said Lowell.

"But it can, it did that day. I don't think I've stopped seeing the beauty in Los Angeles since the day the baby was born."

Sepulveda Boulevard went under the

freeway, and Frank followed the line of the bluff to the ocean. Bluffs, ravines, canyons, hills, gullies, mesas, rivers. The planet on which the city has been imposed. Why did it matter to him at all?

When the brothers moved out of the house and went to college, their parents sold the large house in Bel Air in which they had grown up and bought a condominium on Wilshire Boulevard, looking out over a neighborhood of small apartments in Westwood. The house had been expensive when they bought it, in 1960, for $500,000, and when they sold it, in 1982, they made $8 million. For a million and a half dollars they bought half of the twenty-third floor, nine rooms, three baths, everything new.

It was an apartment in which Frank never felt comfortable. Frank missed the big house, the suite he shared with his brother, their bedrooms, a large playroom, their bathroom, down a hall their parents almost never came. What did he really miss? The pool, the guesthouse, the garden that they pretended was a jungle. The old house looked like a small hotel, in the style of a mission. When his parents took the apartment, it was as though . . . yes, he knew what he resented about the new place, that by leaving the elaborate setting of the house, they had brought themselves closer to the light, and in the apartment they could be easily examined, and appraised, and finding them wanting, as he did, he found himself wanting; in seeing his parents diminished in their new setting, he was forced to see just what it was that he came from. In the house there was something, if not baronial about his father or aristocratic about his mother, something serious about both of them, something admirable. His family, in that great house, and within the circuitry of all the relatives, all the other Gales and Abarbanels and Siegels, was held to be the most important. When they lived in the large house, his father was head of the family. When they moved, he lost his crown. Everyone could see him for what he was, and whatever that thing was, and it was a quality of character that even now Frank could not name, he had lost his place. And Frank knew that this was something his father knew, that his house, this large, gracious, quiet, dark, noble, old, sober, rich, well-built, heavy-walled stone-and-wood house was his great achievement, and selling it, he had given away everyone's dream, everyone in the family touched the house and felt the house as part of their blood, as part of their lives, as a center, even though the Gales had owned it for barely one generation. The sale of the house was a betrayal of the clan. They owned no other house so grand. In the ten years since his parents moved, when the family gathered for holidays, once a year when everyone came from Toledo, Minneapolis, and New York, they came to Wilshire Boulevard, and there was nothing about this apartment that could buttress the lie of the family's superiority, that could make of the family something better than a family, a clan, even a tribe. Even the jealous cousins, who resented the Gales, felt lucky to be at the table in a mansion.

Worse, there was a secret kept from the rest of the family, that Leon Gale's only great investment had been the big house, that he was not the brilliant developer his family believed him to be. He worked alone, without partners, building apartment houses, and he bought land for too much money, and sold finished buildings for too little, and he took bank loans at high rates, and spent too much money on construction. His workers stole tools and lumber. When he built small office buildings, he chose bad tenants, who went out of business. They would owe him money, they would leave their offices or their storefronts filthy, and he would have to wait in line with other creditors when they filed for bankruptcy. He was a man of mild temper, and to the family this confirmed, before he sold the house, their sense of him as someone satisfied, rich, and wise, a man outside the battles of life. With the sale of the house what had looked like calm was now just meek, and without the big dining room and the ballroom and the long swimming pool he was not the king in exile; he was a small man. His cousins, the men and women who had known him from childhood, would tease him in ways the brothers had never seen. They brought lesser wines to dinner, smaller bouquets of flowers. The cousins of his father's generation wouldn't even bother asking for permission to smoke. They guessed, correctly, that Leon's profits from his house went to pay off his debts. He still had a million dollars in the bank, but his income was no greater than any of theirs. He had been humiliated.

Lowell once told Frank that their father's problem was that he expected things to turn out well, that he went through life as though something would rescue him in the end. Lowell's contempt for their father was greater than Frank's, and Frank knew that this contempt extended to Frank for still thinking so highly of their father. Lowell once told Frank that when he needed to make a difficult decision, he would think about their father, and then do what he wouldn't do.

"That's not fair to him," Frank had said.

"Fine. I'll do what you want to do."

There was no contest. Both of them knew that Frank would let Lowell make the hardest decisions, because, after all, Frank was his father's son.

But was Lowell like their mother?

Frank's mother met them at the elevator. She was crying, and when she hugged Frank, Lowell patted her shoulder. Frank was not as good a son to her as Lowell. He didn't think that she loved Lowell more, but Lowell was easier. Had Lowell discovered earlier than Frank that their father was a hollow man, and with their mother's coaching did he beat the disappointment and keep the clarity? Lowell understood something in their mother that Frank resisted, Lowell had compassion for her, and pity. For too long Frank saw his mother as an embarrassment to his father. For a time he hated his father for marrying such a weak woman. There had been a moment at his wedding when he hated himself for marrying Anna, when he knew that he was marrying her for bad reasons, and then hated his mother for loving Anna, and then hated his father for loving his mother, for loving a woman who did not have the courage to tell her son that he was making a bad choice, that if he wanted to be brave, to be the hero of his own life, to succeed beyond Lowell, he would have to be alone, longer, and without the warmth and kindness of a woman, without someone to soften the blows of the world, so that he would be forced to fight back, to be stronger than the blows. He wanted his mother to tell him that he didn't need a woman. He wanted his mother to tell him that he didn't need the kind of woman his father had needed, to tell him that he didn't have to be like his father, all talk. Frank thought his mother had said these things to Lowell, so Lowell was free not to marry, free to start a business and make it succeed, and make himself rich. Or had Lowell known this without their mother's help? Now Frank was without a woman. Would his mother expect greater success from him? Would she expect him to give up the business and go back into a recording studio, without the excuse that he had to be home to be a good husband and father? What would she hope for him now that he was finally free of the woman he had wanted her not to love?

"Your father is taking this very hard."

"And you?" Frank asked.

"What can anyone say?"

His father was on the phone in the living room. In the old house they didn't have a phone in the living room, or a television either, but in the apartment there was a telephone on the table next to the couch, which faced a tall black cabinet that held the television. Frank was sure that his parents watched during the day. Not a lot, but they never watched television in the old house, when the television was in the bar, a room that was almost the size of this living room. And this living room wasn't even a separate room; the kitchen was open to the dining room over a counter, and then the room turned at the corner of the building and became the living room. L-shaped. His father was talking to one of his brothers, telling him what had happened. He reached out a hand, and Frank touched it.

"Lonnie Walter," said Frank's father.

"Who?" asked Frank.

"Lonnie Walter, he's the one who blew up the plane. That's what they think."

No one from the airline had ever officially announced what Frank had been told privately.

"Did the airline call to tell you this?" asked Frank.

"It was on the radio," said his mother.

"Let me tell you about the airline," said his father. "We called them last night because I wanted them to let us know of any late-breaking developments."

"Leon," said Frank's mother, "this can wait." She was like Frank with Lowell, cautioning, trying to keep him from making a scene.

"I had to call the regular reservations number. Nobody there was allowed to say even if there had been a crash. They would not give me the number of the airline's business office. I called the airport, not the airline, and they gave me a general office number, which was closed, of course, it was after nine. Finally, on the ten o'clock news, they gave out a number to call."

"For families and friends," said Frank's mother. She was with him in the story now.

"And I called it, and the thing was busy for an hour. I got through at eleven o'clock, and the woman on the phone told me she couldn't give out anyone's names, nothing had been released yet, but she took my number, and that was last night, and no one has called me yet. And I think that's a disgrace."

"But you know they're dead," said Frank, "so why do you need the airline to tell you? They were on the plane, and it crashed. No one survived. I think they need to keep that line open for the people whose families were on the ground in San Diego, in the houses that the plane crashed into. That's where the doubt is."

"Fine, be on the airline's side," said his father. This came out in a little gust of petulance. "Identification with the aggressor." He said this with a blend of pity for Frank's muddied view of things; were he not so grief-stricken, he would not be identifying with the aggressor, and also hatred for Frank's refusal to share his anger, because Frank was always quietly telling Leon that he was too angry. If Leon said something bitter about a politician, or a bad movie, or a wealthy builder he had known when both were starting out, Frank would tell his father that he was too angry. His mother told Frank that it was unfair of him to stop his father like this, that he had a right to his anger. Frank had told her that what annoyed him wasn't his father's anger, but the free-floating rage that came into view every time he talked about any human being with more power or money.

Lowell screamed at their father, "What? What are you saying? Identification with the aggressor? What does that mean? I don't believe you," said Lowell. "You just lost Anna and Madeleine, and you're arguing about things that you don't know about. This is some psychological term. Identification with the aggressor. You're showing off something that you know? How can you show off at a time like this? Identification with the aggressor? What does that mean?"

"It means that Frank is already defending the airline: They've had him in their hands for the first fifteen hours, and they fed him and gave him a bed, and he's grateful to them, and it's clouding his perception of who they are, and what they really want out of all of this."

"I think they just want good publicity," said Ethel.

"Wrong," said Lowell. "I mean, maybe that's part of it, but the issue is publicity and cost, and also the industry. They have to obscure the event, they have to confuse everyone so that the event is never in focus, and then in a few weeks the only ones who will remember it will be the next of kin, that's what they have to do."

"And why can't they return your father's phone calls?" she asked.

"Because then they would be taking responsibility. And the idea is to avoid responsibility at every level."

Frank didn't know if his brother was right, but as usual, after his father attacked Frank and his mother tried to stop him, Lowell pushed Leon into his corner. Frank wondered if the brothers' early success with the stores had not challenged his father into a competition he never announced but to which he devoted himself and through which he lost his house?

"Does anyone want anything to eat?" said Frank's mother.

"I'd like an apple," said Frank. Anna hated apples and never bought them. It was a funny thing to hate, but she had grown up in Philadelphia, where the first apples of the year announced the end of summer, and the beginning of cold weather. She hated the cold. How cold was it outside when the plane opened up? Almost thirty thousand feet. Higher than Everest. Thin, cold air. Does the shock take the breath away so quickly that you pass out before you know that you're falling to your death? And all the debris, something could knock you in the head, knock you out, or kill you right there, cut off an arm. Falling dead. Or dying in the air, after a fifteen-thousand-foot fall, with fifteen thousand feet to go. A heart attack, a seizure. Asthma. Falling through a cloud of pollen. Hitting a bird. Being followed by a bird. Eyes to eyes. I had a dream last night that a large bird told me how to take care of him. Or answered my questions.

"We should go to the house," said Leon.

"No," said Frank. "I don't want to, not today. I'm going to San Diego this afternoon; I'll go to the house when I come back. I'm taking the train."

"I'll drive you down," said Lowell.

"No," said Frank. For a moment he regretted the decision, he thought he might need the company, but he didn't want to give in to their concerns.

"He's taking the train," said Lowell, as Ethel came back into the room.

"You should go with him," she said. "You can leave the car here."

"No," said Frank. "I'd like to be alone for a few hours."

"Are you sure?" his mother asked him.

He was.

The apple was on a blue plate. She put it down on the glass coffee table and set beside it three green cloth napkins. Frank studied the colors. The luxury of vision astonished him. He saw the dark green, the color of his father's Jaguar, but the green was made of the cloth, and the napkins were made of long strings tied together so ingeniously that they could lie flat, or be folded, or be soiled and then washed and then folded and ironed again. He saw the tight weave, and the fuzz of the ciliated cotton threads. It had been shiny, when it was new; now the cloth was slowly disintegrating, and he saw that decay in the color. The color of the cloth was changing as he watched it. It was so different from the blue on the plate, which was buried under the glaze. The cotton napkin was old; he could vaguely remember a dinner at the house when his mother set the table with the napkins, and he had found a price sticker, a white dot with a handwritten $3. The memory was not vague, it was as clear to him as the shining plate, which was new to him. A gift? Or had she seen it and bought it? Did Ethel hate Leon? Was it beautiful or was it ugly? He voted for beauty, because it existed, because he could see it, because he could imagine a device fine enough to measure the depth of the moist crescents left by the slices of apple as his mother and his father and his brother took their snack from the plate.

Frank watched his parents and his brother eat their apples. Was it a miracle, or was it repulsive?

"Life's a bitch," said Lowell.

"Where do you get your philosophy, from reading T-shirts?" said Leon.

"Fuck you," said Lowell.

"Leon, Lowell," said Ethel, flatly.

"My family is dead," said Frank. "They were killed in a plane crash. If anyone in this room raises his or her voice, I am going to leave, and I will never come back, and you will never see me again."

"Frank," said his father.

"I'm going to San Diego," said Frank. "And I want to go alone. I want to be alone. I'm going to the train station. I'm going to take the train."

He ran out the door, and in the building's lobby he called for a cab. He bought a first-class ticket at the station, and he was in his seat with a few minutes to spare.

As the train passed slowly through the rail yards, Frank concentrated on the sounds of the wheels, the orchestra of couplers and springs pushing and pulling without rhythm, and trying to make sense of the industrial concerto, he found a simple pattern, a few clicks within the heaving frame of the car, but another set of noises intruded on the music, and in desperation, to have something of his own, something private that belonged to no one else, he tried again to separate the sounds. Easier to put smoke in a cage than recreate the shattered harmonies, but he let his mind absorb every vibration, and then, with relief, inside the roar he found something that was constant, determined, and promised at any moment that the train would surprise him, make him suddenly happy as it went at full speed, in a rush that would be the train's pleasure in itself.

They were beside a freeway, and the slowest lane of traffic was still faster, though only by a little, than the train. So he was going, how fast? Thirty miles an hour? It was a doubling that he wanted, and he felt himself urging the train ahead. He thought he could hear a change in the ratchet, a promise that the sounds that Frank could separate into units would soon blur into an indistinct hum that would disappear as the comforting blend of all the little movements of the railroad car gathered together in the one great movement of going forward to San Diego, but nothing changed. However fast it would go, he knew it could never go as fast as he wanted, as fast as a jet plane.

Now it was almost six. The day had been filled with people. The airline had discouraged the next of kin from coming to San Diego, the bodies were going to be returned to Los Angeles as they were found, but a few wanted to go. The flight was short, thirty minutes, but Frank pleaded fear of flying.

"We've got a bus," said Bettina Welch. "You don't have to take the train. The bus is comfortable, and we'll be taking it straight to the hotel."

"Thank you," said Frank, "but I just don't want to . . ." He let the sentence trail off. He meant her to understand that he could not imagine himself on the same kind of plane as his wife had flown, with engines and flaps and retracting wheels making the same kinds of noises she had heard, looking wistfully as she must have out the window at the same coastline. He wanted Bettina to think he was too uncertain now, not just grieving, but also unhappy, and if he could surround himself with the grace of unconditional mourning, he would be safe, protected by the purity of the emotion. Unhappiness was an older feeling, his humor before the plane had crashed, and this feeling was not being eclipsed by the mourning, and so, because there was something of himself lost in space between these two galaxies, he was alone, and he was scared. If pure grief was selfless, his unhappiness was too clearly to him a kind of petulance. In grief he would be with his family, in spirit, in feeling. In grief he would be tender. In grief he would be holding his daughter's hand. In grief he would be begging forgiveness from his wife, and she would forgive him. In grief he would love his brother like a brother. In grief he would be a good son. In unhappiness he thought of himself. In unhappiness he thought of his mistress. In unhappiness he thought about money. In unhappiness he tasted the food he was eating. In unhappiness he looked at women. In the gap between unhappiness and grief, the space in which there was only his consciousness of the difference between the grief and the unhappiness, he was chilled by his solitude in the freezing universe, and it was this enormous fear that kept him from flying on a plane.

"We'll reimburse you, of course," she said.

"Thank you. It's not very expensive."

"We'll buy your brother's ticket too," she said.

He could have said that Lowell was driving, but he didn't want her to give him any more advice. She would tell Frank to stay with his brother.

"Thank you," he said, and that was all she seemed to want from him, a formal closing.

The freeway passed over the train, and as the train came to the concrete pylons of the road, the bridge rose and curved up and over the rails, and there was a feeling of disaster averted to triumph in the sudden uplift of the bridge, a heavy ribbon in the wind, as though it were not set in steel and hardened sand, but that the bridge had made a decision, was in fact a monument to pure decision, a monument commemorating that moment, the act and its monument, to save the train.

Frank recoiled from this, this thinking of crashes.

Through his reflection in the window, he saw the conductor come into the car. When Frank turned to hand him his ticket, he saw a strip of black cloth pinned to the conductor's arm. Another conductor came into the train, and he wore the same band. Neither of them smiled. Now he felt an urge to tell them that they wore the black for his wife and daughter, and that it mattered to him, that it pulled him closer to that grief for which he felt such longing, and that seemed to him to stand like his wife, forever unattainable to him on the better side of a river.

No, he would say nothing to them. If the conductors had been asked to wear black, he didn't want to know that they felt no solidarity with his loss, and if they had asked to wear the black, because . . . why? he wondered now. They must be wearing black because the crash was, what, part of the transportation system? It made no sense. This is not a nation of such deeply linked sympathies. Planes crash often. The country never cries. Perhaps a train official had been killed on the plane, or else one of them had lost someone. Or had Frank missed some news, and was the president dead? If there had been an assassination, the news of the plane crash would recede to the back pages. Frank felt, in his unhappiness again, something like annoyance, that the world would turn its eye from his misery. No, the president was not dead. Everyone in the train would have a loud opinion if the president were dead. Someone always plays a radio when a president is dead. It must be the crash, Frank decided, someone here is connected to the plane in some way, maybe not one of the conductors, maybe an engineer, or the bartender, but someone wanted to share someone else's loss. He gave himself over to the possibility of tears. Nothing. He shook his head in dismay with himself because he could not cry. Now he was feeling sorry for his inability to feel sorry, and he blew a rush of air through his nose, it was the start of a laugh. He had not yet buried his wife and daughter, and already he was coming back to himself. This would be how he passed from mourning to amnesia; the sound of his laughter would cover the pain. He thought, So this is how we come to accept. We forget. He would acquit himself of all charges against his hateful self, he would absolve Frank Gale of the crime of a cold heart. He would plead to the jury of the peers of his inner realm that Frank Gale was only being Frank Gale, a crime for which they, as Frank's peers, should have no trouble understanding, and if they looked into their own hearts, moderated by the juries of their own selves, they would know that Frank really did feel the loss of his family, really did miss them.

The conductor came through the car, calling out, "Fullerton, next stop Fullerton." Frank had lived in Los Angeles his whole life, but how much of the city did he really know? Was Fullerton named for Fuller, or was it named for Fullerton, or was it named by some

Iowan who bought the land, and built the town, and named it for his home in Iowa? At least he knew Culver City, a little. He'd once fucked a woman in Culver City. Why was he thinking of her? Culver City, the drive through in the morning. And the woman, yes, of course. He had met her on an airplane. He smiled, the circuits of his associations! Silly how they do that, charming.

The train stopped at Fullerton. It was an insipid thought, something to say to his brother, a way to keep Lowell's sympathy high. It's an ugly city, he thought, a stain, an ashtray. Well, that's a tired idea too.

What was Fullerton? Frank wanted to know. He thought of getting off the train, finding a taxi, and asking for a tour of Fullerton. Their father could have been wealthy. Lowell would make them wealthy because he did not hate the world. Their father used to tell them that a good developer was an explorer, and his car was his ship, and the roads were oceans and rivers, and he sailed around this world looking for rich harbors, those fabulous intersections where people would want to shop and eat and set up their businesses, places where people would want to live. But it was as though someone had told him this once, when he was young, and it was a lesson he repeated but never seemed to have learned, or if he learned it, there was another lesson that he must have ignored, the lesson of exploitation, of enrichment, the lesson of conquest. While Frank imitated his father, and his fears, his hollow pretensions to an aristocratic equilibrium borrowed probably from magazine advertisements for scotch whisky, Lowell was his mother's son, and from her he inherited an impatience with his father, and her clarity.

The train left Fullerton, and the track went through a neighborhood of small houses before finding its way past factories.

Behind him Frank heard an accordion playing Chopin's Funeral March. He turned around. The conductor with the black armband walked down the aisle in front of four men and one woman, dressed in black, with black armbands, holding a four-foot-long pine coffin over their heads. One of the men was tall—Frank thought he might have been six-and-a-half feet—and he had to bend to keep the coffin level. There was something in the coffin, but not a body; they could never have held a body overhead so easily. At the end of the parade was the second conductor, playing a small electric keyboard on a guitar strap around his neck.

Across the aisle from Frank a man shouted, "No, no!" It was a cry of joyful disbelief. He stood up and shook a finger at the conductor, and said, "Dave, Dave, you didn't. Don't tell me. Dave, do not tell me."

The funeral procession stopped beside Frank. The woman rested the coffin on the edge of Frank's seat. She winked at him. "This'll just take a minute."

"What's in the coffin?" asked the man.

"Dearly beloved," began the conductor.

"That's for weddings, you dork," said the woman.

"The Lord is my shepherd, I shall not want," said the conductor.

"What's in the casket?" asked the man.

"Just open it, you dingleberry," said the woman. She turned to Frank. "Right? Doesn't everybody want to know what's in the coffin?"

Frank nodded.

The excited man across the aisle said, "You guys. You guys."

The pallbearers settled the casket onto the floor and lifted the top. Inside was a birthday cake in the form of a grave, with flowers and a headstone, and the inscription, in red jelly:

HERE LIES THE YOUTH OF
CHRIS BENTINE
1953–1993

Set around the cake on a bed of napkins, paper plates, and stacks of plastic cups, were a hundred miniature bottles of vodka.

"Christopher Bentine," said the conductor, "on this, the occasion of your fortieth birthday, your friends and fellow passengers would like to extend our deepest heartfelt sympathies on the loss of your beloved Youth." The conductor with the electric keyboard held one note, and the pallbearers hummed together, found a note, and then sang "Happy Birthday" in a minor key.

Frank felt that everyone in the car had been embarrassed by the procession, but at the same time were thrilled to have seen it, to have had something in their day that would make a story, something to tell when they got to wherever they were going, and spent the night with whomever they were seeing, and that the spectacle of the party did not throw them back into the role of audience, that somehow they were also in the party too, that they were lucky, that they were privileged. And Frank saw that no one was singing along with the group, because the singers were good, they had the authority that comes from practice and devotion and the love of making music together. They had rehearsed the song, and the melody they had chosen, or that had been chosen by the conductor with the keyboard, was close enough to the tune everyone knew that to sing the variation, in a difficult five-part harmony, without being dragged back to dullness by the familiarity of the major key, was something to respect. The mood in the car changed, and as the singers finished the ditty, everyone could hear the sound of the train, which reminded them, even in a way that the more cynical among them (Frank) would call sentimental and common, of the things that trains in the night are supposed to mean, of all the romances, of leavings and arrivings, of moments that are important. Now even silly Chris Bentine was quiet, staring at the sugar-frosted gravestone, at 1953–1993, at the awful brevity of a life cut off at forty. His face lost all of its stupid vigor, and the pallbearers and conductors stopped smiling at him. Frank saw in Chris Bentine the reflection of a man haunting his own life, suddenly aware that his youth really was over, that if he lived another forty years, he would be an old man, and that if he died even in thirty years, no one would say he had died young. He had become his own ghost.

Something had been violated. Chris Bentine's friends should never have played with him like this. For that moment, before Chris Bentine sliced the gravestone in half and licked the knife and had his picture taken by the woman, and everyone in the railroad car applauded, and the pallbearers handed out the miniature bottles of vodka to all the passengers, Frank was not alone in his complicated stew of feelings, he was not so alone in an icy universe in which everyone is born alone and dies alone. He had company.

The woman handed him the vodka and the plastic cup and a piece of the cake on a paper plate. He got the edge of *9* and all of *3*.

He thought of what his mother had asked him: "What can anyone say?" They could say that chocolate and vodka were a good combination. The cake was heavy, and he needed to drink something to clear his mouth, and all he had was the vodka. He could have told his mother that anyone could say, "I want to tear my hair out" or "Now I know there is no God" or "I want revenge, I want blood for blood."

Blood for blood. Even when they say it, they don't mean it, thought Frank. He rested his head against the window; the glass was cold, and the vibration was unpleasant, not like on a plane, where all the pieces fit together and the window's hum is synchronous with the floor, until the floor drops away and the window shatters and you're strapped to a seat that's sucked backward past the tail and pieces of the plane are burning and falling around you and the air is cold and thin and you have enough clarity to know that in a few seconds, thirty-two feet per second per second, silence. And if a baby was sleeping in your lap, and you lost it in the explosion?

What happens in a train wreck? Frank thought of the awful job of lifting the trains from the side of the tracks, setting the tracks right; the work seems endless and impossible, railroad cars on their sides, sliding down a wet hill, maybe into a swollen river. And the trains don't have to move fast to fall off the bed, just a little too fast, or else for no reason over the rusted legs of a badly aged bridge. No warning. But the impact? So many shredding metal panels, so many windows out of which a person could fall, and then the train could roll over you while you're half out a window, that would hurt, squeeze you like a heel on a worm. There would be no time to say ouch. The slow rolling, not like a plane, how many seconds and you're dead? Thirty-two feet per second per second. What is the law of motion that applies to a Pullman car rolling down the embankment? And the way all trains smell vaguely of cigarettes and farts, and the toilet tanks, burst, that smell, and wet sand, and oil. To be in charge of the rescue, what a job, thought Frank. So many facts and so many decisions, but one clear law: Clean it up, get the trains running again. That man does not have to think. Everything he has to do is obvious.

The pallbearers carried the open casket down the aisle, collecting the plastic cups, the vodka bottles, and the paper plates and plastic forks. Chris Bentine sat on the armrest and braced himself with one foot on the seat across the aisle. People had to step over his leg to get down the car, but he didn't move.

Chris Bentine had no face. Almost no one in the car had a face. What kind of name was Bentine, and when did the first Bentine come to America, and was that progenitor of the American Bentines so aggressively without distinction? Chris Bentine was forty, but he must have been without a face for fifteen years; Frank recognized in him a beer drinker from college, someone neither handsome enough, nor athletic nor rich enough, to get into a fraternity, but someone who still was friendly enough to run with a crowd of other noisy boys. And what was this facelessness? There was nothing to read in his eyes. But a lot of them were married. Somewhere along the way they had met a woman who was not repulsed into sickness, into seizures, weeks of crippling dry heaves, by the idea of committing what remained of their only chance at life to these men with no faces. And they don't live long. They die at sixty. You don't see a lot of old men with no faces in California.

"Rack race!" yelled Chris Bentine.

"Rack race!" yelled the pallbearers, together.

"Not a rack race," said the conductor.

The woman pallbearer unpinned a brooch from her shirt and took off her pearl necklace. "Would you hold this?" she asked Frank.

"Where are you going?" asked Frank.

"I guess you've never taken this train," she said.

"Once."

"But you've never taken the Friday afternoon five-fifty."

"No."

"This is the best party in California."

"Is it like this every Friday?"

"We don't always have a funeral."

She ran to the back of the car and joined everyone else from the birthday party. Chris Bentine climbed on a seat and pulled himself into the luggage rack. The woman did the same on the other side of the aisle. The conductor raised his hand.

Frank looked back and tried to read the faces of the passengers. They were all regulars, he was sure of that. Some hid from the embarrassment of this display of the small scale of the human imagination by burying themselves in newspapers and horror novels. A few stared at their reflections in the window, wearing earphones, listening to music. Others looked back to the start of the race, and many of them, thought Frank, were jealous of the racers, they regretted their own poor social skills, their inability to carouse with a happy group.

The conductor dropped his arm, and the race began. Not too many people were traveling with suitcases; the biggest obstacles were cardboard boxes sealed with tape, but the racers had to pull themselves over small dividers every five feet. Frank was surprised that Chris Bentine was keeping up with the woman, since her small size should have favored her. She had a better reach than Bentine, and she took advantage of the edge of the rail, so that she pushed off against her outside arm, her left, when it was by her waist, and then with her right hand she grabbed the next divider. Bentine had a less developed system, but a stronger grip with his feet. He pressed his inside knee, his left, into the junction of the wall and the rack, then brought his other foot over the next divider. His hands were bent under his chest, the effect was of a salamander crawling around the roots of a tree. By the middle of the car the passengers over whose heads the racers had not yet passed reached up and took down their bags and coats, and the rest of the way was clear. The woman was ahead. The pallbearers were keeping pace with the racers and urged them on, clapping their hands and pounding the luggage rack before them. There were still some passengers who refused to follow the race. Frank, holding the brooch and the pearl necklace, stood up as the woman came closer. He took down his soft suitcase and put it on the seat. There was nothing in front of her now except for one flat cardboard box, which probably held a framed poster.

Frank looked for the owner, but no one seemed worried about it, and he decided not to move it, since the woman, who was now gaining, with a half-length on Chris Bentine, would, at worst, put a hand on a corner of the box, but did not let all of her weight attack the middle.

Bentine called out to her, "Let me win, it's my birthday!"

"No discounts for senior citizens, Chris Bentine!" she cried in return. She was over the flat box, and Frank surprised himself with a little smile when she avoided any contact with it. She was good. She deserved to win. She won.

Bentine stopped when she touched the far end. He was two lengths behind.

"Vodka! I need vodka!" he said, pretending to be a thirsty man in a pitiless desert.

The train stopped in Del Mar for a minute, and then left the ocean. There were lights on the right side; San Diego was near. He put the notebook away. Around him, everyone was getting ready for the end of the line. The party was over now, and people were nodding their good-byes to Chris Bentine as they closed their briefcases or folded up their newspapers. The conductors went down the car, but they were already thinking about their drinks or their dinners, or the next trip, and by their abstract concentration on a duty too involved for the passengers to understand, they were like dead men, and no one talked to them, or even smiled.

Now the train descended from the canyon south of La Jolla, and there was Mission Bay. It was almost pretty. It had the elements of romance; lights reflected in water, water, the silhouettes of masts and riggings, but Frank was overcome with his feeling of hatred for San Diego, which always seemed to him a stupid city. Lowell liked it because it was an easy place to sell records; the navy was here and the sailors bought music, compact discs and lots of recorded tapes. And there were other homosexuals in San Diego, and in Del Mar, and up the coast in La Jolla. What did Lowell do at night? He never talked about sex with Lowell. His brother used to have boyfriends, but in the last few years, though he gave money and some time to help people with AIDS, he seemed to live alone and rarely talked of the men in his life. Frank felt sad for him now, and realized that Lowell was surrounded by death these days, and with so much misery, so many funerals, so many eulogies, so much rage, he still had the grace to shed tears for his sister-in-law, and his niece, and not just for himself. My brother is a better man than I am, thought Frank.

The train passed the airport. If there were signs of special activity because of the crash, he could not read them.

And then downtown, and then the station. Chris Bentine and the marines were already at the door.

5. Lights

Everyone followed an indistinct line, trusting those among them who knew where they were going. It was typical of San Diego not to have arrows or signs pointing the way to the station, or even to name the station, not to have a sign above the station that said, simply, "San Diego."

I am in a foul mood, thought Frank, and I should be careful now.

And then there were no signs in the station, and no one to answer questions at the information booth. He was tired of his dull angers.

He went out the wrong door looking for a cab and then had to pass through

the station again and out another door. On this second time through
he wanted to stay inside, to hide in public, as he had hidden in
full view at the airport, before he had been told of his wife's and
daughter's deaths. He would stay here with the obese and the ancient
and never leave the station, and cause no trouble, and become a
witness. He would ask no questions, beg for no money. He would
start no conversation. He would make no friends of the men and
women who cleaned. He would spend only as much money as he
needed to eat small meals. He would sleep on the benches, until
rousted by policemen with shiny hair, and when they threw him out
at night, to share the misery of the insane and the out-of-work, he
would rent a small room in a motel that he would walk to, where
he could always have a change of clothing. He would stay here
forever, until he died. How long would it take to die this way, if
he gave himself over to a destiny of stubborn silence, day after day
after day after day after day after day after day after day after day
after day, asking only for a cup of coffee and a tuna sandwich,
grilled, with a slice of cheese? No one would find him. He could
tell his lawyer to send him money. If his lawyer said no, he would
find someone who would indulge him this, in conspiracy. He could
set up some kind of complicated system of bank accounts, through
which he could draw funds without anyone knowing where he was
living. Money from Los Angeles would be wired to an account
in . . . where? . . . somewhere, even Switzerland, and then wired
back to . . . to . . . to a bank in Tijuana, and he could cross the
border once a month to get enough cash. If he had an account in
Tijuana, he would not have to give his Social Security number. That
was the way to stay hidden in America, never to give his Social
Security number to anyone. And what would this scheme give him?
He would be able to live in suspension in the San Diego train station,
and there, perhaps, learn something about something. He didn't
know what, but whatever it was, he felt that the reason for this
impulse to make such an arbitrary hermitage would be, over time,
revealed to him. He felt this as a calling, almost as something filled
with light, to stay inside the San Diego train station until he died,
or until he knew for certain that he had learned something important.

He would pay attention to the life of the station. If he concentrated on the station's life, he would be closer to God, he thought.

Outside, three black cabdrivers asked for his business. Again, this was so typical of San Diego; there was no organization to the line. The drivers were Africans or Jamaicans, he couldn't tell. What difference did it make? None.

One of them touched his arm, having won Frank in some kind of competition that was over quickly. Frank went with him to a car without official emblems, and for a second worried that he was going to be murdered, but he got into the car anyway, thinking to himself, Maybe he'll kill me.

He was asked where he was going.

"I want to go to where the plane crashed," he said. He wasn't sure until he said it that this was what would come out, but it was the truth.

"Cohassett Street," said the cabdriver. "But they got that closed off. They won't let anyone near for a mile."

"My wife and my daughter were on the plane."

The driver looked at him in the rearview mirror; Frank supposed he was looking in his eyes to see if this was true. Frank turned his eyes away, in case the driver would see something else in him, but that was also, he knew, some fear of what he imagined was a black man's superior wisdom, that the man would see the grief, and also all the other things, the weakness, all the bad reasons for doing everything he did, and then the fear of losing his privileges.

"There's nothing that you'll be able to see over there now—why don't you go to where all the people in the neighborhood who had their houses burned are? There's a school near the crash, and they have it set up for helping the people." So the man believed him.

"I want to go to the crash. I want to see it for myself."

The driver nodded, and then they were on the freeway, following the signs to the Mexican border.

A few minutes of silence. There was the harbor, and battleships and an aircraft carrier. He wondered what it was about the species that needed grief. There was something so useless and old-fashioned about the grief he felt now, if this was grief at all, a thin layer of resentment and then another one of tenderness, and then longing, and then old pictures that came up to him from childhood, of losing something to a bully, or picking a fight for no reason with his mother, and slamming the door, that kind of violent, self-pitying love of loneliness, making a religion of his loneliness, biting into the windowsill and tasting the dust and dry paint, and the surprising freshness of the pine underneath, after all these years, after all these years, and hiding under a desk and hugging the reluctant dog.

They left the freeway near Coronado and turned east. He knew the exit, one of Lowell's new stores was near, in a mall on a parallel road. It was a small store, Lowell supplied it with only the most popular disks, no more than a hundred titles, for impulse buyers with pocket money. Frank liked the idea and wanted to design the racks that would hold the titles. Lowell wanted to buy a modular system from a catalog, but Frank had insisted on his right to supervise the design. If the store did well, Lowell wanted to open more in every mall in Southern California, and then sell the idea to people who would buy distribution rights for different territories in the country. Their mother told them that one of their cousins, Julia Abarbanel (mother's sister's daughter, middle of three, about thirty, attractive in that side of the family's sullen way), had complained about this, that Lowell and Frank were doing something evil by selling only those records that were popular, by not supporting more obscure music, that they were fouling the whole idea of freedom of choice, if the choice offered was only the choice made by millions of others whose choices were established by a music industry that wanted to limit the choices to only a few, not to invest in so many unpopular records, so many dry holes. Frank and Julia had been best friends, as cousins, for a long time, since they were children, but then he and Lowell started making money, and something happened. The friendship ended. Julia became angry about things that shouldn't have mattered to her. The color scheme of the stores, gray and blue. She was angry with Lowell for not telling the record companies that the oversized packages in which the compact discs were sold wasted paper. Lowell had always hated Julia, and it was obvious to Frank why, because Julia had always favored Frank. And then Julia turned on Frank. Because he had come under his brother's shadow.

He could have slept with Julia; one Thanksgiving in Yosemite, the two families stayed at the park's grand rock-and-timber lodge. Frank and Julia watched the moonlight on the rocks after dinner. The pines made their whispering sounds, and the river made its own noises, and the two cousins were drunk. It would have been easy. And she was pretty then. He had a fabulous erection; it was maybe the last great erection of his youth. It would have been interesting to kiss his cousin, someone he had known for so long. She would have been the only woman he kissed whom he had liked as a friend first, whom he had thought of as a friend for a long time, and not as someone to get naked with. There was something disgusting, he thought, some sign of weakness, when all the women he had slept with had been women he had wanted to sleep with from the beginning. But he had done nothing that night. Lowell would have done everything. They would have laughed about it. But she didn't like Lowell. Well, she would have if they had been under the Yosemite moonlight. She would have liked him more than Frank, if she had seen how really wonderful he was, how brilliant. She hated him for his faith in reality, in the basic truths of the marketplace, the laws of supply and demand. Lowell loved demand. He loved how people spent their money on things other than food and clothing and shelter. People made a necessity out of music. They could not live without the music they had heard on the radio. Now someone was inventing a store where a kid could grab a tape, could walk in blind from the street, could reach into a bin filled with tapes, and pull out music that lots of other people already liked. How could anyone not want to try this kind of business? It could make them wealthy, millions and millions.

But now he was going to be wealthy from the plane crash. Ladies and Gentlemen of the Jury, the airline's security was so remiss that a fired worker with a gun . . . et cetera, et cetera. It would be worth a few million dollars to him. Three or four.

"There," said the cabdriver. There were fire trucks beyond a barricade, and two policemen waved traffic away. A crowd stood at the barricade, watching the street. The cabdriver brought the car to one of the policemen.

"You have to move the car," he said.

"His wife and daughter were on the plane," said the driver. The policemen gave Frank a close look.

"My name is Frank Gale," said Frank, in the voice he used to announce himself to the maître d', going up at the end just a little, as though reminding the policeman of his lapse in forgetting the name of someone he should have recognized. "I just drove down from Los Angeles," said Frank. He wasn't sure why he didn't mention the train.

"I'm sorry."

"Can we go through?" asked Frank.

"We've evacuated half the neighborhood," said the policeman, "and there's no traffic."

"I'll walk."

"Your wife and daughter."

"Yes."

"We don't know how many people have died," said the policeman. "The plane tore into the middle of a block, and took about fifty, maybe sixty, houses with it, and an apartment house, fifteen units. There might be three hundred dead."

These were the bleak facts, the facts that Frank had avoided all day, the facts that he had turned away from when he was in a room with a television, the facts that he had not wanted to know.

The policeman continued, "Go to the Red Cross command center at the high school. There's people there to take care of you, Frank."

It touched Frank that the policeman had remembered his name.

"That's the best thing for now," said the driver. "You should be with other people who have the same suffering now, to comfort your heart."

"I wanted to see the plane," said Frank.

"You can't get into the neighborhood. And there's really nothing to see. Go to the high school." He asked the driver if he knew where it was. The driver said that he did.

"I'm really sorry," said the policeman. The driver turned the car around.

On the other side of the line, beyond the fire trucks, Frank watched people walking in the middle of the street, and he thought of block parties or street fairs, with everyone given freedom to walk wherever they wanted, on the sidewalk or in the middle of the street, and how much fun it is just to do that, just to step off the sidewalk as though the sidewalk is nothing very special, how walking in the middle of a street, with a crowd, is a way of feeling rich. Wasn't the entrance to Disneyland nothing more than a street? So you could step off the curb in the middle of the block and no one would punish you. The city as playground. Join the parade!

There was a crowd on his side of the line, and he was aware of them looking at him, something in the policeman's posture told them that Frank was in some way important. Before he was turned back, they would have wanted him to be someone whose house had been destroyed, someone whose family had been killed. And were they disappointed when the car left? The people who live in the houses on the border of the crisis must be jealous of the people who live inside.

"We'll go to the high school now," said the driver.

"No," said Frank. "Take me around the corner." His flowing tenderness was dissolved in the heat of a plan.

"Mister Gale," said the driver, "let me take you to the high school."

"No," said Frank. "Just drive me to the middle of the next block." They were around the corner from the barricades now, and there was another barricade at the next intersection.

"Stop," said Frank.

The driver turned around to look at him. "What are you going to do?"

The meter was now at forty dollars. Frank took out his wallet, wondering if the driver would reject the money. Frank had a fifty and four twenties. He gave the driver seventy, and said, "Keep the change." The driver kept the money.

"I have to see the plane," said Frank. "I just have to see it, I
have to know."

"Good luck," said the driver, and then he gave the money back
to Frank. "I can't," he said.

The cab went away, leaving him on the sidewalk, and Frank
walked up the path to the nearest house. He rang the bell and heard
a two-bell chime, high-low, and then he heard someone walking.

A man inside the house said, "Who is it?"

"My name is Frank Gale," said Frank. "And my family was
killed in the plane crash. The police have the neighborhood blocked
off, but I have to get through, and I was wondering if I could climb
over your back fence, so I can get to the next street, so I can be
inside the police line."

"And the police won't let you through?"

"No," said Frank, "they want me to go to the high school."

"Dear God. Haven't they let you through to your house yet?"

It took Frank a second to understand the question. The man
thought that Frank lived in a house that had been hit. If Frank went
along with this, it would be easy to make up a story about the
confusion of the police, but he wanted to tell the truth. "I'm sorry,"
he said, "but I don't live in the neighborhood. My family was on
the plane." He felt odd calling Anna and Madeleine his family; two
seemed a small number for family. He would have needed two
children to have a full family, or better, three. More connections.

The door opened. The man was younger than Frank expected,
thirty, probably, and slim. A five-year-old boy was at his side,
holding on to the man's belt, and swinging his weight from it.

"You really should go to the high school," said the man, and
he studied Frank before telling him to come into the house. He
introduced himself. "Dan Burack. And this is Dennis."

"I know this is crazy," said Frank, "but I don't know what else
to do. I just want to see where they crashed, it makes a difference
to me, I need to see it, to know that it's real."

"It's real. Dennis was home when it happened."

There was no mention of Burack's wife; Frank supposed she was
at the market. Maybe with their other child, if they had one.

"He lost a friend. We lost a few friends. But friends aren't the same thing as family."

"If you love people, what's the difference?" asked Frank, but he was sure there was a difference.

"Come on through," said Burack. It was a comfortable and undistinguished house. Frank would not have noticed it, but Anna always made fun of wall-to-wall carpets in a living room; she thought that there was something too suburban about them, that a wood floor with even a mediocre rug, something with an uncomplicated design, was better than carpet. Frank thought that above all reasons, it was for just this kind of distinction that he needed her, because her eyes were set on the world, and his were so clouded with his own shit. Or did he hate her because this kind of distinction left him with a catalog of sins against which he measured everyone, and without the guidance of his now-dead wife, would he have halted his affection for Dan Burack because he had a carpet?

Burack took him to the backyard. "Can you smell it?" asked Burack.

"Yes," said Frank. It was there, clearly, the smell of a fire, of gasoline and wood.

"It's about five blocks to where the plane hit."

"Why do you believe me?" asked Frank. "How do you know I'm not going to break into an empty house?"

"Are you?"

"No."

"There you have it."

The back wall was only five feet tall, and the lights were off in the house beyond it.

"Thank you," said Frank. He pulled himself over the wall and dropped to the other side. There was only a patch of lawn at this far end of the yard, and then a long swimming pool surrounded by a fence. Frank trotted beside the pool, and when he came to the driveway found a lock inside the gate. The gate was wood, and about six feet tall. He hoisted himself once again, this time bracing himself against the house. He stood up on the gate. There was a window just beyond it. He bent over to reach the sill, and with a firm grip on the window he jumped to the ground, with only a light insult to his ankles. Now, on the other side of the police line, all he had to do was follow his nose.

There was a pale half-moon. Cypress trees with dry needles moved in a light wind, which came with the rumble of the heavy engines of fire trucks on the next block. The sound of the trucks passed away, but the light wind continued. No matter what the weather, he thought, it would feel appropriate. Full moon, no moon, crescent on the wax or wane, light wind or typhoon, he could have read into any of them a fitting judgment on his grief, on the universe, on his silly goal to see the plane. What did the light wind mean, was it indifference or comfort? Did the passing fire trucks play a threnody just for him, or even not just for him, but for everyone? The sound reminded everyone of what had happened.

When Frank passed the corner of the front of the house, he saw the barrier from which he had been turned. He was in the middle of the block, and he walked to the next corner and then made a right turn up the empty street. Ahead to the next block, some fifteen or so houses away, he saw a knot of people in the light of something large that was hidden around the corner. The light shifted, and then he heard the sound of a crane or bulldozer. He walked, but then he found it easier to run.

Men shouted directions and responses, and gears were shifted, and engines changed pitch, and as he came to the corner, he could smell a dead fire, water on charcoal making the air damp. Around the corner he saw that two houses had burned almost to the ground. The nearest house was half-destroyed; the wall closest to him was fine, but the roof was off, and a section of the second story was still complete. The fire had been at the next house, and there was nothing left of it. The bulldozer was prodding at the rubble while a crew of workers took it apart more gently with shovels. Each wore a white mask that covered his mouth and nose. There was an ambulance parked across the street, and a table with a tall steel coffee jug. Frank walked to the edge of the circle of light. The ambulance driver watched, coffee in one hand, a cigarette in the other. He was about fifty, with deep creases and dry, freckled skin. Frank hated him.

He had the look of those Californians, those San Diegans, for whom boredom and hostility blend together into smug silence. He flicked his cigarette with such practiced attention to the ash that it was not beyond the possibility that this tic was a large piece of the man's character.

"One of the engines went down here," said the driver. "The first house burned and set the second on fire. And this is three blocks from the worst of it. There's bodies in some trees out of the evacuation zone, but the real bad part is up ahead."

"The plane exploded in the air?" asked Frank.

"Not completely, the engine may have ripped off as it was coming down, but more than likely it flew off the wing when the plane hit Cohassett. Have you been over there yet?"

"No," said Frank.

"What a mess."

"Why are they digging here now?" asked Frank. "Can't this wait until morning?"

"There's three bodies left in the house. The guys with the masks got the masks on because of the smell."

The men with the masks sifted through a layer of drywall, smashed furniture, and what remained of a second-floor bathroom. Satisfied that nothing, or rather no one, was in there, they let the bulldozer pick it up. When the bulldozer moved the pile to the lawn, they went at the rubble again.

"Does anything survive the fire?" asked Frank.

"Oh yeah," said the driver. "The fire doesn't last that long or burn that hot. It's not like a car crash. A car crash is rough. If the gas tank is full when it explodes, you can get a concentrated fire, and they have to go back to dental records to make the I.D. But with this kind of fire, usually what kills is the smoke. The bodies from the plane, some of them are all fucked up, the ones that fell from high up, people out of their seats, but the ones that were in seats, or were in the sections that hit intact, they're broken, but they're not cut up. The people on the ground look worse than the people from the plane. I just finished a run from Nimitz Street, and that was bad. There was this family getting out of a car just when the plane hit. The joke is, they'd just come from the airport. The tail section skidded down the street right into the garage as they were getting out of the car."

"How do they know?" asked Frank.

"The little girl across the street saw it happen. The whole house came down, there was nothing left of it, but it didn't burn. What a mess. Pieces of bodies." The driver flicked his ash and then repeated his last words. "Pieces of bodies." This time he lowered his voice, because, Frank thought, he was suddenly aware that Frank was probably not on official business, and that if he was on this side of the barrier, he was from the neighborhood, and for him this was not an opportunity to test the strength of his professional detachment.

Frank realized that there was no law compelling him to stay. He wanted to see if they would uncover the three bodies, but he knew that there would be others, and better. He said good-bye to the ambulance driver.

"Have a good one," said the driver.

He wanted to see the plane. He wanted to see the dead. But which dead? A flight attendant stuck in a tree, or a postman crushed by the tip of a wing? As he thought of the dead, he discovered himself grading the dead, giving them more points if they were passengers, giving them no credit if they were on the ground. The passengers were the ones to blame, of course, but if there was something noble in their deaths, there was also something stupid and annoying about the deaths of the people on the ground. What was noble? The sudden catastrophe immediately recognized by everyone on the plane. But did he mean noble, why noble? Because of a better vantage point, higher station. Elevation. In the air. And what was seen from the vantage point? Why, life, of course. And what about life? Its brevity. And from this knowledge of life's brevity, what lesson are we then free to take to heart? Why, to act on impulse, to act without fear, the freedom of the nobility, the freedom of power, of seeing through the collective futility of the masses.

And what was so insipid about the deaths on the ground? To be on the plane was to be part of a bomb, to be the bomb, to be the killer. And to be on the ground? Was to be another stupid innocent victim. Another victim of massacre.

And if someone on the plane was sleeping when the plane exploded? Or is nobility reserved only for those who see their deaths coming to them?

Yes, only that.

Frank walked back to the street he had come down on, the name stenciled on the curb, Dana Street. So he continued along on Dana, parallel to the main road, the next block. There were big dump trucks rumbling along in formation, and overhead there were helicopters searching the ground with strong lights. It was impossible not to feel excited by all of this, and in the excitement, which was the sheer thrill of being a part of something large, something military, something that was better than entertainment. The little run he had given himself had awakened something in his body, and the numbness of his sorrow, and the boredom of the train trip, were small now, disappearing. There was smoke in the air, and the sounds of a hundred different engines. People shouted to each other. There was purpose to everything around him. No further danger could touch anyone inside this zone now, no other planes would crash, and so everyone was like a surgeon, brilliant with determination in this operating room that was also a neighborhood. And if it was like his neighborhood, it had never really been that, either, it had just been a place with a lot of houses next to each other, but it hadn't been a community. That would change. Everyone who came back to their houses would be friendly with their neighbors now, they would treat them with respect, and if they saw each other in distant parts of the city, they would wave, stop, chat. There would be a community here after the crash. Frank was happy with his thoughts; they were clear and moved forward with an agility he had forgotten. He was having a good time.

He heard himself say, "Madeleine. Anna," to bring them back.

Dana Street led him to Cohassett, two blocks away. He thought of the house destroyed by the engine as a small junior college compared to this great university, this Harvard of lights and noise

ahead of him. Dana had been spared, and there were families at
home, some of them eating dinner, others watching television. The
older children were out with their fathers, and the fathers were
talking to each other in their driveways.

Frank fell in beside a few men and women. One of the men
looked at him with doubt. "Are you from here?" he asked. Frank
understood. The man didn't recognize him, and knew, didn't guess,
that Frank had jumped a wall somewhere to get past the police,
that he was here to see the gore. But Frank held the better card
than this man's pseudo-cop pose, no one could trump him tonight.

"My name is Frank Gale. My wife and daughter were on the
plane."

Behind him he heard a woman say to someone else, "His wife
and daughter were on the plane."

"Dear God," said the block's protector. He said it with force,
and Frank thought that the man must be a Christian, a true believer.

Frank wanted them to introduce themselves, but no one did.
Maybe they think I'm lying, he thought. It was odd, all that suspicion, the preparation for a fight, or a lynching—*This man is not
from here!*—or would they have just denounced him to the police:
Officer, arrest this man, we don't know him! The officer says, Who
are you? Frank says, Frank Gale. The officer says, So what is that
to me? And Frank repeats the story of the day, but already the story
sounds old to him, and the policeman, hearing Frank's stale delivery,
seeing Frank's annoyance at being trapped in this story, doubts it,
and doubts Frank. The policeman screams at him, You prey on our
sympathy! And Frank says, Pray? And the policeman hits him. No,
says the policeman, you come here to see what you have no right
to see. And what is that? asks Frank. That is all this death, says
the policeman. This death is our privilege! It belongs to the people
who live inside the police barricades. But those lines were drawn
arbitrarily, says Frank. They could have been a block farther or
closer in each direction, and the plane hit the neighborhood ran-
domly, did not choose to fall here. The policeman hits Frank again.
The neighbors put away their video recorders. A group of children
chants: It is our luck to have been spared, and if it is our luck,

then we must be deserving! And Frank asks them, And did my wife and daughter deserve to die? And the children chant, It is our luck to have been spared, and if it is our luck, then we must be deserving! In this mild reverie the street disappeared for a moment, but the trance passed, and Frank settled again into his body.

They walked together, like a crowd on its way into a stadium, with the occasional strangers trading speculations. Someone, anyone, could have lost friends in the crash, all those families wiped out, and told Frank that he had no special claims on anyone's sympathy tonight, but no one did. Well, it's a neighborhood, thought Frank, and who really knows anyone in their neighborhood, except the kids? And these days, aren't the kids told not to ride their bikes too far?

They wore T-shirts with the pictures of the famous, or dirty jokes. A man wearing a SHIT HAPPENS T-shirt carried a small videotape camera. Frank wanted to ask him if this was the Hi-8 kind, with the improved resolution that made the tapes almost broadcast quality. Frank had been thinking of getting a new camera, but he supposed there was no need for it now. There would be no more birthday parties filled with screaming little girls.

They came to the barrier, and the man who believed in God showed his driver's license to the policeman standing guard. Frank saw the license: The man's name was Tim Westerberg, and his address was 2851 Cohassett. They were on the 2700 block, and there were no houses standing from the middle of the block on for the next two blocks, on the other side of the street, which was odd-numbered. The policeman stepped aside. Frank passed him. Now he was in the zone of devastation. They turned at the corner, one house away, and saw it all.

There was an engine in the middle of the street, the blades of the fan six feet long. Pieces of a wing were on the sidewalk. There were suitcases everywhere, spilled from the burst containers. And the shells of the houses. The friendly smell of wet charcoal. Bad smells, carpets made of nylon, and pressboard kitchen cabinets cured in formaldehyde had burned. Cars had burned, and there was that gasoline smell, and the paint in garages too, and the stacks of bundled newspapers, most of which had not burned, and were now soaked from the spray of fire trucks. And the smell of the airplane's burned fuel, heavier than gasoline smells, or was it broader? All those smells, layered like a rotting club sandwich (or pastry? a pastry). It was an exciting smell. Yes, and wasn't part of the thrill the knowledge that each breath carried with it a little lung damage? Frank had heard of the sweet smell of decaying bodies, or worse, a disgusting smell, from the exploding intestines, the rot of meat eaters. He looked for that smell here, but the bodies were only thirty hours old, and the weather had been cool.

The circling helicopters threw their searchlights on the ground. Two trucks from the county animal shelter, and men and women, Mexicans and blacks. They carried baited traps, cages with doors that dropped down. A few cats had already been picked up. A woman from the neighborhood quarreled with one of the women from the shelter. Frank heard her wail, "Every day is Auschwitz for the animals."

They came to the end of the block, and another police barricade, yellow tape strung between Stop signs on opposite corners, with a warning not to cross the line. There was a water-filled crater in the middle of the street. One of the neighborhood experts explained. "He must have been alive, because you can see that he was trying to set the plane down in the middle of the street, but his wing hit the ground, and the plane spun over to the left, here, and then cartwheeled along the block."

Someone else said, "He could have already been dead."

"No," said the first man, "because he was lined up with the street."

"That's just chance," said someone else.

"Well, I would prefer to see some heroics in this," said the first man. "It gives me comfort. Is that all right? Does anybody object to my wanting something positive in all of this? One thing? Is that too much to ask for?"

"But why?" asked a woman. "What difference does it make? They're all dead."

Steam rose from the burned houses, where the helicopters had

dumped water the night before. Large lights on tall cranes were set
around the block. There were few shadows inside the light.

Two blocks is really a small area, thought Frank. When you
take the houses away, what do you have? The area of a football
field. You can build thirty houses on a football field. We live in
such small rooms. Fifty feet from the front of the house to the back
door is generous. He thought of his parents' house in Bel Air. But
that was twenty thousand square feet. These houses were probably
two thousand square feet. Yes, his parents had a large house. Even
Julia Abarbanel liked it. The Abarbanels were just far enough outside the Gale orbit not to feel so threatened by the move to the
condominium on Wilshire. Julia's father owned a printing business.
They made most of their money printing annual reports for big
companies. How large was their house? Frank wondered. Eight
thousand square feet? It was something like that. And they were
temple Jews. He was the president of his synagogue. Her father was
an angry man with a good sense of humor, and because he dressed
neatly and walked quickly, with the happy look of a man delighted
by the attention paid him in the performance of his responsibilities,
he was often mistaken, by Jews, when on vacation, as a doctor.
Julia's sour contentiousness, her tendency to quarrel, was a mis-
reading of her father's wit. He was a bore about Israel, and naturally
she took the Palestinian side, but without any effort. What she knew
of their issues she had learned from newspapers and television; she
was not full of facts. And for this her father seemed to hate her a
little, that she could not muster an argument worthy of his intelligence. The Abarbanels and the Gales shared Passover seders a few
times, and at the last one they had held in Bel Air, as conversation
wafted into the usual mess of gossip and movie reviews, Julia's
father banged his spoon on the table, to remind everyone that this
was not a family reunion but a religious service. Maybe I am praising
him too much, thought Frank. Was he really so spiritual, or did he
just like to drag everyone into a wallow of tribal self-congratulation?
Maybe Julia was sour because she had seen through her father's
pretensions, including his charade as cardiologist, and hated him,
and her mother, his aunt, for denying her, as a child, even the

strength to make a strong enough character so that her parents' flaws would not remind her so terribly of her own failings, so that she could make of herself something in the world, which she had not yet done, and knew that she would never. Aaaah, I should have just fucked her, thought Frank.

A large van drove past them and stopped before the crater, where the pavement was shredded by the plane's impact. The driver got out of the van and opened the back, and then he leaned against the truck, to smoke a cigar.

Men in orange jumpsuits, from the Coroner's Office, came across a backyard and around the rubble of a demolished house. There were five teams of them carrying black zippered sacks with bodies inside. From where he stood, Frank could not see them load the bodies into the truck.

Someone behind him said, "Yesterday I saw them plucking a few out of a tree."

Someone else said, "They say a lot of them aren't in one piece. A lot of people in the plane got shredded up, and a lot of people on the ground too, and were burned up."

Someone else said, "A lot of times people just die from smoke inhalation, but the bodies aren't really all that damaged. On the ground. In the fires in the houses, when the houses, when the plane hit the houses, and the fires, what caused the fires in some of the houses wasn't getting hit, it was the fires from the house next door, and that caught, and then on, to the next house, the whole block, like that. And that fire was hot."

Frank wanted to get beyond this final barricade. He left the group and walked back up the block into a shadow. A coroner's truck came by, slowly, and Frank ran beside it, and then behind it, across the street and into the debris of the first burned house on the block. The damp charcoal squeaked under his feet, like new snow.

He was able to walk through five houses, or what had been five houses. Nobody stopped him, nobody saw him. I'm invisible, he thought. He kicked a pile of bricks, and saw a metal bed frame.

He walked on, and passed a vinyl cylinder, someone's record collection, fused by the heat. Rooms are so small, he thought, houses are really so small, compared to the size of the world. He picked up a soup ladle and then put it down, having learned nothing from it.

I miss them. Right now I miss them. I have no one to share this with. He watched himself have this feeling, and wanted to banish the watcher, just to be unhappy about it all, without knowing that he was unhappy.

A luggage container, resting on its top, was just behind the base of a fireplace. This was what was left of the wall of a house; the chimney was gone, the wall was gone, the second floor was gone, but here was the fireplace, in all its annoying resilience. A thin-walled metal luggage container lay next to it, upside down, the cargo spilled out in a horrifying parody of cornucopia. And here was another pile of suitcases in front of him. Nothing had shaken the luggage tags off. Someone would pick them up soon, and then one day, in a week, two weeks, the airline would call the relatives of the dead, and the suitcases would be returned to them. Someone would have to unpack each bag, each bathing suit, each pair of sandals, each silly T-shirt, each tube of suntan lotion. Maybe I'll just give them to the Salvation Army without opening anything up. Closer to the container, he saw his black suitcase on top of Anna's.

He stepped on a sports bag made of rip-resistant nylon, bending a tennis racket. He threw aside a makeup case in the way, and tugged at the handle to his bag. There was his name! And below his bag, there was Anna's, with a piece of red yarn she tied to the handle, to make it easier to find. It was like seeing someone famous; he was almost dissolved by the excitement, the shock.

He pulled the suitcases out of the container and threw them on the ground. They were in perfect shape, there was no sign of damage. He smelled them. They didn't even have the aroma of smoke and kerosene.

He opened Anna's bag, and when he did, he was caught in the light from a helicopter a few hundred feet above him. At the same time, a National Guardsman called out to him, and Frank turned and saw that he was in the man's gun sights. He was told to put his hands up, and he did.

"My name is Frank Gale," he said. "My wife and daughter were on the plane. I just found her suitcase. Isn't that incredible? I can't believe it." He raised his hands slowly. He was told to walk forward. Two police cars came down the block.

"Really," said Frank. "They were on the plane. I came down to . . ." But Frank couldn't finish his sentence. Why did he come down here? he wondered. To find their bodies. Could he say that? Or just to see. Wasn't that enough—could he be arrested for wanting to see? He was told to put his hands on the police car, and when he did, they were pulled behind his back, and then a hard plastic band was pulled tight around his wrists. He was pushed against the warm hood of the police car. The engine was running. He had never listened to a car so closely.

6. Among the Dead

He was handcuffed by a black policeman who shoved him into the back of a police car. He knew there would be no trouble once he got to the station; his first call would be to Lowell, who would call the airline, and Frank would be released before the morning. He was afraid of having his picture taken with a number across his chest. Now he would have an arrest record. What would be the charge? They would accuse him of looting, even though his hands were clean of any of the soot that covered anything that might have been worth taking, if anything worth taking had not been burned, or soaked with water and ashes.

He did not want to tell the cop that his wife and daughter had been on the plane. He felt bad that already he had won so much sympathy for this, that he had earned interest on the deposit of their lives. In the burned-over houses he thought of the pain of everyone who had died, everyone who had heard the engines falling so quickly and so closely, who thought, This is for me, and then thought, No. When you see it coming, is there any time to say to yourself, calmly, "So this is it"? And then the plane hit, broke up, all those pieces, this enormous pomegranate bursting with human seeds and suitcases and first-class seats with their reclining backs and the videotape machines for the in-flight movie and hundreds of miniature vodka bottles and fiery jet fuel and wall modules and bulkheads, and killed them. How odd for a ball of fire to suck all the air from where you live, and then burn it all. He asked the cop, "What's the worst way to die?"

The cop looked at him in the rearview mirror. "Burning to death."

"I used to be afraid of drowning. But I guess that's kind of a psychological thing, the great mother, the ocean." As usual, his voice rose almost to form a question, to invite the cop to join the party of his view of things.

"I wouldn't know. I don't cover the harbor."

"But people drown in swimming pools."

"Very few. Hot tubs sometimes, but usually they pass out from drugs and alcohol, and have a heart attack after soaking in the hot water for hours."

"You've seen that?"

"It happens. Not so much anymore. People know the dangers."

This was another cheap discussion, and Frank stopped it. What had he meant to say? What did he want to know from this policeman, the second black man to drive him tonight?

At the police station he was taken to a room where he was fingerprinted, and then his picture was taken, full face, and profile. Then he called Lowell, who came to the station and posted his bail. Lowell tried to get them to drop the charges, but now that Frank had been arrested, only a judge could do that.

"My brother just went through the worst experience of his life," said Lowell. And the dead? Lowell posted the bail, ten thousand dollars, and Frank was free.

Outside the police station, Lowell smacked Frank on the arm, an old gesture. "Let's go home."

"No," said Frank. "I want to go to the hotel."

"Which hotel?"

"Whichever hotel the airline has, the hotel they're putting the survivors in."

"Why?"

"Because I want to be with all the other families. I need to be."

"No, you need to be in my house, in your bedroom in my house. I'm your family. Not the others."

"But I need to know what's going on."

"Frank, please. Come home with me."

"No, Lowell. I want to go to the hotel. I have to find Bettina Welch. She may have more information."

"Listen to me. I don't know if you can hear me, but listen to me. You've gone through a terrible trauma. You can't be left alone. I have to be with you. No one expects you to behave in any way other than the way you're behaving now."

"Which is what?"

"I don't want to get into this."

"Into what?"

"You shouldn't have taken the train. You should have driven down with me. You shouldn't have gone to the crash site. You should have been with me, or with Mom and Dad."

"But I had to see the crash site. And I had to take the train alone. I had to be alone for a little while. And now I want you to take me to the hotel."

"Okay," said Lowell, without enthusiasm. Frank felt the pointlessness of checking into a hotel at one in the morning; no one would be awake to take care of him, but at breakfast he could find Bettina. What would he ask her? Anything.

In the car Lowell called a number that the airline had given him. *The Flight 221 Hot Line.* A man answered. Lowell told him who he was, who he was related to, and the man told them to go to a Marriott, near the airport.

When they got there, Bettina Welch was in a small conference room with a hand-lettered posterboard sign on the door that said OPERATIONS CENTER.

"Frank, oh Frank," she said. "What were you thinking?" Of all the things she might have said, this seemed to be the most perfect, the best expression of the corporation's union with her. What else could she have said? It was reprimand but not condemnation. To assume friendship and still be impersonal!

"I just wanted to . . ." His voice trailed off.

"Of course, who wouldn't?"

Lowell put a hand on Frank's shoulder. "Okay, Frank, I'm going home. I'll be back in the morning."

"Sure," said Frank. But he didn't care about Lowell coming back. What difference would it make? He was tired of everyone's compassion.

Two women were at a table with phones. Did they work for the airline, or for the hotel?

Lowell walked away. Bettina Welch called the hotel's front desk. She identified herself, and then explained that she had another guest with her. Then she thanked someone and put the phone down. "I've got a nice room for you upstairs. It has a view of the bay."

"That would be nice," said Frank.

"And anything else you want, remember that the airline is here to help you. I'm here to help you. And if I'm not here, you can speak to Kelly or Chris." And then she introduced him to the two women at the desk.

"But you won't need them," said Bettina, "because I'm always available."

How many times today had she said all of this? Two days ago, in Los Angeles, there had been something fresh about her little speeches; even though they were written, she had not yet wrapped her mouth around each word a hundred times. But now the show had been on the road for too long.

Someone led Frank to a room on the ninth floor. He opened the curtain and turned off the lights, and looked at the bayside traffic in this city he hated. How many places in the world are as pointless as this? How many people are this pointless? Do I have a point? he asked himself. What was lost in the crash? Who was lost? What was lost beside the predictability of a set of lives? Someone assuring someone else of a certain amount of time spent in some semblance of dedication to the other. We know each other, and we will probably continue to know each other. And money, that too, always. I make money, and we share it, and so we will have money together. And now death, and the threat of no money. And what else? Love? Well, who wouldn't be thrilled, after such a spectacular, divinely decreed divorce, by all the possibilities? I am thrilled, thought Frank, with what I can now do with my life. He looked at boats in the harbor, the lights on top of the masts of the sailboats at the marina next to the hotel. I can go to islands now, with women who are better-looking than my wife.

It was a bad hotel room. He wanted to check his answering machine at home, and when he tried to carry the phone from the side table to the bed, the cord's short line caught him by surprise, and the phone crashed to the floor. When he took a shower, the steam rose to the bathroom's low ceiling, and after a few minutes the condensation fell back on his head in large, cold drops. And the water temperature was hard to adjust. He used a hand towel on the floor instead of the shower mat. The hand towel had no grip, did not absorb, was too thin, too light, and when he stepped out of the shower, he slipped and had to catch the toilet for balance. Then he saw the bath mat, folded on the towel rack. He dropped the mat on the floor, but it fell on the other towel, and he had to bend down to move them both, and he didn't like getting his hands wet with the water on the floor, because it brought up old piss that had settled into the grout. He washed his hands again in the sink and then dried them on the remaining bath towel. Next to the sink was a little tray stocked with soap, a shower cap, a small sewing kit (needle, thread, a few buttons), and a small toothbrush and toothpaste. The sink, too shallow for the strong water pressure, became a fountain, splashing onto the counter, staining these little, what, not gifts, they're paid for, these little . . . things. But they're nice to have, the conditioner, the lotion. The things of the hotel. He brushed his teeth and wished he had some floss. He would have made his gums bleed tonight, he would have liked that, the pain, and the next day, his gums tender, and swollen, not so much that anyone but a dentist would notice, and yet enough for him to feel them, enough to warrant an aspirin he would not take.

When he called home for his messages, the machine picked up on the first ring, which meant that there had been calls, but when the cycle shifted to rewind, he heard a few clicks, but no messages in reverse.

The outgoing message on the tape, Anna. "Hi, this is the Gale home. We're not in now. Leave a message at the sound of the tone, and we'll get back to you when we can." We. Madeleine, in the background, singing. And anyone calling would think about that word, that "We." Maybe I will leave the tape unchanged, thought Frank, just to bother whoever calls me.

When the machine started from the beginning of the tape, there were blank spaces, and then the long tone meaning that the messages were finished. A few people had called, but left no messages. The living checking the dead, of course. To hear the voice, knowing that Anna, and the little girl trilling away behind her, were dead.

He went to bed and turned off the lights. Amazing, to feel so unglued just by sleeping in a hotel room alone. In the dark he stroked his penis a few times, but let it go. He wondered if Bettina Welch would understand the freedom his grief gave him. Why jack off, when he could fuck a whore, or rape someone? Not rape, not really, he thought, but then, yes, he supposed so, the fantasy was there. Bettina Welch in a stairwell. Fuck her bloody and leave her in the basement. But not to die, only to forgive him, to understand, because she *would* understand. No, she would never forgive him. And she wouldn't like it. It might wake her up, though. No, she

would cry. She would PRESS CHARGES. She would FEEL VIO-
LATED. She would learn that it was NOT A SEXUAL CRIME, but
a CRIME OF VIOLENCE. But then she might forgive him if she
considered that to be so violent, HE MUST HAVE BEEN TREATED
VIOLENTLY AS A CHILD. HE MUST HAVE BEEN BEATEN
AND RAPED HIMSELF. And the man who blew up the plane? HE
MUST HAVE BEEN BLOWN UP AS A CHILD. His father must
have put a hose up his ass and pumped air into him until his
intestines ruptured. And so he must have pursued a crisis in his
life that would JUSTIFY ACTING OUT his scenarios of distension.
Or could he pump air into Bettina's ass with his own lungs? Was
that the sort of thing homosexuals do with each other? Rimming. A
tongue in the middle of that face that can't talk back. Someone
wears the right color handkerchief in the pocket of choice, and
someone else knows that he likes his ass sucked in a certain way.
He played with his penis as he thought about Bettina's ass. Was
Bettina wearing something that told people who knew how to read
such things that she liked to have a man play with her nipples while
lightly circling her asshole with his pinkie? Was there something
in the way that Frank dressed, or in the way he spoke, or held his
shoulders, or his arms, or in the way he polished or did not polish
his shoes, or arranged his clothes in his closet, that signaled to the
attentive world that he had a specific fantasy? Or did he signal to
the attentive world that he did not, in fact, have any particular
fantasy at all? That he was dull, or dull to those whose fantasies
were involved, specific, bold. Did hard muscles, tight clothes, and
an obsession with fashion bring someone closer to ecstasy? The gold
chain on Bettina's ankle: There was someone in the world who saw
her when the bracelet was all she wore. He felt the shadow of a tall
man, with a big American face, someone with ambition but little
discipline, and the voice of someone on the radio, late-night disk
jockey on an oldies station, someone who lived in utopia. He lives
with Bettina, and they talk sometimes of marriage. What if the three
of them went to bed together? Would that bring back his wife and
daughter? If he fucked Bettina's boyfriend while he fucked Bettina,

on the grave of his family, would that help turn back the clock? But there never was a saint who altered time. A demonic ritual, all of the impulses, larger impulses than mass murder and terrorism. Fuck them all! That's what they say. Fuck 'em all! And to do that? To really fuck them all? Every one of them, in every hole, happy, angry.

And Mary Sifka, well, yes, with Mary he was almost a good fuck. She liked him. She wanted him. But that had taken a little time, for both of them. And if Mary loved him, and also loved her husband, did she ever want to fuck them both, fuck them all? Which one of them would get her ass first? Or her mouth while the other one fucked her? Would she suck Frank while her husband fucked her ass? Or would the husband claim seignorial rights, and dictate to Frank what he could and could not do? You can drink her piss, but she won't drink yours. Yes, the yellow handkerchiefs that homosexuals used to wear, golden showers, actually to sit on a toilet in a bar, an open stall in a bathroom with five seats in a row, your pants around your ankles, your dick in hand, trying to come, while strangers line up to piss their beery piss into your mouth. Frank had never been to that kind of party. But once he knew about these bars, he couldn't look at a crowded room without wondering, Would you? Do you? And Lowell, how far down was that creature of abandon, how close were the memories, or the anticipations, of licking someone's butt in a men's room? Was the pressure of such impulses the force that stopped the talk at dinner tables? Look at the not-too-crowded party, everyone posed about the room, and the boredom over it all, the exhaustion that makes each word a screaming effort. All that food, something to keep the teeth busy, away from skin.

Or murders too. Let's fuck each other and bring down an airplane! Come on, guys, let's pee! Could he fuck Mary Sifka and then have her husband lick her juices off his stick? Frank wondered if people thought like this a thousand years ago, or fifty years ago, or twenty years ago, or was it new?

His brain spinning away, Frank fell asleep. His dreams were a continuation of his last conscious thoughts. He had never known this before, that he could watch himself dreaming. How could he call himself asleep, if he knew that he was dreaming? On any other night these dreadful images would have catapulted him awake, and he would have grabbed his wife, and told her about the nightmare. But this was not a nightmare, this was meditation. Bodies falling around him, a dark street with the houses burned, a ride in a police car, the conductor on the train. There was nothing hidden behind a screen, nothing repressed. And there was no fear.

He lay in this hypnagogia for a few hours, until the sun came up. At seven in the morning, he called Mary Sifka at home. He needed to talk to her, to tell her that he was alive.

Her husband answered, as Frank thought he might, but they had never spoken, and what was so odd about early calls to a woman who worked?

"Is Mrs. Sifka there?" Frank asked.

"She's in the shower," said her husband, which seemed like a piggish thing to say, giving a stranger permission to think about water running down his wife's naked body.

"I'll call her at work. This is the New York office calling, Ed Welch, I'm about to tell the printers to go ahead on the spring proposal, and I need to check some last-minute figures with her." He hoped this sounded reasonable, and dull. Doesn't everyone have to deal with a spring proposal?

Mary's husband turned away from the phone, and Frank heard him call to his wife, that there was a phone call for her, from the New York office. "One second," he said. Frank supposed she was getting the phone in another room.

She picked it up, and said "Hello?" and then the husband put the receiver down. They were alone.

"I know I shouldn't call you at home."

As soon as he said this, she screamed. "Oh, God, I thought you were dead."

"I missed the plane."

"Your name was listed in the paper this morning. You're listed among the dead."

"Well, here I am."

She started to cry, and then her husband came into the room. Frank heard him. Muffled, "Honey, what's wrong?"

Is that all to say? What else?

She hung up. What was she telling him right now? Why did I call? I should have had someone else call. My voice, I was a ghost to her.

He felt a smile growing. This is fun, he thought. This is actually quite amazing. This will be legend. Who else can I scare? He got out of bed and went to the door, to see if the hotel had left a courtesy copy of the newspaper outside. They had, but not the *Los Angeles Times*, only the stupid local paper. The crash was the only news on the front page, with four pictures; the largest was an aerial view of the burned-out blocks, and the other two were of children crying at the neighborhood's high school, because a favorite teacher had been killed. The third was titled CRASH INVESTIGATORS SEARCHING THROUGH THE RUBBLE. The fourth picture was of Lonnie Walter, the former airline employee suspected of causing the crash. The photograph had been taken when he had been given his job for the airline. Frank could tell nothing from his expression. He wore a white shirt and a tie, but no jacket. He was forty-five. The article said that little was known about his background, beyond a few dates. He had been born in Texas, and the family had moved to Los Angeles when he was seven. He was divorced. He had a son. And he had been fired by the airline a few days before the crash, by Nick Burdett, an operations supervisor who was on his way to Acapulco to a meeting there at the airline's aircraft-maintenance center. Walter had left a note at home, for his ex-wife, telling her that he was never coming back. Well, that was true. Frank could not connect the man's face, or his story, to the death of his family. He closed the door and looked for the list of the dead.

The airline, or the newspaper, divided the dead into categories under three headings. The first heading was PASSENGERS. The second heading was FLIGHT CREW. The third heading was ON THE

GROUND. The paper cautioned readers that the lists were incomplete. The Flight Crew list separated the *Cockpit Crew*, the pilot and first and second officers, from the *Cabin Crew*. Frank could further break the passenger list down by nationality, since a third of the names were Mexican. The rest were tourists or people going to Mexico for business, but that distinction was harder to read. He could separate all single men from the list and assume they were on business, perhaps all single men over forty. How many fifty-year-old men would go to Mexico for a vacation by themselves? But then, how many of them were attached to women whose last names they did not share? For example, Anna, who had kept her maiden name, was separated from Frank on the list.

Between Fogel, Mark, and Gallegos, Luisa B., were:

> *Gale, Frank*
> *Gale, Madeleine*

Then, down the list, between Levy, Lawrence, and Keith, Darnelle, was Klauber, Anna. Someone reading the list with an eye toward solving the puzzle of the relationships, would assume that *Gale, Frank,* and *Klauber, Anna,* were strangers to each other. If that breakfast-table detective tried to dissect the list for all the single men and women, to stack them together again in couples, he might put Levy, Lawrence, with Klauber, Anna, but it was also possible that he would create for himself an Anna Klauber heading for Mexico to drink margaritas at lunch and fuck the cabana boys. He would follow this Anna down in flames to the ground, thinking of her underpants, her bathing suit, her vagina.

The list of the dead on the ground was short, only twenty, but the police had not yet notified all the next of kin, which might take days. The police expected the list to grow to at least a hundred.

He picked up the phone. Who to call? He could call Lowell, but if his brother was annoyed with him for last night's stunt, then why call him unless he meant to apologize? And if he apologized, would that give Lowell the power to

BRING FRANK TO HIS SENSES?

Now with an apology, Frank would have to
ADMIT THAT HE'D BEEN OUT OF CONTROL.

And with that, Lowell would trundle him out of the hotel, bring
him to his house, and help Frank
TO PUT THE TRAGEDY BEHIND HIM.

It was too soon for that. He called his mother instead.

Lowell had already told her about the arrest, which meant that
he was awake and had called them early, or had called them last
night, when Frank was roaming the zone of death.

"Your father and I couldn't sleep last night."

"Is he okay?"

"We'll never be okay."

"I'm sorry."

"You're not supposed to bury your children or grandchildren,
that's not the way God wants things."

"He wanted it this time."

"Don't be bitter."

"Mom." He said this quickly.

"What am I saying?" she asked. "Be bitter. Be as bitter as you
want. It might be good for you. You could stand to cry. Have you
cried yet?"

"Last night. I cried when I got home."

"What were you doing out there? They could have shot you, for
looting."

"I wasn't looting. I was looking."

"And what did you hope to see?"

"I don't know."

"I do. And I shouldn't say this, because I know what kind of
pain you're in, but you were hoping to see their bodies, Frank.
That's what you wanted to see." The way she had said this, the
words she had chosen, the comma after bodies and then his name,
and the quick, short sentence after that, told him that she had gone
too far, and knew it, and wanted to negate the first intention, which
was to brutalize him with the strength of her insight, her honesty,
to show off that she knew things about him to which he was blind.
She was punishing him with his own motives.

So why didn't I tell her the truth? he asked himself. Why not just come out and admit that I wanted to see their bodies on the ground? Because I did not want to shock her. But she knew anyway.

How much had she known about me when I was growing up? How much had she withheld from me, how many of her insights did she keep to herself? And do I wish she had been truthful, or am I glad that she let me be? Or was she afraid of telling me the truth, for fear that I would turn around and make her suffer the indictment her son had crafted for a lifetime?

"Yes, you're right," said Frank. "I wanted to see the bodies. I needed to know for myself that they really are dead."

"THE GUILT OF THE SURVIVORS," she said.

There was a knock on the door. "Frank?" It was Lowell. "Frank, it's me."

Frank called out to him, to wait a second, and then his mother said, "What?"

"Lowell is here."

"Let me talk to him."

So she wanted to talk to Lowell about the problems baby brother was having, how to take care of him, how to help him

GET OVER THIS.

Lowell was there with a brown paper shopping bag. Frank saw a few bagels, and a plastic container with cream cheese, and a plastic bottle of fresh orange juice. He told Lowell that their mother was on the phone, and that she wanted to speak to him.

"I didn't want you to have that shitty hotel food. Let's eat this." He handed Frank the bag, in a gesture that meant, Accomplish this small task, the setting of a table, and reenter the world of the living. Your therapy begins now. But the effort to so quickly help him

DEAL WITH THE PAIN

only pushed him further away from Lowell, since he was expected to start his recovery. He opened the bag and put the bagels on the round table near the balcony. There was nothing to cut the bagels with, only plastic knives for spreading the cream cheese. He tore an onion bagel in half and daubed the cut ends with the cheese.

While Lowell talked to their mother, Frank went to the bathroom for the drinking glasses, and poured the orange juice.

On the phone Lowell assured their mother that Frank looked fine, Frank was going to be fine, and that he, Lowell, was fine. Then his mother said something to Lowell, and to respond he grunted a few times. She was telling him something, and she didn't want an articulate response. What was she saying, that she was worried? Maybe she was talking about their father. No. She's telling him something about me, thought Frank.

Lowell offered the phone to Frank. "Dad wants to say something."

Frank took the phone. His father's voice was heavy, wet. "I'm going to temple, Frank. I'm going to say kaddish today."

"Thanks, Dad."

"You should too."

"I'll think about it." He didn't want to pray, or he did, but he didn't want to go to temple, he didn't want to have to park his car, think about finding a space, or reach for his keys when the service was over.

"Your mother wants to go to San Diego. The airline says there's going to be a memorial service, and they think it's going to be in San Diego, because of the people on the ground. There may be a service in L.A., though. We'll go to them all. These things, these prayers, these services, that's why we have them, to help us through the hardest times." Frank could detect, in his father's gush of sodden theology, the notes of capitulation to reality that, transposed to the sphere of business, became the shudders of doubt that made him pull short of what he was afraid to do and brought his business down.

The phone call ended. "Do you know anything about this memorial service?" he asked Lowell.

"There may be something in a few days. The airline is setting it up. I hate to say this," said Lowell, and then stopped.

"What?"

"Well, it's a publicity stunt, it's the airline managing the news.

They'll come across as the chief mourner, they'll set up something in the public's mind, so that juries will feel sympathy for the airline, so it'll be harder to get a big judgment against them. For the money. We have to find a good lawyer. I don't know whether we join a class-action suit, or if we do this alone. Maybe we find a few other people and sue with them."

"I could sue my limo driver for getting me to the airport late."

Lowell used a laugh at this to pull up a chair and tear apart a bagel and drag the cut end through the cream cheese, piling it against the leading edge. "Let's go back to my place."

"No," said Frank. "I want to see Bettina Welch. I want to find out what else they know."

"I'm not going to say that I know how much pain you're in. But I am going to say that you're only going to make that pain worse."

"If what?"

"By hanging around here waiting for whatever it is you're waiting for."

"Where should I go? What should I do?"

"We should go home."

"But what about the bodies? I don't want to go home without the bodies."

"We'll stay here until we can bring Anna and the baby home. I promise." He always called Madeleine "the baby." Frank thought it was because he wasn't quite sure of her name.

For the second time in two and a half days, they left a hotel room to see Bettina Welch.

She was in the conference room, on the phones. The airline representatives all wore identification tags, with their pictures. The photographs were of the same dull style as the picture of Lonnie Walter, a head shot in front of a cream background. A few of the other survivors who had been in the hotel in Los Angeles were there, getting breakfast from a buffet table. The spread was not so lavish as in Los Angeles, three steam trays, one chef, a few busboys. There were eggs, sausages, and pancakes. Beside them, on large plates, were cereals and breads, and then a few pitchers with orange and tomato juice, and milk. The coffee cups were small.

The woman with the copper-colored hair sat at a table, reading the paper, while her husband brought her a plate of scrambled eggs. A Mexican family ate sausages and drank orange juice.

Bettina Welch left her table. She approached Lowell with her hand out, because he had been so difficult in Los Angeles, and she had to win him over. He took her hand as she said, "Hello again, Mr. Gale."

"Lowell," he said.

She gave Frank another official hug. "How are you feeling today?"

"I don't know yet."

"We have to talk. Can I get you something to eat?"

Frank wanted a pancake with syrup, but said nothing. She took him by the arm and they sat at a table away from others.

"Frank," she said, and he knew there was trouble. "The press found out about you."

"What did I do?"

"Two things. You weren't on the plane. And then the arrest last night. They want to talk to you."

"Why?"

"Because you weren't on the plane. They say it's everyone's nightmare."

"Not dying on a plane?"

"Missing a plane that crashes. I don't know why. People have such horrible things, sometimes." Have things. What things?

Lowell put himself between Frank and Bettina. "Listen to me. I don't want the press bothering my brother, do you understand that?"

"You know, Mr. Gale, you're also suffering through this."

"Is that supposed to make me happy, your concern for me, Miss Welch?" Nothing had changed. Lowell would never try to be nice to her. Lowell blamed her for the crash.

Frank put a hand on Lowell, the familiar way to bring him back from his rage. "We just won't talk to them. That's all. I just won't talk to them."

"We need a lawyer," said Lowell. "We need a lawyer today."

"Let's wait," said Frank.

"No," said Lowell. "And we're not going to join anybody else's suit. I want to make a separate case out of this."

"Do we have to talk about this now?" asked Frank. "Can't we wait until after the funeral?"

Bettina Welch interrupted. "There's going to be a memorial service for everyone in two days, here in San Diego. We'll have limos to take you."

"Limousines. As if that helps," said Lowell.

"We're trying."

"Bettina," said Frank, "my brother is very upset."

"I know that. And thank you. And now I have to get back to work."

"What's next?" asked Frank.

"In what way?" she said.

"Where do we go next? What are we supposed to do now?"

"I've given your name to the County Coroner's Office. They'll be calling you as soon as they can. I'm sorry, Frank, but you'll have to identify the body. I'm sorry, I mean the bodies."

"Is there anything left of them?" asked Frank.

"Don't think about that," she said.

"I can't help it. It's a natural thing to think about. Do you know?"

"I don't, no."

"She won't answer the question," said Lowell. "She doesn't want to say anything that would cause you more distress, so you could sue."

"As a matter of fact, Mr. Gale, that's exactly right." And then she turned and went back to her desk.

"You dick," said Frank.

"Fuck her," said Lowell, in a way that sounded more like a command than a curse.

The copper-haired woman looked up from her sausages and waved to Frank and Lowell. Lowell led Frank to her table.

"I'm Brenda Cohn," she said, "and this is Geoffrey. We lost our Danny, and his new bride, Angela. They were married last Sunday. I guess we're still in the anger stage of all of this. We weren't in denial very long."

"I lost my wife and daughter," said Frank.

"We heard. We're terribly sorry. You're the fellow who missed the plane."

"Does everyone know?" asked Lowell, but his belligerence was under control. Frank thought that only he knew the meanness inside the question.

"I think so," said Geoffrey. He seemed less a ruined man than on the night of the crash, when defeat was so much a part of him that the crash loomed over him as only the most recent attack on his life, or the necessary conclusion to a series of disasters. "It's going to be hard for you."

"It's hard for all of us," said Frank.

"But for you," said Geoffrey. "We'll have a little privacy. But for you, no. You'll never have privacy. This is going to stick with you, forever."

"I hope not," said Frank.

"Yes," said Brenda. "For the rest of your life you'll be the man who missed two-twenty-one. You'll be marked by this. It won't be easy for you to remarry."

Frank expected Lowell to jump in, but he stayed silent. Frank looked to him for support.

"That makes sense," said Lowell.

"Why?" asked Frank, knowing this was the wrong question, because it brought him into their game.

"Because you'll be cursed," said Geoffrey. "Every time a woman who loves you leaves for anything, any trip, she'll worry about her safety. She'll worry that she'll be the second wife to die. Your wife, she was your first wife?"

"Yes," said Frank.

"And if she gets on a plane without you," said Brenda, not finishing the sentence. The implication was there: If she gets on a plane without you, she'll be sure to remember how you were widowed.

"But only if she gets on a plane without me when I was supposed to be on the plane," said Frank. "Don't forget, I didn't not take the plane, I missed the plane. A million people don't take a flight that their wives or husbands are on. That happens every day. But this was different. I didn't not take the flight. That's normal. I missed the plane. I was late to the airport. How many people miss a flight their families are on, and then the plane crashes? How many people? You can't say that happens all the time."

"I don't know," said Brenda. "You might be right. That's an interesting opinion."

"Why were you late?" asked Geoffrey.

"Traffic," said Frank.

"We dropped them off at the airport," said Brenda, "and the traffic wasn't that bad. Which way were you coming from?"

"I don't know."

"Of course you know," said Geoffrey. "Everyone knows the direction they're coming from."

"Hollywood," said Frank. "I had lunch with a friend, and then I was running a little late."

"Your friend saved your life," said Brenda.

"Who was it?" asked Lowell.

"Actually my insurance agent."

"What insurance agent?" asked Lowell. "Jack Ney?" Jack Ney was Mary's boss.

"No," said Frank. This was going to be a bad lie, but it was too late to stop. A name spilled out of his mouth. "Mark Sifka."

"Is he with Jack Ney?" He meant: Does he handle the company's insurance? "Is he ours?"

"No, mine."

"What. Car, life?"

"Not car. House and stuff. Life."

"I thought you used Jack's office for that. Why'd you stop?"

"I don't know. This guy kept calling. I don't know. I met him at a party."

"Whose party?" asked Lowell. Frank thought Brenda Cohn suspected something in his reluctance to answer.

"You don't know them, friends of Anna's." Now I am using Anna as an alibi for my mistress. This is out of control.

"Whatever," said Lowell. Frank thought that he had threatened Lowell with the possibility of independence by finding his own insurance agent, without asking for permission or advice. It had never occurred to Frank before that Lowell needed him too.

"Did you buy life insurance from him at lunch?" asked Geoffrey.

"Not then. A while ago."

"Wouldn't that have been something?" said Geoffrey. "Although it wouldn't have been in effect when the plane crashed."

Throughout this, Brenda watched Frank, but he couldn't tell what she was thinking. He thought a stranger might have thought she hated him, the way she looked at him so impatiently. The stranger would have thought that Brenda was keeping a running tab of his errors, and everything he said was wrong.

"Mark Sifka," said Lowell. "And you had lunch with him." Meaning: It's not like you, Frank, to have lunch with an insurance agent, since you are a snob and can't see past someone's job as easily as I can, you can't appreciate a good salesman as well as I can. And since insurance salesmen are so reviled in the culture, it is not likely that you, Frank Gale, would talk to one for any time longer than it took to buy the minimum amount of insurance he was selling, suspicious of his rates, and merciless in not wanting to give the salesman any moment of joy, thinking that his happiness, his satisfaction with the sale, would only mean that he had triumphed over another sucker. "So this Sifka, he knew you were going to Mexico. He knew what time you were leaving."

"I guess so," said Frank.

"If he reads the papers," said Brenda, "he thinks you're dead."

"I should call him," said Frank. This was perfect, the excuse he needed to leave the table.

"Did he insure your wife and daughter?" asked Geoffrey.

"Yes," said Frank. He didn't know what else to say, and the stupidity of the lie crashed around him, like an airplane on fire.

Geoffrey matched his wife's hard, unpleasant study of him. "You better call him. He's preparing the settlement on the claim. He's probably waiting for someone in the family to call him. He insured you too."

"Yes, we had a lot of insurance with him. I did."

"You better call him," said Brenda. "Maybe your brother should call him."

"That's a good idea," said Lowell.

"Why?" asked Frank.

Brenda kept her stare. "Because if you call him, he'll think it's a ghost."

"Even if he doesn't believe in ghosts," said Geoffrey.

"People get heart attacks that way," said Brenda.

"What's his number?" asked Lowell. He took a pen from his jacket, and then a little notebook he always carried.

"I don't know," said Frank. "I'll call him, I think I should."

"You don't need to," said Lowell.

"Let your brother call," said Brenda. "It would be a blessing, for your friend to hear about this from your brother. Then you could call him. You could even be in the room with him."

"That's a great idea," said Lowell. The issue of Mark Sifka was clearly his first relief from the catastrophe in three days; he had a focus for his anger that did not call out for more anger, but compassion, and at the same time gave him the privilege of belonging to the heart of the story, to be a part of the disaster. "Let's go upstairs."

"Can I ask one question?" said Brenda.

Frank said yes.

"How much were they insured for?"

"That's kind of a personal question," said Frank.

"Listen," said Lowell, "we're all going through this together, it may help them to know."

"My wife was insured for one million dollars. I was insured for two million. The baby wasn't insured at all."

"Of course not," said Brenda.

"Well," said Frank, trying to stop all of this.

Geoffrey offered his hand. Frank took it, and held on. "You know," said Geoffrey, "I have to say you seem a little ahead of yourself."

"How so?" asked Frank.

"I think you've raced a little too quickly from anger into depression. Maybe you need to go back to denial for a bit. After the period where you tell yourself it isn't true, you get really mad. I think you need to be really mad at the airline, at God, at everything."

"Maybe," said Frank. He thought this might be true and, thinking back, could not recall any real anger yet. So perhaps he was still denying.

"Let's go," said Lowell.

In the elevator Frank had a clear vision of what to do. When they got to the room, he called information in Los Angeles, and asked for, and spelled, Mark Sifka. There was only one Sifka, an M. Sifka. That was Mary, of course. He then made up a number and wrote it down on the hotel's memo pad. He gave it to Lowell. Lowell dialed the number.

Someone answered, and Lowell asked for Mark Sifka. Lowell then said, "Are you sure?" And then he read the number that he had dialed. He had dialed correctly. He thanked the person and hung up. "I got a wrong number."

"I don't know," said Frank. "We'll call him later."

"No," said Lowell, dialing again. Then he said, "Yes, I'd like the number for Mark Sifka, please. In Los Angeles, or West Los Angeles." After a moment he was told, as Frank knew, that there was only one M. Sifka. "That's it."

This time he dialed again, and this time when the phone was answered he said, "Is Mark Sifka there?" There was a pause. Frank couldn't hear the other's voice. "I'm sorry," said Lowell, "I called Information for Mark Sifka, and they gave me this number. I'm sorry to bother you." He hung up. Then he dialed again. He looked at Frank while he waited for someone to answer.

"What happened?" asked Frank.

"The wrong Sifka. I'm calling Karen." Karen was Frank's secretary. "She'll have the number in your address book."

"I don't think so," said Frank. "I just met him, I mean we just started doing business together. I don't think I ever gave her the number."

"Jesus, Frank." Meaning: What kind of a businessman are you? Meaning: Is this chaos, this disorganization, typical of how you run things when I am not around? Can I trust you?

"Sifka's not going to do anything with his company's money until someone files a claim."

Lowell moved away from the phone. Frank was safe. Then the phone rang. Frank rushed for it, in case Mary Sifka had found him. He didn't want Lowell to ask who was calling, and hear her last name.

"Hello," said Frank.

"May I speak to Frank Gale?"

"Who's calling?"

"This is Ron Godfrey."

"What is this about?" asked Frank.

"Is this Mr. Gale?" Neither would give anything away.

"I need to know what this is about?"

"I was calling to tell him how terribly sorry I am for him."

"Are you with the airline or the Coroner's Office?"

"I'm with the *Los Angeles Times*, the San Diego bureau. I wanted to talk to Frank Gale."

"Yes."

"Is this Mr. Gale?"

"Yes."

"I just wanted to tell you how terribly sorry I am for your great loss." It was interesting to Frank, this new perspective, to be in the center of things, and see how human everyone was, how much trouble they had saying what they meant, how they lied to protect themselves from the shame they felt at the things they did in order to survive. Here was a reporter, a man doing his job, and his job called for him to speak to the victims of cruel fate. And he was repeating himself, because it hurt him to violate the victim's privacy, but he persisted, because that was the nature of his job. Frank thought of sad-eyed Republicans, and how they live in Olympian distance from the mob, which gives them greater knowledge of the mob. And if knowledge is power, to know the mob is to control the mob, and so Frank would be able to control this reporter. Frank would become a Republican.

"Yes," said Frank, again. Lowell asked him who it was. Frank covered the mouthpiece and whispered, "Newspaper."

"You know that you were listed as having been on the plane."

He waited five seconds, which is a long time to be silent on the phone. "Yes." Leave him hanging.

"We understand that you just missed the plane. That they took your ticket downstairs, but they made a mistake, and you were at the gate as the plane was pulling away."

Another five seconds. He counted to himself, and then just made a sound. "Mmm-hmmm." Frank didn't even have to say anything now.

"I should call back," said Ron Godfrey. Whatever he had expected, this wasn't it. He was probably used to hysteria, someone to whom he could offer comfort. But Frank would accept none from him.

Another long wait. "Yes," said Frank.

"Maybe there's someone in the family I can talk to," said Godfrey.

"No, my family is dead." He said this quickly, without hesitation. Then he held his hand over the phone, because he wanted to let out the laugh that was building inside of him. He wanted to cackle into the phone.

"I'm sorry, I shouldn't have called."

Frank said nothing, but breathed into the phone. What did Ron Godfrey think of this?

"Mr. Gale, are you all right?"

"What do you think?" and then he hung up.

"What did he say?" asked Lowell.

"He wants to know how I feel about missing the plane. Maybe I should have told him the truth."

"Did he know about the arrest?"

"I don't think so."

"You should probably talk to them, just say something short and don't think about it."

"But why?"

"Because you got arrested. If you just go along with them, you'll disappear in all of this, but if you cause them trouble, they'll come after you, they'll think you have something to hide, they'll make a freak out of you."

"How did you get to be such an expert in this?"

"I read the papers."

"Does it have an effect on a lawsuit?"

"Why?"

"Because that's why you want me to play along. Not to hurt a lawsuit."

"Maybe a little."

There was another phone call, from Dale Beltran, the grief counselor.

"Mr. Gale, I've just been contacted by the County Coroner's Office. They're ready to begin the identification of the bodies."

"I'm ready," said Frank.

"But I have to warn you," he said, "not all of the bodies are ready now. You may have to go back a second time."

"That's okay," said Frank. "It's something I need to do."

"Yes," said Beltran. "The denial of the reality of the situation only prolongs the healing process. At the same time, some of the more gruesome aspects of the results of a crash can be so horrifying that they linger in the mind, and we develop a morbid obsession with what we've seen. Then we exhibit the symptoms of POST-TRAUMATIC STRESS SYNDROME. And that requires an even longer time to heal."

"So I shouldn't go."

"It's your choice, Frank."

"I'm coming. And I'll bring my brother."

"That's a good idea, Frank."

Everyone gathered in the command center, where the chefs stood behind a display of salads, fruits, and cheeses. Bettina and her deputies, Chris and Kelly, handed red passes to the mourners, tickets for the transportation.

Frank and Lowell joined the crowd. People talked quietly, Lowell joined in a few little chats, but Frank said nothing. The names of a few lawyers were mentioned.

Downstairs at the hotel entrance, the group was led to a tour bus.

"Where's the limousine?" asked Lowell.

"What limousine?" asked Bettina.

"You promised us a limousine would take us to the coroner."

"I said there'd be limos to the memorial service, not the coroner."

Frank touched Lowell's shoulder. "That's what she said."

They got on the bus. Frank recognized in Lowell's hesitation upon entering the bus, and seeing the relatives of the dead in their printed T-shirts, a little fear of contamination from the mob. The bus could have been carrying tourists, nothing about the way they looked as a group, except for their eyes, most of them red, tired, swollen, suggested the terrible landscapes waiting for them. Lowell's pause at the top of the stair, which could have been read by some on the bus as the normal surveillance for a good seat, was a second too long, and his dismay was obvious. Frank whispered to him, "We don't need the limo. Let's sit down."

There was another bus behind them, and the mournful caravan left the hotel, the grieving survivors shielding their eyes from the press. The papers would report on the GRIM TASK.

The bus drove through the entrance to the naval yards, and the mood of the passengers changed as they came to the docks. None of them could continue to play with their reflections in the windows, as the road took them through the shadow of an aircraft carrier. The driver reached for his microphone and announced, over a public-address system that was surprisingly clear and free of static, "That's the *Kennedy*. Thirty-five-hundred sailors call the *Kennedy* home for voyages that take them out to sea for as long as a year. The refrigerators in the *Kennedy* are ten times the size of this bus." Then he pointed out a destroyer, and a small house on a hill where Douglas MacArthur had been billeted. Across the bay was the Coronado Island, "and that grand old lady, the Hotel Del Coronado, where Marilyn Monroe and Jack Lemmon made *Some Like It Hot*." Lowell rolled his eyes, but Frank was grateful for the information.

At the end of a long pier was a refrigerated warehouse that the Navy had given to the Coroner's Office. Bettina Welch made a little speech about following the coroners, and staying together as a group. Frank wanted to say, "Doesn't this feel like a high school field trip?" But he thought no one would appreciate the humor.

A delegation of coroners met the buses, and the mourners gathered in smaller clusters around their assigned guides. They were given heavy white jackets and taken inside.

The warehouse was cold, like a day early in the winter, before the snow, after the first real freeze, and the jackets were welcome. Frank played with his buttons but saw that the workers in the room kept theirs open. So he kept his jacket open too, and came to appreciate the chill.

His guide, Dr. Kashiwa, told them that the GRIM BUSINESS of identifying the dead took place around the clock. For some of the dead identification would be impossible. Kashiwa described the condition of the bodies in the cockpit as being "the consistency of strawberry jam." Some of the dead on the ground may have been incinerated when the fuel tanks of the left wing exploded in a MASSIVE FIREBALL. Several large sections of the fuselage remained intact, including the rear of the plane. The pilot had turned off the Fasten Seat Belt signs, and though it is unlikely that many passengers were in the single aisle of the 737, most of the passengers had unbuckled themselves. As the plane crashed, they were tossed out of their seats.

The coroner told them, "Even with their seat belts on, the bodies were not protected from violent distress. Some seat belts held firm while the passengers they embraced were torn in half by the force of the crash. Unfortunately, some of you will have to come back here again, but our systems are not yet so refined that we can tell you in advance who is ready for identification and who is not."

The group came to a table of small arms and legs. How could he choose among them, which were his daughter's?

A few sharp chemical smells rose from the tables of body parts in the large, cold room, partly of chlorine, from the bleach with which the floor was washed, and partly from whatever soup they sprayed over the tables. A row of a dozen left arms was being matched with right arms. Many of the dead lost their feet as the metal sheared their legs. Right feet and left feet, on separate tables. Frank learned that most clothing was burned off, or blown off, as the bodies tumbled.

Though the attendants washed and drained the blood from the arms and feet, pieces of legs, the torsos in shallow plastic caskets, they could not erase the burns, the deep gashes, and the disgusting mutilations within mutilations, the fingerless hands without arms, like chicken breasts ready for the frying pan, which Frank could identify only because someone had collected these puffy shards on one long tray, unmistakable with their stumps of wrist or thumb. And on every piece of flesh someone had taped a strip of paper with computer bar coding, so that as each piece was identified, the system would eventually reconstruct as much of the body as possible. The computers knew where each piece of a body had been found, and then to which bin it had been remanded.

"The reconstruction will be simple," said Dr. Kashiwa. "After the crash we laid a detailed grid over the entire crash zone. Each body, or each body part, was then labeled according to the grid, so that we will be able to simulate, precisely, the dissemination of the bodies across the crash zone, and since we know the seat assigned to each passenger, eventually the computers will be able to replay the entire crash, in any speed we want, and we will know exactly how each person was affected by the destruction of the plane."

They all died, thought Frank. That's how they were affected. And those on the ground too. And I was affected, but if I say that, they'll make fun of me.

"It's amazing, isn't it?" said someone else. "What they can do. The crash won't have been in vain."

"Yes," said a man, "they'll have the whole crash on computer, and they'll know how the plane broke apart, which will tell them what they have to do to strengthen the NEXT GENERATION OF AIRCRAFT."

"That's her," someone cried, and everyone watched a dark-haired woman in her twenties as a coroner covered a body on a steel table. Frank wondered who she had seen, a sister or a mother. The woman seemed too young to have lost a daughter on the flight, since Acapulco was not a destination for teenagers traveling alone, or even in groups with other teenagers. Unless of course the woman had found her own three-year-old, who had been on the plane with the woman's ex-husband, who had visitation rights this week, and he was taking his kid on a trip where he could let her hang out by the pool during the day, and then at night he could get her a baby-sitter while he went out looking for action. So it could be a little girl, thought Frank. But I doubt it. The story would have been in the news, and so far nothing has taken the spotlight from me. So I'm still the most famous person in the disaster.

Everyone handling the bodies wore long rubber aprons and heavy rubber gloves, to protect themselves, the coroner said, from the threat of contamination with plague-infested blood. Was there a bucket with penises? Frank wondered. Or were there two trays, hidden even from this room of total exposure, marked PELVIS: MEN and PELVIS: WOMEN?

In another room, jewelry. Plastic envelopes, each with a bar-code tag. Every fingerprint had been taken from every hand or finger recovered. Teeth were being photographed, and jaws were being X-rayed. The names of doctors and dentists had been taken from next of kin. Frank was asked and gave the names. And there were rows of computers linked to each other, sharing all of this information.

What might have taken a month only a few years ago could be accomplished in twenty-four hours now, said Kashiwa.

The teams of coroners assigned reconciled all the pieces with each other, to be separated later into their own bins and stacked on shelves. Then three special machines, robots, now sitting idle in a corner of the huge room, would be programmed by the computers to roam the aisles, collecting the separate pieces from the shelves on one side of the room to stack them, body by individual body, on the other side of the room, leaving the job to a few workers of putting all the mangled pieces into their final containers, into their coffins.

Imagine the destruction to a body, to a face, exploded out of an airplane, and bounced against the roof of a house, or slammed into a chimney. What happens to a ten-year-old when he's blasted through a hole in the wall, and then a thin sheet of metal from the plane's tail catches him across the shoulders? How many pieces are left? What remains?

They told Frank that his wife and daughter's seats were in the tail section. When the plane broke up, the roof peeled away. At the same time the tail flipped upside down, crushing the fin, nothing to brace the inverted fuselage, and the passengers, unbuckled, fell. Here comes the plane, scraping the passengers along the road and into first one house and then out the backyard and across the next backyard into another house. These bits and pieces of people, squeezed into nothing by the weight of the plane, masticated by metal bed frames and stucco walls, and nails, and chimneys, and the jumble of stuff that a second before had been a car filled with children and groceries, now packed tall metal drums lined with plastic. There were probably things other than ruined human body parts in the drums. Anything fleshy had been collected for examination, classification, and that would include what was left of dogs and cats, the meat from freezers, and pieces of the dinners from the airline's kitchen, choices of fish, chicken, beef, or cheese, now fused by the heat with the skin of burn-ravaged flight attendants. Let the coroner's sophisticated laboratories divide the blended proteins from each other and say with great assurance that this was passenger and this was enchilada.

Frank heard a worker joke with another worker as he pushed one of those barrels in front of him, "Come on, honey, let's eat out tonight, I'm tired of leftovers."

Frank went back to the hotel. He knew he was in that state of grief that was denial. Knowing this, could he still deny?

7. Public Relations

Frank watched himself become famous on the news that night. The story was the same on every channel: Man misses plane, evades police barriers at crash site, is arrested for looting on Cohassett Street. As he listened to them talking about this man who had been arrested, as he felt the thrill of fame, a disturbing high-pitched tone vibrated through their reports, linking the basic elements of the story, implying a relationship, an intention, some subtle marriage between the crashed plane and his walk through the ravaged houses, his arrest. He wanted to know what they really meant by the implicit connec-

tions—PLANE CRASHES; MAN WHO MISSED PLANE
SEARCHES THROUGH RUBBLE; ARRESTED—and why they
were frightening him. He wanted to call up the radio and television
stations, and the newspapers that would print the story in the morning, but he couldn't think of anything to say that would help his
cause. Don't they care how it makes me feel? What do they mean
when they say I was *searching* through the rubble? Searching? As
though I had a goal.

He wanted to tell the reporters covering the story that in his
distress he had visited Cohassett Street to see for himself where the
plane had crashed, and that of course he had not been looting. He
could tell them what he told the police, that he had found his wife's
suitcases. He hoped that anyone hearing about this would put themselves in his place. He hoped they would understand that there was
nothing to loot. But who would believe that? Too many people
crowding the police barricades that night wanted grim souvenirs.
But who would blame me for wanting something that might have
been touched by my daughter? What if I said I was looking through
the awful zone hoping to find her favorite doll? Yes, if it comes to
trial, he thought, and my lawyer sees the jury running against me,
he will claim that my search through the wreckage could hardly be
called looting, since by definition looting is theft, and by definition
I was looking for what I had lost. And I found it.

No jury will go against me, he thought. But there won't be a
jury. And how important is my story in the larger story? I will be
lost in all the other news. There were so many pieces of the event
now. The flight attendant whose dogs were waiting for her. The pilot
who was going to retire in six months. The three couples killed on
their honeymoons. The destroyed families. The reports of eye-
witnesses.

In the Flight 221 Crisis Center at the Marriott, Frank waited
with the families of the dead, while Lowell was at the airport, meeting
their parents. The airline was flying them down, for free.

Minutes would pass while he watched Bettina Welch on the
phones, or Ed Dockery talking to the press who tried to get through
the cordon into the room with all of the families, and Frank would

have no thoughts. He was aware of nothing, really. Occasionally some consciousness would surface, like a fish stirring itself to a bit of food, alert only to the moment of hunger and the moment of placation, and then he would settle down at the bottom of this ocean of no feeling, and he would stare into nowhere, thinking no thing. Something within him, or something that he was within, marked the remote distance of his large emotions, saw them, absorbed them, and forgot them. Whether everyone in the room felt this way, or only those called survivors, or just Frank, well, who could say? Not Frank. This was not a feeling of peace, because there was still the electricity of grief, of regret, of mistake. No, he rode on the inevitability of the crash's effect on the rest of his life. As soon as he said to himself, "Everything will be different," something like darkness came up around him, and he had only to give himself a push into this, and he would collapse. Frank saw his fate and was stunned by it.

After however long he sat there—three hours like this?—he found himself standing, but he didn't know why, or for how long he had been up from his chair. In his daze he had been blind, without knowing it, but now he could see again. Something had impelled him to stand, but the reason behind the move was gone. A few people watched him. Are they watching me because I have been standing here for twenty minutes, asleep, or because I am the man who missed the plane, or because I am just one more place in the room, not even a person anymore, and as good as anything else for them to look at? Look at a curtain, look at Bettina Welch, look at me. When he sat down again, he tried to find the sensation that would bring him again to the pleasant isolation of the last three hours. But then he heard his brother's voice, and knew that Lowell must have called his name a second before, and that out of habit, because he always wanted to stand when Lowell found him at his desk, in the office, thinking about what he would rather be doing, he had jumped at the familiar, truly familiar, sound. Even when Lowell called on the phone, Frank would put his feet on the floor, if they had been on the desk. And yet sometimes he saw Lowell behind his own desk, with his feet up, while he argued with the

presidents of record companies trying to get them to see things his
way, trying to wrestle a little more money from them without making
them an enemy. Often he even won those battles. To win, and stay
friends! And still with your feet up! To be casual about the battles!
And when Frank, in a negotiation, never as important as his brother's
since Frank had no authority to feud over something that the stores
could not do without, tried to relax like Lowell, and put his feet on
the desk, he lost the line of his thoughts, and panicked, thinking
that he would soon lose the deal. So when he kept his feet on the
floor, he felt safer but, too aware of his safety, congratulated himself
for learning to concentrate. How to measure successful concentration
except by waking up to a mountain of unconsciously completed
brilliant work, and time passed? To fly through the business day,
making money the way a bird finds columns of warm air rising. But
some birds must be better at flight than others? In all their Dar-
winage. This one flies higher. Stupid songs about soaring hearts.
Some soar higher. Another kind of flying. And what goes up must
come down. Like a plane.

Here came his family. Each of them took one of his hands, and
his father gathered him into a hug with them. They had never done
this before, the four of them, close like this. Lowell with his hand
on Frank's shoulder, something shy in the touch, afraid to admit he
needed to join in. Ethel, crying, and Leon asking Frank, not in
words, but with the pressure of a hand, to give something to her to
help her, and that helping her would be good for him, would take
him out of himself, that anyone could see that Frank was too inside
himself, that he would ruin himself by staying so close to his grief.
So many hugs in the last two days, and bodies, and hair, and skin,
Leon's smooth wrists, and his mother's perfume. Even today, she
put it on. It was a heavy perfume, something he had once given
Anna, who refused to wear it because she said it made her smell
like Ethel. The comfort of the closet in his mother's bedroom. In
the mansion. What adheres to clothes over time. The memory of a
social life.

But I should love them now, he thought. I should finally forgive
them. I should see their humanity now. I should see that they love

me with all the complicated feelings that I love—loved—my own
child. They may have hurt me at times, yes, yes, but I was no better
with my own. Or I thought I was better, but what challenges had I
faced with her? So my parents shamed me when I was young, or
even later, just by being themselves, but what have I done to bring
honor to them?

Or is this crap, these feelings, should I not see that the events
of the week, events that, in the future, I will see with dispassion,
have clouded my resolve, and that the dangerous, heroic gesture
now is to not let go of what I think about them. Just because they
need me now, or think they need me, does that create a special
indebtedness? I will not cave in, thought Frank. Not collapse like
the ceiling of a plane when the walls are crushed, and hundreds
die screaming.

"How were you treated by the police?" Leon asked. "If they
hurt you . . ." If they hurt me, what? Frank wanted to say. What
are you going to do? Shoot a cop?

"We've got a lawyer now," said Lowell. "Aaron Waramus, he's
very good."

"Is he the best?" asked Ethel. Frank hated this in his mother,
because he hated it in himself, always to think about the best, not
to buy unless he could afford the best, or to know what the best
was, and then, when buying something that was not the best, thinking of it only as a temporary substitution until he had the money to
buy the best. And did he really need the best lawyer for this case?
Wasn't the case so obvious?

"As good as they come," said his father.

"But the arrest, is he a criminal lawyer? I thought he was for
the lawsuit." So there had been discussions between Lowell and
Leon from which Ethel had been left out. She was used to playing
catch-up with their conversations.

"They'll let me off," said Frank. "I wasn't looting. There was
nothing to loot."

"Don't be so sure," said Leon. "There's a lot of money at stake
here."

"What difference does that make?" asked Frank. He didn't

understand what his father was saying. That because the airline might have to pay out millions of dollars, or an insurance company would have to, therefore the police, in collusion with the forces of authority and capital, would put Frank on trial, and that this trial, successfully pursued, would somehow diminish the obligations of the immense financial combines that own airplanes and insurance companies?

"We'll probably need a psychiatrist's report to clear you," said Leon. "I don't see how we can get around that."

"But what did I do?" asked Frank.

"You were caught where you shouldn't have been. I don't blame you, Frank, don't get me wrong." Everything sounded stupid now, everything his father said. "But these things get tried out of court, in the press. And the press needs to think of you as crazed with despair."

"As though I'm not."

"You have certain tendencies," said Leon.

"What tendencies?" asked Frank.

"This isn't the time," said Ethel.

"Great," said Frank, "so you'll provoke me the way you usually do. You start to say something to me about how you really see me, and then just as I want to know what you're thinking, you pull back, so I don't get to hear what you had to say, and I have to make it up myself, something that's usually worse than what you were about to tell me."

"You know what I mean," said his father, "and it isn't a terrible thing about you, but you do wander a little. You have a *tendency*," and he underlined the word, "to kind of go off by yourself, and you did it yesterday when you took the train here."

This was Leon's attempt to prove that the family still had a commander. Since he had no direction over his sons' business, and little over his own, he had nothing left to play with but their emotions. Lowell was immune to him, even liked him, but Frank hated Leon in these moments.

"I don't want to go to a psychiatrist," said Frank.

"You don't have to," said Lowell, trying to finish this.

"I'm not crazy," said Frank, and tears came to his eyes, and he felt pathetic. "Everyone is dead."

Ethel hugged him, rocked him. She loves me, he thought, she knows who I am, and she still loves me. She loves me because I gave them their only grandchild. And now that grandchild is dead. And she doesn't really know who I am. She doesn't know about Mary Sifka. So he broke the hug, he broke another hug.

Ed Dockery walked toward them, and it made Frank happy to see him. What he had hated in the man two days before, his class ring, his shuffle, now seemed to Frank emblems of a deep sincerity, an empathy, even a real compassion so rare that no one he had met since shaking hands with Ed had made any similar claim on Frank's respect. Behind Ed was another man. Ed shook Frank's hand, and then introduced him to Piet Bernays. Frank then introduced them both to his parents. Ed regarded Lowell with a bit of suspicion.

"Are you with the airline?" asked Lowell.

Bernays said that he was not from the airline, that he was with a public-relations firm hired by the airline. Frank thought that he might be homosexual. A Republican homosexual. Why? He was fastidious beyond the culture of this airline. He liked his clothes too much, he liked his hair. He was trim. He had a thin gold watch on a lizard band, with the watch on the wrong side of his wrist. He was beautiful, in a way. Was this what Lowell felt with men, to see their beauty and not run from it? But I hate this man, thought Frank.

Bernays explained that the airline was aware of pending lawsuits and wanted to do nothing to stand in anyone's way of them. That there was a procedure for the lawyers to follow, and that everyone knew the protocols. Rather, he said, it was his job to make the *survivors* available to the press. He wanted Frank to speak to them.

"No," said Lowell. "And I want you to get out of here, now. Just get the fuck away from us."

Ed Dockery shook his head, and in his look to Piet Bernays Frank saw the confirmation of an earlier warning. Bernays tried to say something to Lowell, but Lowell would have none of it.

"You're trying to take control of the propaganda here," said Lowell, "that's what's going on."

Bernays said that he only wanted to help Frank.

"How does Frank's going to the press help him, if you do the handling?" asked Lowell.

"That's a good question," said their father. Ethel put a hand on Frank's shoulder, and the four Gales stood in a line, this bulwark.

Bernays said that he had hoped only to stop the kind of mad speculations that drive the press into frenzies and make everyone's lives difficult. Better, he said, for everyone to be as direct as possible than to hide something.

"But we have nothing to hide," said Frank.

"That's right," said Leon. "Nothing to hide."

Bernays said that he knew of the arrest, and that the press knew of it too.

"Maybe we should get our own press agent," said Lowell. This seemed to Frank to be a good idea, and immediately he saw the advantages to this, how their press agent would speak for him, and arrange interviews, if everyone agreed that they were useful, with only those reporters who would be sympathetic to Frank, and would not press him to talk more about his trespass on Cohassett.

Piet Bernays said that hiring their own press person was a good idea, and that he could find one in San Diego if they wanted. This man will run the airline someday, thought Frank, and if not this airline, then another one. I am looking at a man who is brilliant at what he does. Any other functionary, even while encouraging the Gales to hire a press agent, would have conveyed some tremors from the corporation's anxiety. When Bettina Welch and Ed Dockery stood for the airline, one could still see pieces of their flesh behind the masks. Bernays, practiced in the art of transparency, wasted no time putting on a cover.

"Look," said Lowell, "I'm a businessman in San Diego. I deal with the public all the time. Don't you think I have my own resources here? Don't you think I'm capable of finding my own press agent if I want one? Are you suggesting that I don't even have my own publicist already?"

Bernays apologized if anything he said had implied that he did not respect Lowell's place in the community. He even smiled as he admitted that he often bought records in Lowell's store.

Bernays gave Lowell a boyish, shy smile, and Lowell patted him on the back.

"What a fucker," said Lowell, with respect, with envy. "You've really done your homework, haven't you?"

Bernays said that the airline was just doing what it had to do, and as a businessman, Lowell would appreciate that they should be expected to do no less. Frank saw that with this Bernays had brilliantly and deftly raised Lowell's business to the stature of any important business, to a level equal to the airline.

And their father relaxed his posture, and even their mother, she relaxed, and sat on the back of a chair. When she did this, Bernays pulled a chair from a table and sat down. He was so finely tuned, and he used himself brilliantly, his breeding; quietly appealing to Frank's mother and father that they compare their sons to him, with his posture, how wonderfully relaxed he was with himself, so unlike at least one of their sons. And then they all sat down.

It was maddening to Frank! They liked him, this dry Republican homosexual, this catamite to industrialists, this pet of bisexual investment bankers. He could imagine Bernays dressed in nothing but suspenders clipped to a jock strap, with his fucking horn-rimmed glasses on, pouring gin martinis for a senator whose campaign he had just successfully managed, in some CIA condominium in Santa Barbara. And the senator, in a pink alpaca sweater, smoking menthols and nattering on about how we did it, we did it, I'm a senator! I'm in the club! I made it, we made it, you helped me make it! And then what would they do?

Frank asked himself what it was about Piet Bernays that made him so unhappy, so jealous. He was tired of putting these questions to himself, tired of comparisons, tired of jealousy, tired of the way his family made him feel.

"Fuck you," he said to Bernays. He had meant to keep this under his breath, but it came out.

Bernays gave him a quizzical look, hurt puppy, hurt angel, more fraudulent compassion.

"Frank," said his mother.

"It's over, Frank," said Lowell. "This is one of the good guys."

Bernays raised a hand in peace and told Frank that he understood anything Frank said or felt now.

"We know you do," said Ethel.

Frank got up and walked out of the room. Lowell ran after him, but Frank pushed him away. He didn't want to say anything, and he left Lowell behind, calling his name in frustration. Some rage surged in Frank, something new, something that felt like the energy he had always missed in his life, the thing he never had when he played games in school, the thing that makes the basket, or kicks the ball or strikes out the batter, this focus of all emotion into a single beam. He was ready to talk to a stadium filled with losers and tell them how to win. Who was this Piet Bernays, this negligible faggot with queer suspenders? Who was this Dockery, this Ed? Who was this Bettina Welch, this weak-chinned nothing, this wage earner, this uneducated processed-cheese eater, this fool who thinks that in exchange for her dedication, the airline actually gives two shits for her? Losers, losers, losers. All of them. And his brother too, and his father. And Ethel? Beside the point. No, a loser too. She married Leon, and the bet was wrong. Apartment dwellers, mansion sellers.

Here in this hotel corridor, past meeting rooms with names evocative of San Diego history, the Nimitz Room, the Dana Room, the Serra Room, the Coronado Room, the Drake Room, Frank, running better than he had ever run in his life, wove in and out of the knots of men and women in suits who were going and coming from different conferences in all these rooms, regional sales managers, local medical societies, the boards of trade associations, men and women with jobs in a world so far from his, and Frank looked at them, and thought, losers also, all of you, losers. At the end of the hall, where it joined the next wing of the hotel, was a small sitting area with a couch and a table, and he jumped over the couch and landed, he felt, with the grace of an African, a runner from Kenya. When the hall turned, he ran down the corridor and then into a fire escape and down the stairs to the lobby, and then out the lobby to the street. Sudden change of light. Late afternoon. The sea air. The sound of cars on the freeway nearby, a kind of heavy, tired breathing.

Was anyone watching him? Did he care? Fuck them all, he thought; again he had that thought, and this time the thought, his disdain, his perfect scorn, rose inside him the way great waves build off the north shore of Hawaii, scooping up the old shattered waves returning in defeat from the beach and then piling them into another massive wall to roll across the reefs and try again to tear down the island. All these puny beings who tormented him today, the police, his brother, his parents, Bernays, the airline reps, none of them could ride for long on the massive waves of energy that collected inside this thing that used to be Frank Gale. None of these fuckers can surf on me! I am *tsunami*, the hundred-year wave, killer of sharks, destroyer of whales, widow-maker, orphan-maker! I eat villages whole!

And so he ran on, in this convention zone in San Diego, past the Marriott, the Holiday Inn, the Ramada, the Sheraton, the Embassy Suites, the Days Inn, the Hilton Inn. How many executives unpacked their bags behind him, in front of him, beside him, and, bored, turned the pages of the *Guide to San Diego* with the picture of the trained dolphins at Sea World, and played with themselves, or poured a drink from the minibar, or made a call to their families, or looked up old college chums in this big navy town, and did all of this without knowing that outside their rooms Frank Gale ran like a hero?

He ran along the curving drive that linked the hotels, and as the road turned back toward the Marriott, something in him sagged, and then his ankles hurt, and he stopped running beside a long planting bed of ground cover, in purple bloom.

The hotel looked so far away, and he was so tired. He lay down on the ground cover and looked up at the setting sun. If the family had not died, he would be in Mexico now. If Anna had not found the letter as she packed, she would have read it as he had intended. He wondered if he really would have given it to her, or if, at the last moment, or not even the last moment but any moment, he would have decided that taking her to Mexico with contrition in his heart made sufficient amends. Hadn't he broken up with Mary Sifka? Would he have needed to give Anna the letter? By the second full day of the trip, today, she would have known that something was different with him. She would have seen his love for her. And it would have been love. And he would have proved it by making love to her, slowly, wonderfully, letting her come first. Oh, how he would have set a slow pace, starting with a back rub, massaging her feet, taking time. And then, when she would have expected him to pull out, or to reach for a condom, he would have stayed inside her, he would have risked—no, not risked—he would have thrown himself into pregnancy. No blow-jobs, no coming anywhere but inside, toward the womb! That would have been the seal of the new contract, that would have been the rededication, the proof, better than any declaration of love or any confession of his crime. A new baby, a child, more to love.

He wondered where she was in that cold warehouse on the docks, and in how many pieces she had finally come to rest, and whether something of her had mingled with something of their child. I should have been on the plane, he thought. I should have crashed with them, I should have died with them. And as he thought this, the phrase GUILT OF THE SURVIVOR poked into view, and his mind went blank, and he got up and walked back to the hotel.

The sun was almost gone as he reached the lobby, where his brother waited for him.

"Let's talk," said Lowell.

"There's nothing to say."

"No, no, there is, there is. We've been expecting you to behave in a certain way, and we've been wrong."

"What was the certain way?" asked Frank. Someone took his picture from across the room, a woman. She wore a vest with a lot of pockets, and a name tag on a leather loop around her neck. So she was a press photographer, thought Frank. She looked around the room for someone, and found him, the reporter she'd been sent out with.

"Reasonable," said Lowell. "We thought you'd be reasonable,

but you're not, and you don't have to be. This is not a criticism. Behave the way you want."

"So I'm being unreasonable. That's not a good thing." Frank watched the reporter and photographer approach them.

"Don't take it that way."

"But what other way is there to take it?"

"And this is why I'm here. I'm here so we don't fight. There's nothing to fight about."

"So now you're humoring me." Frank knew that he really was being unreasonable now, and worse, cruel to his brother, who meant him no harm. The photographer took another picture.

"Don't put it that way, that isn't fair."

Frank wanted to tell his brother that he was right, to say, Yes, I'm being unfair. Instead, he asked about Piet Bernays. "Where did he go?"

"He had things to take care of."

"I shouldn't have yelled at him."

"Maybe you were right."

"What did Mom and Dad say?"

"They're in their room."

"Drinking?"

"He is, she's trying not to."

"But she will," said Frank.

The photographer took more pictures. Frank pointed her out to Lowell.

"We really should get a publicist," said Lowell. "We can't keep getting mad at everyone. We have to be cool. Elaine Swofford handles stuff for the stores here. She's okay. I'll call her."

"What will she do?" asked Frank.

"She'll talk to the press first for us. She'll set up the interviews, or tell them why we can't be interviewed. She'll keep them away from us if that's what we want."

"That's what I want," said Frank.

"And will you come back to my place tonight?" asked Lowell.

"No," said Frank. "But I'll behave myself." They crossed the lobby to the reception desk, and Frank asked for his messages. The desk clerk gave him another pile of message slips. The first was from Mary Sifka. Frank quickly moved it to the bottom of the pile, but Lowell didn't seem to notice his nervous speed. Five were from different reporters, asking for interviews.

"Let me handle these," said Lowell.

The reporter and photographer were next to them now. The reporter introduced himself, "Mitchell Hefter," he said, holding out his hand. "I'm a reporter." He named a press syndicate, and showed his identification.

Frank took a quick look at the other message slips, to see who had called, and also to avoid eye contact with Hefter. A few cousins had called, also his secretary.

"What do you want to know?" asked Lowell.

"We just wanted to ask about the night your brother was arrested."

"It was a mistake," said Lowell.

"Yes," said Frank. "I saw my wife's suitcase."

"Was there anything you were trying to get from it?" asked the reporter.

"Not really," said Frank.

"Were you aware that it was against the law for you to have opened it up?"

"I wasn't thinking about that," said Frank.

"What were you thinking about?" asked the reporter.

"He was thinking about his family," said Lowell.

Frank wanted to disagree, but held himself back. Besides, he couldn't remember. The reporter thanked them and walked away.

Frank told Lowell to go home, and Lowell said good-bye. Frank read the message from Mary. She gave him a few specific times to call, ten in the morning, which had passed, and then again at one, and then seven. The message said for him to call only at those times. So she was hiding this from her husband and from her work. He had an hour before he could call her. If it was time to connect again with the world, he would begin by returning the other calls, to tell the people who cared enough to call, whatever their motives, morbid curiosity or true concern, that he missed his wife and daughter, that he needed and welcomed the support of his friends. He would say that he was fine.

The first call he made was to his parents. They were on the same floor, and his mother told Frank he should come to their room. He said he wanted to take a shower first and return a few calls. His mother said they should go out to eat, just the three of them. "I think we should go to a good restaurant," she said. He knew that she meant something expensive, the kind of rich man's restaurant they used to go to when he was a child, and he wanted that too, a martini, and carrots and green olives in a little tray filled with ice, and cheese toast, and the salad made at the table by an old waiter. They would have two rounds of drinks, and then they would order a bottle of good wine, and talk about the past. They would not ask Lowell to join them. The club of three. At the end of the meal, on the way out, Frank would filch a handful of mints from the large glass snifter at the maître d's station, and eat them all in a few minutes. He would be a little boy again, when his father was wealthy, the year he bought the house in Bel Air. The kind of meal that lasted as long as a summer. He would order a steak for dinner, or else a rack of lamb and split it with his mother. There would be mint jelly, and he would dab the meat into the green sauce, and then scoop some of it against the creamed spinach. He would eat a few of those olives during the meal too, for the lost pleasure of ruining, with that overlay of vinegar and salt, the taste of the wine and the meat. And he would butter his bread. How long has it been since I have buttered my bread? Frank asked himself. Tonight I will not abstain. I will not worry about calories. Tonight I will order what I want. I will have the shrimp cocktail if I want it! And the chocolate mousse! If he couldn't bring himself to hug his parents and feel their love, at least he could fall into the embrace of what was left of their money. He called the front desk and asked the receptionist if there were any old, expensive restaurants in San Diego that had strolling violinists.

"We have an excellent dining room right here," said the receptionist.

"I want to leave the hotel," said Frank.

"You're looking for French food?"

"What I'm looking for is probably called Continental."

"Let me ask someone who might know, and I'll call you back."

Frank thanked him. He started to undress for the shower, but stopped. A shower would only delay his next responsibility, which was to return phone calls.

Mary Sifka still needed another forty minutes before he could call her. He would talk to Julia Abarbanel first. I can probably fuck her now, he thought. She's probably thinking that too.

He didn't recognize the area code of the phone number. It might have been Massachusetts, or Chicago, he wasn't sure. He dialed. Someone answered, a man. Frank asked for Julia. The man asked him who was calling. Frank told him. The man mumbled something, Frank thought it was "I'll get her," but he wasn't sure. So the man knew who he was, and why he was calling.

Julia was there. "Frank, it's Julia." This was good, she didn't start by wailing at the injustice of it all.

"Where are you?"

"I'm in Colorado."

"Where?"

"I'm staying with a friend in Denver."

"What are you doing there?"

"She's my roommate from college. She had a baby." Julia said this trying not to sound excited or happy for her friend, not to hurt Frank again with his own loss.

"So that was her husband."

"Yes, Howard."

"Where are you living now?"

"I'm still in Minneapolis."

"And what are you doing these days?"

"I went back to school. I'm getting my law degree."

"No kidding. That's great."

"It was time to grow up."

"Oh, don't do that," said Frank. He wondered how to take advantage of this situation. Maybe he could turn her toward a rude conversation, so they could masturbate while creating a scene.

"Frank, I'm so sorry."

"Thank you."

"If there's anything I can do." What could she do? She could tell him if she would have fucked him in Yosemite. Why can't I ask?

"Nothing now, really."

"I want to be direct with you." Another one testing herself.

"Yes."

"You're going to need help at home, aren't you?"

"I don't know."

"Yes. Cleaning the house. Packing all of their clothing. The baby's toys." The way Julia said "baby" made Frank think that she wasn't sure of Madeleine's name. And Madeleine wasn't a baby anymore; she was a dead three-year-old.

"I haven't thought about that yet."

"I think we're all coming out for the funeral."

"I don't even know when it is." I don't even know if there's anything to bury. But he couldn't say that.

"You know that you have all of our love," she said.

"It helps a lot." No, it doesn't. When will you fuck me?

"Thanks," said Frank. He could say anything, and the best thing to say now was, "I have to say good-bye now."

"Good-bye Frank."

He hung up and dialed the number Mary Sifka had left. It was a number he wasn't used to, neither home nor office.

There was a high whine when the connection was made, and then Mary said, "Hello?"

"It's me."

"Oh, Frank."

"Where are you?" he asked.

"I'm at home."

"I didn't recognize the number."

"It's my fax machine in my office. I told Stewart I had to work." Had he ever heard his name before? Stewart.

"So that was the sound I heard."

"They're dead?"

"Yes."

"And you missed the plane because you were with me."

"No, the traffic was heavy."

"No, you didn't leave enough time. If you hadn't had lunch with me, you would have gone to the airport with them. Right?"

"Unless I had business. I was busy all morning."

"Frank, no. You were seeing me. That's why you didn't go to the airport with Anna and Madeleine."

"I guess."

"It's true."

"Then it's true," he said, not knowing what to do with this. If she was guilty for the affair, then she was guilty for the long lunch, the last kiss that delayed him, and then she was guilty for saving his life. Or was she guilty for the affair, because the trip to Mexico was his bid to save the marriage from the affair, and without the affair there would have been no trip? He wanted to ask her what kind of fax machine she had; he had been thinking about getting one for his house.

"I don't know who to talk to about this," she said. "I'm afraid of telling my friends."

"Didn't anyone ever know about us?"

"Sort of, at the beginning, but once we started, I kept it a secret. How many people did you tell?"

"No one. That was one of the things I liked about it. That it was a real secret."

"I told one girlfriend that we'd had lunch, and kissed, the first time. She'd broken up with a married man. She told me not to go ahead with this, so I told her I didn't."

"Maybe you should see a therapist."

"I've thought about that. I don't know how I'd justify it to Stewart."

"Tell him you're unhappy."

"Then he'll want to know what he can do to help me. He loves me."

"You could talk to a priest. I mean a minister." She was a Methodist, although he didn't know what that really meant.

"This is too complicated for that. And it's over."

"So see a therapist."

"I suppose."

Mary's reluctance annoyed Frank. She had taken his grief, equated it with her guilt, and forced him to goad her into seeking help, when it was his loss, and not the inconvenience of the long-held secret of her affair, and the intrusion of the disaster, that demanded the greater attention. Maybe this was why they had broken up. Maybe he had stopped liking her. And if he had not stopped liking her? Then they would not have broken up, and they would have continued seeing each other, secretly, happily, and he would have never taken his family to Mexico to make things better. There would have been no plane to miss. He would have been in Los Angeles now, fucking Mary Sifka in a motel.

"I don't know what to say to you," she said. "Anything I say will sound stupid."

"Maybe that's all you need to say."

"I wish I could make this all better for you."

"I know."

"When my brother died, well, you know." She had a brother, two years older, who had died when she was twenty, killed in a car crash. He had been drunk. She told Frank about it one afternoon, in bed. The usual stuff: a year to get over it, always a little pain in the heart. Hard to look at any BMW 320i, the same kind of car he was in. Frank tried to comfort her when he said that the 320i was an old model, and disappearing from the roads.

"I've been drinking a little," she said. "I had a vodka an hour ago, and then another one just before you called. Stewart saw the first one. He thinks I'm relaxing, that I want to make love tonight. I guess I'll have to."

"I don't think it's a good idea to drink, I mean for me to drink. I want to stay on top of things."

"I can't even come to the funeral."

"Well, we know each other from business. So you can come for that, you know, as business."

"I have to tell her I'm sorry. I'll go to the grave alone, after."

When she said "grave," she added, so softly that Frank wasn't sure if he'd heard it, a slight z, the afterthought, to make the singular plural. Graves. Mother and daughter.

"You didn't do anything."

"Maybe not, but I can tell her I'm sorry she died. Did she know about us?"

"No," said Frank.

"You're lying. I can hear it in your voice."

"Maybe she did."

"She did, didn't she?"

"She knew. I told her."

"What did she say? About me."

"Nothing, really."

"Yes, she did."

"Mary, why do we have to do this?"

"I need to know."

"Think about how I feel for a minute."

"Think about how I feel for an hour."

"She knew it was you. We were going on vacation to pull things together. She knew that was what the trip was for. And I really was trying to pull everything together."

"And she didn't say anything bad about me?"

"No. She had no reason to. It wasn't about you, anyway, her anger. It was about me."

"So she was angry."

"Yes."

"She was angry at you."

"Yes."

"And did she forgive you before she died?"

"I hope so."

"She didn't say it."

"That was what the trip was for."

"Oh, my God. I'm sick. I feel sick."

"Maybe you should lie down."

"Maybe I should die."

"I'm sorry," said Frank. "I don't know what else to say."

"When's the funeral?" she asked.

"I don't know. There's this memorial thing here tomorrow. For everyone, for all the people, the families and friends. From the plane and the ground."

"Will there be something in L.A.?"

"I don't know."

"I'll ask the airline. They'll know. And I'll be there, Frank. I'll come to that."

"Thank you, Mary." But it was just something to say.

They hung up. He supposed he did love her, there was something that they knew about each other, something in each that was unsettled, that wanted to travel but was afraid to go. It was the thing in her that had glowed for him, and the thing in him that she had liked, or needed. So it was with Julia too, and it was really nothing more than the predictably feverish anticipation of sex with a new woman. And even as he told himself that this need for something wild was nothing more than a frenzy of despair, he asked himself why Lowell was permitted to heed the call of the orgy, and he was not. If homosexuals see something in each other, recognize the signs, then why couldn't he, as this unsettled thing, recognize the signs of the same condition in unsettled women? It was the call of the orgy. Harder to just duck into an alley and grope, but not that much harder. How difficult had it been with Mary Sifka? They met twice for business, in his office, and then, at the end of the second meeting, they talked about marriage, and then sex. He had said something like, I'm horny all the time, something that bold, and she had said, Your wife is lucky, and he said, What about you? and she said, All the time, and then they were both dizzy and quiet for a moment as he watched her knees; she was sitting in her chair and she opened them and squeezed them, so she suffered the same tension as he, and then he got out of his chair and kissed her, and then he had his hand under her skirt, and he knelt on the floor, and she spread her legs, and he never saw her underpants, he just gave her a hand-job while she unbuttoned his shirt and kissed his chest. Then she unzipped his pants and gave him a blow-job, and then they kissed, and that's how it began. The unsettled. Men and women with pornographic imaginations. She forced the kiss on him, his semen on her tongue, so he had to taste himself. And she smiled at the end of this kiss and looked him in the eye, and he could tell she was surprised that he accepted the dare, and that this amused her in no small way, because she gave her husband this test, to accept a swallow of his own sperm, and he always refused. Frank kissed her again.

When he was off the phone with Mary, the front desk called to give him the name of a restaurant, L'Epicurean. He was encouraged by its pretension, but the number yielded a phone-company message that the phone had been disconnected. He tried Information to see if he had the right number, and there was no listing. So L'Epicurean was out of business, and the hotel had it still listed on its register. And had no one been referred to this expensive place since it had closed, and had no one complained? He supposed they had, but then did the hotel erase L'Epicurean from whatever lists it kept for guests? This was another sign of San Diego's stupidity, and he thought of calling the front desk and ranting about the place, but he hadn't the energy. He took his shower, where, again, he dodged the cold condensation from the ceiling, and considered that since he wasn't calling the desk to tell them L'Epicurean is dead, then in similar moments perhaps dozens of other hotel guests had not bothered to bring the bad news to the concierge of the hotel, and perhaps for years to come guests would call to make reservations, find out the place was closed, and then, exhausted from a day spent convincing themselves that this stupid city was actually interesting, they'd call for room service. Where would he go with his parents? He would let them decide. He put on the shirt and jacket that Lowell had given him and went to his parents' room.

In the hall he wondered to what restaurant had the headwaiter of L'Epicurean gone, or was it an ancient restaurant that closed because its habitual patrons, the retired admirals and emphysemic politicians, had died?

He knocked on his parents' door; they let him in. His father was reading the afternoon paper. His father said, "Here, you should see this."

There it was, on the second of three pages devoted to the crash: LOS ANGELES MAN, LISTED AMONG THE DEAD, MISSED FLIGHT, ARRESTED FOR LOOTING. And the article, brief. No interview. No picture. There would be more tomorrow. A few of the articles on the page had jumped from the first. There was one, just two paragraphs, the ending of a story headlined LETTER *(continued from page 1)*. The story referred to a letter found in the wreckage. An airline official was complaining that the letter was released without authorization, and the paper was defending its right to publish it. Frank turned the paper to page one. Under the headline LOVE LETTER FOUND IN WRECKAGE, and then a short introduction, saying that a name had been mentioned in the letter, but was being deleted for reasons of privacy, there it was, the entire letter set in type, to be more easily read.

I love you. You asked me a few weeks
ago why I was so desperate to take this
vacation and I said that I needed to get
away from the office for a while, and
that's true, but there's more. For six
months you've noticed that I've been dis-
tant, and I have been. You asked me if
there was another woman, and I said no,
but I was lying. I had an affair with
[name deleted]. It's over now. I wanted to
take this trip so that we could find a way
to heal ourselves. I don't know how you'll
take this, and all I can say is that I beg
you to forgive me, but if you don't want
to, I will understand. I love you.

"That's so sad," said his mother. "I hope she read it before she died."

"They're holding the name of the woman he was fucking."

"Leo," said Frank's mother. "That's not fair."

"They shouldn't have printed it at all," he said. "It's an invasion of privacy."

"It's on all the news now. It was on the national news already."

His father pointed to the picture of a black man on the front page. "There's your Lonnie Walter. The cocksucker who killed your family. They found his note too, but they're not releasing it. They say he carried a gun onto the plane, he used his airline security pass to sneak a gun through."

"Did he sneak onto the plane?" asked Frank.

"No, he had a ticket. The gate attendant knew him, and he told her he was taking a vacation. And she knew that the guy who had fired him was on the plane, and she mentioned that to a friend."

"She was worried that Walter was going to kill him?"

"No, just that it was going to be embarrassing for the supervisor, to see this guy he'd fired on the plane with him. They think he shot the supervisor, grabbed a stewardess, and then he got into the cockpit and shot the crew."

Lonnie Walter was forty-five, light-colored, bald. He had little dots around his eyes that were like raised freckles, or beauty marks. The picture was from an airline file. So he was dead too. Frank wondered if he had been listed among the dead in the long lists, if he had paid for his ticket. Of course he had, thought Frank. He had sneaked the gun past Security at the employee entrance to the airport, and then again at the terminal. He had entered the main terminal from backstage, but they wouldn't have let him on the plane without a ticket. Now all airports were sure to change their security systems. Everyone working at the airports would have to pass through those metal detectors. It would cost a lot of money. The price of travel would go up.

How long will it take them to find me? he wondered. Of course they'll find me. And they'll find Mary Sifka. The paper assumed the letter writer was dead. "I guess he's dead," said Frank.

"Lonnie Walter, he's in Hell as we speak," said Leon.

"Not Walter," said Frank. "The one who wrote the letter."

"Oh, God, of course," said his father. There was no reason to believe the letter writer had not died on the plane. And there was no clue yet to let them connect this thing to Frank. That six months' distance was something only Anna complained about. To his mother and father he had always been distant. The attachment to Mary, which for so long gave him comfort, finally corroded all of his connections, even to Madeleine. This distance became a punishment. What else could he have done but confessed? But now everything was fucked up. How soon would everyone know everything?

Why did Anna keep the note after reading it? If she had put the note in her handbag, which surely exploded with the crash, the paper would either have burned with the passengers or else would have been lost in the wet muck after the fire trucks had finished spraying the area down. But the existence of the note meant they would easily trace it back to Frank, because the police, or the crash investigators, or the County Coroner had found it in his suitcase.

And then Frank felt a terrible sadness for Mary Sifka, because even if the letter had been separated from the luggage, there was Mary's name. It didn't matter that the letter was so coyly unaddressed and unsigned; unless a little piece of hot shrapnel grazed the note card, scorching, beyond recognition, only her name, they were looking for her.

"It was on the national news?" asked Frank.

"The crash? Of course," said his father.

"The letter."

"That's going to be the big thing from all of this," said his father. "You'll see. We'll know the girlfriend's name by tomorrow. They can't keep that stuff out of the news for long. It's the papers that are holding back the names, I guess until they notify the next of kin."

Frank thought of telling his mother and father that the letter was his. What would it cost him? He had an answer: He wanted more than anything to keep their sympathy, for however many hours he had until someone restored the deleted name, because they would hate him once the world could say "Mary Sifka." For the rest of their lives shame would dog their mourning. The mother and father of that man who wrote the letter. The adulterer. Mary Sifka's real in-laws.

"Let's go somewhere," said his mother. "I'm hungry."

Frank said he didn't know where to go. His father said that Lowell had made reservations for them at an Italian place he liked. Awful San Diego Italian food, with rancid oil, and badly chopped stalks of parsley drowning in the salty tomato sauce.

"Is he coming?" asked Frank. Frank didn't want Lowell there, since his brother was sure to be obsessed with the letter and would want to talk about it.

His mother said that he wasn't. I should tell them the letter is mine, thought Frank. His feet were cold. COLD FEET. It was true, the blood was somewhere else. Where? What was the evolutionary function of cold feet? Where did the genius of adaptation decree that some protection from predation derives from cold feet? How could he run from danger with cold feet? And what was the danger in the truth, if he told the truth now?

His HEAD WAS SPINNING. And just as something in him shrieked when he made the leap into the first pornographic tableau with Mary Sifka, now the ice floe moved from his feet up his legs, and then, without warning, he was SCARED SHITLESS. So even that exhausted phrase came from experience: Before he could look down, he knew that he was standing in a puddle of his own shit.

His guts had opened. Everything inside of him was sliding into his underpants, his boxer shorts, not even jockey shorts with an elastic at the thigh to hold the crap in, like a diaper. So the shit dribbled down his legs, and out his cuffs, over his shoes.

He cried, "Mom!" and his mother looked down at his feet, trying to understand.

"Frank?" she said.

"I don't know what's happening to me," he said, lurching into the bathroom a few steps away. His parents rushed toward him, but he shut the door.

"Frank, what happened?" asked his mother.

His father said, "Jesus."

"I'm sick," said Frank. He wondered if they were standing in his shitty trail. Someone would have to clean it up tonight, it would smell, or else they would have to change rooms. He could go to a market and buy rug cleaner, the spray kind, and a sponge or paper towels, whatever the directions on the rug-cleaner package said was best for cleaning it up. Maybe there was something in a pet store for cleaning up cat and dog shit, deodorizing a carpet. He would let his parents sleep in his room tonight, he would stay here. The shitty imprints of his shoes, like the shoe shapes used to diagram dance steps. And what step had he described? A straight line. A cha-cha without the return. A cha!

He stepped into the bathtub and turned on the shower. It was hard to adjust the temperature, and he settled for too cold, something to wake himself up. He had to untie his shoelaces, smearing his fingers, but he washed them off. His mother or father had taken a shower already, because the little bar of soap had been unwrapped. He took off his pants and tried to wash the legs out by putting the shower head through the top, but the pressure wasn't strong enough. SAN DIEGO CONSERVES WATER. So he changed the stream from shower to faucet, and pulled the pant legs inside out. He opened the COMPLIMENTARY SHAMPOO, and worked up a lather. Glops of loose shit collected in the tub's narrow drain. He used a washcloth to scrape the pants clean, and the job was done. He washed his shoes out, cleaned the soles, and put them on the rim of the tub. Then he turned the handle to change the stream from faucet back to shower, and, taking off his shirt, he washed himself. He made the water warmer, and when the temperature drifted to cold, he turned it up, letting the water burn him, so he could sterilize his skin, so he could soap, and soap again, and rinse off, and soap again, using the hotel's inexhaustible supply of hot water, to make himself clean.

One of them knocked on the bathroom door. His mother.

He told her he was feeling better.

She asked for his room key, so she could get clean clothes for him. Did he want a doctor?

"No."

Was it something he ate?

"Maybe, yes. But it's over."

He apologized.

She asked him why.

"Because you wanted a nice dinner tonight."

She said it had been selfish of her to think of going out.

He said they could still go out. Whatever it was, was over.

No, she said, she had already ordered from room service. And she had spoken to Anna's parents, who were coming in to Los Angeles tomorrow, from Philadelphia. Her two sisters were already there. Somehow they had missed the news that Frank was alive. When he could, they wanted to talk with him. They sent their love. They were so sorry for him.

"Take my room tonight," said Frank.

His mother asked him why.

"Do I have to explain?"

"But you were sick, Frank. Everyone gets sick."

His mother was silent, and he could hear her mumble or whisper something to his father. His father probably wanted to accept the offer of the clean room.

"We'll get you a doctor," said his mother. So Leo was thinking of Frank's health, not his own comfort? So they were being parents now?

His father came to the door. "Frank?"

"Yes, Dad."

"Don't be embarrassed about this."

"Thanks for saying that."

"It's not food poisoning, is it?"

I can say it now, thought Frank. Easily. I can say, No, Dad, I'm scared shitless by what's going to happen when you know that I wrote the letter. But he said, "No."

"It's everything."

Frank said it was.

"We'll stay in this room. It's really not bad. Did you clean up in there?"

"I tried to. I think you need fresh towels, though."

"I'll call."

"What will you say?"

"Nothing, I don't have to explain myself to these assholes." This was Lowell's voice too. So his father wasn't a complete loser. Why didn't I learn those lessons? Frank asked himself. What did Lowell see that I didn't, why does Lowell love them more than I do? Look at what they're doing for me now, the love, the care.

"I'm sorry," said Frank.

"I told you not to be," said his father.

"I'm sorry for everything," said Frank, and he meant: everything that's going to happen.

"We love you," said his mother.

"For now," he said.

"The key," said his mother. It was in his wet pants. He gave it to her, opening the door just wide enough for his hand, and then closed it. He sat on the edge of the tub and waited for his mother to bring him clean underpants.

8. Family

When he was dressed, he went back to his room. A man and woman were in the hall, next to the elevators, arguing. They were both dressed expensively; his suit was dark gray, and she wore blue, and a white shirt with ruffles at the neck. They were probably in their late twenties, and they were angry with each other.

"This is my floor," said the man. "I got here first."

"You can't claim it, you don't own it," said the woman.

"I hate to cite precedence, because I'm sure you don't understand the concept, but there's a long-established principle of finders, keepers here."

"It isn't finders, keepers, that's not it at all. It's more like the claims of imperialism."

Then they saw Frank, and they stopped talking.

"Is there something wrong?" Frank asked.

"No," said the woman.

"Have you made a choice yet?" said the man.

"What do you mean?" asked Frank.

The elevator came. The woman said, "We have an agreement, you know, not to fight for the same one. You can check it."

The man seemed to know what she was talking about, and they both got into the elevator.

Frank wasn't sure if he understood what he had seen, but it would have been something to discuss with his wife. She liked to hear abstract anecdotes from the world, and try to complete someone's story with only a fragment, a glimpse.

Back in his room the message light on the phone was blinking. There were two messages from his brother, one from Bettina Welch, and another dozen left by reporters, including two from Ron Godfrey.

While he looked at the messages, the phone rang. It was Lowell.

"Mom and Dad said you were sick. They asked me to find you a doctor."

"I'm okay now."

"Are you sure?"

"All systems go."

"Yeah, all systems go over the rug," said Lowell, and he laughed. "What happened?"

"I think everything just got to me."

"Everything's just getting to you." Lowell sounded a little bit drunk. This astonished Frank and then left him feeling lonelier than ever. His brother, after all, had not lost his own family, and with a few days passed already, Lowell was slipping back into the general drift of life. Lowell could afford to take an evening off from managing Frank, and like the camp counselor who makes fun of the weakest boys in the bunkhouse after they've gone to bed, Lowell needed the release.

"That's right," said Frank, hoping that his brother would hear something sullen in his voice. "Everything just gets to me."

"You know what I mean," said Lowell, not coddling him anymore. He meant: not just now, but always. What was he drinking? Beer or champagne. Lowell likes champagne. "So should I get the doctor for you?"

"You don't have to."

"You're sure."

Frank said he was sure.

"Fine then," said Lowell. "Tomorrow they've got that memorial thing, and then we'll go back to L.A."

So they said good night to each other, and then Frank called Ron Godfrey, who thanked him for returning the call. He asked Frank if he was ready to say anything.

"About what?" asked Frank.

"About surviving the crash."

"But I didn't survive the crash," said Frank. "Nobody did."

"Yes, sir," said Godfrey. "I was just wondering how you felt when you first saw your name on the list of the dead."

"I couldn't believe it," said Frank. In print, how would that look? "I still can't."

"Are you suing the airline?"

"I suppose," said Frank.

"Do you know which suit you're joining?"

"I didn't know I had a choice."

"There's a few different lawyers, or law firms, trying to pull together as many people as possible for suits."

"I didn't know that," said Frank.

"Well, it's early still," said Godfrey. He didn't seem to have many more questions. "You were at the airport?"

"Yes, I was waiting for the next flight."

"What time was the next flight leaving?"

"Six."

"And I understand you were held up in traffic."

"That's right."

"You took a cab?"

"Yes." He lied, but why let the world know he was in a limousine, why stimulate envy from strangers?

"On your way from work?"

"From lunch, from a business lunch."

"And you called from the restaurant to say you'd be late?"

"No, from the car."

"There was a phone in the cab?"

"I meant we had to pull into a gas station. I called from the gas station."

"How far from the airport was that?" asked Godfrey.

"A few miles."

"Do you remember the name of the street?"

"Mr. Godfrey, don't you think you have enough information?" They will uncover all of my lies, thought Frank.

"Thank you, Mr. Gale."

"That's it?"

"For now, yes. Thank you."

"You're welcome."

"And you have my sympathy. I—my—my mother was killed in a car crash when I was in high school. I was supposed to be in the car with her, she'd picked me up from school after we'd finished putting the high school newspaper to bed, but I had a fight with her, and I swore at her, and she told me to walk home."

"So you know how I feel."

"A little."

Frank wanted to ask him if he knew so much, why was he bothering him with these questions, but he didn't.

Godfrey was gone, and then Frank called Bettina Welch. And then. And then. And then. Ever since the crash, nothing but loose moments tied together by time. He had no family anymore, the thing that kept time away from him, love, even the faltering love of his three-year-old daughter. Now he had nothing but time, since all of his responsibilities had died.

"Bettina, it's Frank Gale."

"Yes, Frank, how are you?"

"I'm hanging in there."

"I'm sure, I'm sure. Frank, I was just calling to remind you of the memorial service tomorrow morning. The buses will be here, or you can take a cab, or your brother can drive you, or you can rent a car from one of the local rental agencies, and I have lists down here in the crisis center."

"Thank you, Bettina. Will there be coffins there?"

"Oh, Frank. No. No, this is not a funeral. This is a memorial service. So we can begin the healing. But there will be a funeral. By the way, most of the bodies have been identified."

"That seems pretty quick."

"Those guys are working around the clock. And the robots, of course."

"And then I go down to the morgue?"

"Or you can send your brother."

"And then we can go back to Los Angeles."

"You can go back to Los Angeles anytime. You didn't have to come here."

So quickly, life boiled away everyone's intense compassion, their respect for him.

He said good-bye to her. How many people had he said good-bye to since the plane crashed?

He called his parents' room and asked his mother if she had a number for Anna's sisters.

"You don't have to call them now," she said.

"Why not?"

"Because they'll be here in the morning. They're coming down. No one expects you to be a good host now, Frank."

This was odd from her, he thought she would have liked him to call them, but she was thinking, he was sure, of the crap on her rug, and she wanted him to rest, to protect himself, and probably her, as well, from the possibility that he would erupt in other ways, again.

"They want to stay at the house," said his mother.

"Why?"

"They want to help you get everything together." This was such
a bland thought. What did that mean, get everything together?
Everyone would have their own cycle that began with grief and awe
and ended in irritation. He would have to deal with the two sisters'
need to start at the beginning. And then Anna's parents. He needed
a publicist, not for the press, but for all these relations, someone
paid to talk to them, to explain his behavior.

Was he still related to Anna's family? If Anna had died, but
Madeleine survived, there would still have been some kind of genetic
connection, through the little girl, but now? What held them together
but an obligation to remember? And if I want to forget?

Anna's sisters were Barbara and Andrea. Barbara was three years
older, Andrea, five years younger. Their parents, Peter and Margot
Klauber, lived in Philadelphia, where Peter was a real estate attorney. Barbara was a lawyer in Boston; Andrea managed a bookstore
in Seattle. It was not a close family. There were cousins, mostly
centered around Philadelphia, and most of them on Peter's side of
the family. Margot's family, the Van Raaltes, were Dutch Jews, and
only Margot's parents had escaped Amsterdam before the war.
Everyone else was dead. The Klaubers were a more refined family
than the Gales, and this was something that had attracted Frank to
Anna, something he thought of as European, cultured, complicated.
Anna, for her part, was at first delighted by the mercantile Gales.
There was a kind of vulgar Jew that Anna always pointed out to
Frank, someone in his late forties, or older, even into his seventies,
with a creased, pendulous face, and long earlobes, and an open
shirt, and gold chains. She would find them in crowds, in other cars
at stoplights, and on beach vacations. Frank asked her once if she
wanted him to wear a gold chain, and she said he needed to put on
weight to look right. She had meant, he knew, the kind of weight
that came from a Bacchic, orgiastic need for more. She didn't want
a fat man who was stuffing the lonely child within. A concept taken
from psychology. And she wanted him to be fat only if he was rich,
and rich in the right way. Money he had stolen himself, not money

his father or brother had stolen. And she might have been disappointed that the Gales were finally not vulgar enough, not Oriental enough. So her marriage to Frank did not insult her mother and father and provoke their contempt for her, for her conscious degradation of their bloodline, a hatred for her that might have challenged Anna to complete the break with them and choose a path for her own life that needed neither their approval nor disapproval. This was a subject to which she returned often, her family's sense of its own importance, the family curse. In the first years of their marriage, Frank listened sympathetically to Anna's minute dissections of her family's morbidity. Was it the discovery of Mary Sifka that poisoned his interest in his wife's family? He came to hate the calls from Anna's parents, because after she talked to them, chatting pleasantly, she would hang up the phone and swear she would never talk to them again. He told himself that Mary Sifka would never make such a promise unless she meant to keep it, but that she would never, at this age, give her parents, or give anyone but especially her parents, the authority Anna had given hers. And since meeting Mary, he had stopped complaining about his own parents to Anna, although his feelings for them hardly changed. He just didn't want to do anything that would make him sound like Anna, so full of blame.

Still, though neither of them really loved their own families, or each other's, they could not afford, emotionally, to tell the other that they were bored with each other's tired feelings. Mexico might have changed this. Since the crash he had not allowed himself, or had the time, to think beyond the first fantasy of Anna's discovery of the letter. Even while writing the letter, he imagined nothing beyond the first conversation with her in the room when he returned from his walk on the beach with Madeleine. But if the letter worked, if Anna had forgiven him and fucked him deeply—to make another baby!—then for the next week they would have felt a closeness that perhaps they had never felt with each other, for each other. Anything would have been possible after a few days. They could have said, Now let us tell each other every thought we have ever had. All the worst thoughts. About ourselves, about each other. What we want in life. What we want in bed, now.

What a way to seduce. What a name for a perfume, the Truth. What are you wearing? The Truth.

And then, where else could this orgy of truth have led them? To freedom, to holy edification. This might have been the great project for both of them, a new mission for their lives, launched by ten loving days in Mexico. Let go of the past. Burn the past. Burn all the baggage. The purge of the mother and father. Finally to let go of all that. And if this sounded like something that a celebrity couple would confess to in a magazine, well, so what? Wouldn't you like to be so free? He could have told her everything about his feelings at work, about Lowell, about his disappointments, the failure of his career as a record producer, but to really tell her how he felt about it, how awful it was. Or would she be reminded by this that there was something in life for which he wasn't quite good enough? Successes she could have shared. Parties to which she would never be invited. Would she prefer not to think about this? Well, but isn't that what they were testing? That they could trust each other not to use these secrets as weapons. To let go of it all, let go of failure and frustration. Let go of ambition and expectation.

And what would she have said to him? What if they fell in love with each other for a few days, and continued to confess, and explore, but reached a moment in which one of them said something harsh, or more painful than even the rules of trust and honesty could contain? For example: I don't really love you. Or: I always wanted to be with someone more beautiful. What if one of them said something that had been hidden for a long time, and that the relief of this revelation was short-circuited by the truth's imperative to act on this feeling, and that the only action capable of sustaining that relief was divorce? For example: I want a husband who works for himself, not his brother. Or: I want a man who knows languages, and can explain the world to me. Or: Life is too short, and all of this honesty is a device to leave us in a deep embrace with our fates, and I want another fate.

What if he had not missed the plane, and the plane had not crashed? When he talked to her on the car phone, she was mad at him, but she was still getting on the plane. He had consoled himself with this, because she could have canceled the trip, but then Madeleine would have been confused and disappointed. So was she continuing ahead only for their daughter? As the plane went down, was she thinking with bitterness that if she had acted for herself, and not for the daughter she had with this worm, then she would be alive, and on her way to a lawyer, to settle the case and be free, finally?

And if the plane had not crashed, and Frank had gone to Mexico and met them, what would that have been like? Gone to Mexico knowing that Anna had read the letter. He would have called from the lobby when he checked in. They would have been expecting him. Yes, Señor Gale, we're sorry you missed your flight. We've taken very good care of your wife and daughter. The little girl, she's so bright. Would you like your complimentary margarita? He would. And always the same routine: without salt, no ice. Or ice, yes, but no salt. No, make that with salt too, and lots of ice. Thank you. Then to the house phone. Hello, Anna. Or, not even that. I'm here. Well, I made it. Hi. Anna.

Then with the bellboy to the room. Or would he have needed a bellboy, since all the luggage had gone with Anna? No bags, just a toy bought for Madeleine at the airport store. Under his arm. The bellboy doesn't need to show him the way to the room. Yes, he does. I'm too tired, too scared. I need the company. So the bellboy walks with me. He speaks a little English. He knows I missed my flight. He shows me the door. Who knocks? I do. I give him a few dollars, too much, but I need someone to like me now.

So I knock. Madeleine, in the background, shrieks out "Daddy!" Anna opens the door. I stand there, don't cross the threshold until invited. Don't meet her eyes, look down, think of contrition. I say I'm sorry. That's all. I don't come in. She has to invite me in. I say nothing. I wait for her to talk. This is a strategy that will either work or end the marriage now. Either she will let me in, and with that invitation forgive me, or she will see through the device, and make me go back to Los Angeles, now. A minute while she studies me. I do not look her in the eyes. She can see me clearly now.

Come on in.

So I do. The baby jumps up, and I pull her into my arms. I give her the doll, which she takes shyly and then hugs. I tell her that I missed her. I ask her about the flight. Questions that Madeleine cannot answer. She shows the doll to her mommy. Her mommy says hello to the doll. The human drama is so obvious to me now, how to direct it.

We have a suite. We put Madeleine to bed. I tell her a story. Once upon a time there was a frog and a centipede. And the frog fell asleep, and the centipede crawled into the frog's mouth looking for a warm place to rest. And the frog closed his mouth and swallowed the centipede, and the centipede tickled the frog from the inside and said, Let me out, and the frog opened his mouth, and the centipede came out, and then they were friends.

And Madeleine is just barely satisfied with the story, but she lets me kiss her on both cheeks, and she holds the new doll—a penguin? a teddy bear? a bunny?—and lets me leave her in the strange new room with the door open just a bit. And then her mommy goes into the room and stays for a long time, half an hour, until Madeleine is really asleep, and then she comes out of the room, with a smile back at her daughter, and then she slaps me across the face, one hand, then the other hand, and tells me she wants a divorce, that I'll never change, that I'm a loser.

And I tell her what does she know about losers? She hasn't crossed the fucking police barricades, she hasn't walked through the devastated houses.

I'm fine the way I am, and I like myself, I yell at her. And I could hit her, I could slap her face too if I want, but I don't. So she slaps me again, and she tells me she never really loved me, that from the day we met she wondered who I really was, and that a week doesn't go by when she doesn't ask herself why she stays with me, sometimes that is the only thought in her head, for days, maybe she never has another thought in her head except that one, not since the wedding. Well, you're dead now, I say, so I don't have to listen to this. And she says, Yes, you do.

I go back to the knock on the door. Put the baby to bed. Finish with the frog. Anna follows. She comes out of the room and looks at me. Again, I keep my eyes away from hers. She says nothing for five minutes. A long time. I say, I can't stand this. I need to know. I need for her to tell me what she's thinking. She could say, The letter must have been hard to write. So I can shrug. I don't know if I could have written that, she says, if I had fucked around. The word hurts. Is she building up to something, the attack again, the slapping? I shrug again. The little boy. Is it really over? she asks. Yes. And were you having lunch with her? Yes. Did you kiss her good-bye? Yes. On the tongue? Please. But would Anna have asked that? No. Because she wouldn't want to know? Or because her imagination did not search for humiliation? How well did he know her? How long were you seeing her? A while. Six months. Why did it end?

He liked these questions, they were honest and begged for honesty. All he had to do was keep his bargain with the truth. It ended because I wanted to have a real marriage. Because I wanted to be a father again. How do I know I can trust you? You can't. What an answer! How do I know you won't fuck another woman again? You can't. So why should I stay with you? I don't know. Did you mean it about having another child? I think so. Not a definite yes? I can't be definite about anything right now. Then why are you here? I want to try. So you're trying something with me? Yes. But then you're really just experimenting with yourself. I hope not. But you might be. Yes. Then I'm just an experiment, and if the experiment fails, you'll have me pregnant again, or with a second child, before you realize that this was all a mistake. I don't know. But you do know. I don't think so. Then if you don't know, you're asking me to take all of the risks, because if you back out, I'm the one who loses. I suppose so. That's right, you see it, I'm right. Yes. So there's no reason to stay together, because I can never trust you. I'm sorry.

I'm sure you really are sorry, I'm sure this tears you apart, I'm sure you feel miserable. I do. I know you, of course you do, but look at this, here I am, feeling sorry for you, and you're the one who broke his vows. I am admitting the affair; are you telling me that you haven't slept with anyone else? Never. Is there any hope for us? Probably not.

Frank is silent again, but this time without any kind of plan. They sleep in the same bed but do not touch. He is careful not to try.

In the morning they have breakfast in the dining room that looks out over the beach. Madeleine brings her doll but spills marmalade on it and cries. The pineapple is dry. He drinks three cups of cinnamon-flavored coffee, and his stomach burns. Anna arranges herself prettily, in profile to Frank, knowing that he hates the affectation of the pose, and she watches the sea. Frank eats too much from the buffet, three servings of a spicy omelet with peppers and chorizo. This hurts his stomach too. Madeleine drinks her juice and flirts with a six-year-old at another table.

Everyone goes to the beach in the morning. Frank rents an umbrella and chairs. He orders drinks from a cabana boy. Anna has a margarita and reads magazines, *Vanity Fair* and *Architectural Digest,* which she bought at the airport in Los Angeles.

Madeleine plays with a few little girls. Frank drinks too much and falls asleep. Anna drinks and sleeps. Someone wakes them up, the cabana boy.

There has been an accident.

Please come.

Frank sees a crowd at the water's edge, in a circle. The crowd shifts, and Anna cries out. Madeleine is dead. She had been playing in the water, no one was watching her when the wave knocked her down, it happened so quickly.

No one was watching her.

There is nothing to be done.

The parents STAND BY HELPLESSLY as the police take the body away, and then the hotel's manager helps make the arrangements to return home. They fly home with the body in a tiny coffin.

Lowell meets them at the airport in Los Angeles. Everyone asks them how it happened. They tell the same story, that Madeleine was with a baby-sitter, and the sitter couldn't swim, and when Madeleine was caught by a wave, she was gone before help could save her.

Everyone tells them to sue. Frank's mother forces them to see an attorney. The attorney advises them of the difficulty in a lawsuit. Who will they sue? The hotel? Or the Mexican baby-sitter? Some *campesino*'s daughter who lives in a house with dirt floors? This is one of those things, says the lawyer. If this had happened in America, and they had contracted for the sitter through an American hotel, then they might have had a case. He is sorry. So are they.

They go back to the house, put the baby's things away, and then Frank moves out, to a motel. In three months they are divorced.

Or he did not miss the plane. And Lonnie Walter forgot his rage, in the parking lot, he put his gun away and thought of his family, thought of his sister, and could not bring himself to so dishonor them, and returned home, and found a kind psychologist, and rebuilt his life, and trained for a new job, and made peace with himself. And Frank buys Madeleine a toy in the airport gift shop, a key chain with a plastic surfboard ridden by Mickey Mouse. He helps her with a coloring book on the flight. He gives her gum to chew for the descent into Acapulco. There is time for a swim in the afternoon. While Anna is in the shower, Frank tucks the letter behind the extra pillows on the shelf in the closet. Everything is just as it should be. That night they have a pleasant dinner looking out at the sea. He makes love to Anna, starting with a slow massage of her feet and ankles. They exhaust themselves. He makes a lot of noise when he comes, like a buffalo, a heavy grunt, and then a series of strangled cries. When he's finished, he laughs. In the morning he takes Madeleine for a walk, leaving the letter behind. When they return, the room is empty. On the back of the letter he had left for her, Anna has left her own note. It reads:

Dear Frank,

*I have gone home to Los Angeles. We
took a vow of fidelity when we married.
You broke that vow. I have decided not to
forgive you.*

Anna's flight back to Los Angeles crashes. Wind shear, whatever that means, though the weathermen on television try to explain. Some freak of nature, a sudden shift in the air, and the plane loses its lift. And Frank is now a single father. He sues the airline. He makes a lot of money, enough to build a recording studio in his house. Through a friend at a record label, he is introduced to a singer, and helps the singer make a demonstration tape of one song. The label likes it and hires Frank to produce the singer's album. The record sells well. Frank meets many beautiful women and is happy. Or he would be happy, but he learns how weak he is at being a father, how inadequate. Madeleine will not let him forget that she misses Anna. Nothing helps her, because she knows that her father doesn't really love her. That her father would always rather be someplace else, doing something for himself, not for her, not with her.

He tries to find someone to marry, but no one ever really loves him. He calls Mary Sifka a few years after Anna's death, to say hello, to tell her he has survived, and she is pregnant and happy. There is nothing between them anymore, or rather, he tests her and finds that she has no feeling for him, other than a genial good cheer, which Frank believes is proof that she once loved him, and that he should have left Anna for her. After the call he can never quite stop bothering himself with the scenario of a life that turned on a passion. He asks himself, What if I had told Anna that I loved another woman, that whether or not I married this other woman, the love itself, a real love, proved to me the death of my marriage, that I could not be a model to my own daughter if I stayed married against the instinct of every cell in my body? He thinks, Well I wouldn't have said that part, about the cells in the body, but what if I had said the rest?

He starts to drink. Madeleine becomes a withdrawn and confused child, and even with the help of psychologists her somber and arid character cannot be changed. Frank sends her to a private school that specializes in offering paid sympathy to the damaged children of the rich. Her grades are only average, and the friends she makes are colorless, bored with each other. They protect themselves by mocking each other's enthusiasms. After three years at an expensive but mediocre college, she gets a job, with the help of a friend's father, working as an assistant to a casting director in Los Angeles, who encourages her to see all the movies and plays she can. Madeleine buys the tickets, or accepts free tickets from the theaters, but never sees the plays. The casting director gently talks to Madeleine about ambition, and finally Madeleine tells her that she prefers the routine of the job. She explains to the casting director that she has no interest in running a business. At some point in her thirties she goes into analysis, at her father's suggestion. In therapy she discovers that she has blocked herself at work because her father provided so few lessons in life for her. With deeper examination she analyzes the complex structure of her family and discovers that Frank, as the always self-deprecating brother to the tycoon, never trusted his own abilities. Far from hating Frank for his weakness, after a few years on the couch, Madeleine defends her father's contribution to the business, in ways that would make Frank cry if he could hear, since her compassion for his loss, the death of her mother, his struggle with a domineering and difficult brother, reveals something like love for him. Finally she tells her father that she knows how hard it must have been to raise her without a wife, and that she knows that he did the best he could. He wants to tell her that he could have done better, that every time he left her for something else, every time he could have read three stories to her instead of the one he did, every time he could have spent another half hour with her on the floor, coloring, instead of letting her watch cartoons, he knew what he was doing, that he was sinning against her. But he does not say this.

Following the paths along this circuitry of possibilities made Frank happy, but then he heard the analyst ask Madeleine, How did your mother die? Madeleine tells her, In a plane crash. And where was she going? She was going back to Los Angeles, from Acapulco. And why did she leave before you and your father?

Yes, this is the issue in his daughter's life, the great unanswered recurring question. The analyst comes back to the same questions: How did your mother die? She was killed in a plane crash. Where was she going? She was going to Los Angeles. We were in Mexico, and she had to go home early.

Frank watched sadly as Madeleine learned the truth.

For the second year of her analysis this comes up often, her mother's death, around which grows an aura of rage, which the analyst understands as the natural surfacing of long-repressed feelings, blah blah blah. But the analyst herself has a dream of the mother's death, and then she asks Madeleine why the mother was alone on a plane from Mexico to Los Angeles. Madeleine cries, and for three sessions she refuses to talk. When she does, she says, One of my cousins, on my father's side, my cousin Julia, told me that my parents were having a fight, that my father wrote a letter to my mother telling her about an affair he'd been having, and that my mother left without saying good-bye.

Frank could never have kept that story a secret; he would have shared it with someone.

So the story ends not with the daughter forgiving the father for his sins, but, through the analysis he has paid for, perhaps paid for out of the trust fund established with the insurance settlement from her mother's death, his daughter finds the courage to reject him totally, without apology.

Clear of the foggy past, Madeleine can advance at work, find a man to love, without using him to play out scenarios of revenge against her father. The analysis ends with Madeleine asking the therapist if she is obligated by some standards of psychological health to reconcile with the father, and the analyst assures her that she is not, unless she wants to.

Perhaps some years later she comes to Frank to apologize, but perhaps not.

In this projection into the future, Frank assumes that Los Angeles muddles along without the big earthquake, that America muddles along without a military coup, that life goes on as it usually does. Frank dies, and the nurse in the next room hears his last word: "Mary."

The phone rang. Frank said hello to Julia Abarbanel.

"Frank, it's Julia."

"Why did you have to tell her?"

She asked him, "What do you mean?"

"The letter."

"What letter?"

Frank wondered how Julia had even known about the letter, since he had torn it up and flushed it down the toilet. Anna had written her note to him on the back of the letter. But of course, she had seen the letter in the newspaper, when the plane crashed. But which plane had crashed? The one going or the one coming home? Why had he bothered telling his wife the truth? The truth had destroyed his life.

"Nothing," said Frank. "I was having a dream."

"A nightmare."

"I guess."

"At Auschwitz the prisoners in the cell blocks wouldn't wake someone up if he was having a nightmare, because reality was always worse."

"I didn't know that." What else was there to say?

"I'm sick over this," she said.

"It's hard on all of us."

"I'm glad you said that. Nobody in the family really knows how to talk about this." At family dinners, at Passover or Thanksgiving, when there were fifteen people at a long table, he could talk to Julia, even with Anna there, and a bubble would form around them, and inside this bubble they could say anything about anyone at the table, and they couldn't be heard. Now he was free. He thought they would be fucking soon. How was her body? She was what, thirty-five? Did she exercise? Was she firm?

"Are you coming in?" he asked. He wanted to see her.

"Tomorrow. Your mother said there's this thing in San Diego, but I can't get in to L.A. until the afternoon."

"You don't need to be here. The airline is throwing it. It's not a funeral. It's for the cameras."

"What do they know about the guy with the gun?" Her questions were getting almost too casual, and Frank, as much as he wanted to scrape the crust from every facet of the event, wanted to set the limits, to maintain the family's respect for his sorrow.

"I haven't actually followed that."

"Every airport in the country is putting security checks at all the employee entrances now."

"It's a little late."

Julia was quiet. So she was embarrassed, he thought. She returned to Lonnie Walter. "They recovered the flight recorder," she said.

"I hadn't heard that."

"They haven't played it yet, but they have it. There's a report that the control tower has it all on tape. I heard on the news that he came into the cockpit."

"Was it a bomb?"

"A gun, that's what they think. And he knew where to fire it, where the fuel lines run through the walls, where to blow out the windows, so he turned the plane into a bomb."

"Everyone must have seen it." If he had said this to his mother, she would have told him not to think about it, because she didn't want to have the picture of a terrified Anna and an ignorant-of-the-crisis Madeleine watch the crazed black gunman forcing his way to the cockpit with a flight attendant. But it was something he could say to Julia, and a way of exciting her, getting her ready for bed.

"What a shitty way to die," she said.

"At least it's fast," said Frank. "That's the only blessing I can

find. You can't even imagine how scared they must have been, but
then it's over. It's not like starving to death in a lifeboat."

"Did you see the letter?" she asked, skipping to another
subject.

"Which letter?"

"There you go about letters again," she said, lightly. "The letter
this husband wrote to his wife?"

"Oh, yeah, Mom and Dad said something about that."

"This guy took his wife to Mexico so that he could try to get the
marriage kick-started after he'd had an affair."

"What was in the letter?" This was a stupid question to ask,
and he knew it would come back to him.

"I don't have it in front of me, but it was, like, darling, I love
you, I'm sorry I hurt you, and I fucked this other woman and it's
over and if you don't want me, fine, I understand."

"Did they say anything about names?"

"No. Can you imagine? If he hadn't had the affair, maybe he
wouldn't have taken his wife on the trip, and then they'd both be
alive."

"And their daughter?"

"There was nothing in the letter about any children. Did you
hear something?"

"I don't know. I'm confusing this with something else. I know,
the people who were killed on the ground."

"A lot of people were killed on the ground." But she didn't say
this to force him to clarify his meaning, only to show her awe.

With the letter's resurgence into the conversation, Frank thought
he would stop breathing. He tried to swallow, but panic choked
him. "I have to go," he squeaked.

"Where?" Why did she have to ask that? What business was it
of hers?

"Some kind of prememorial service downstairs."

"Good luck," said his cousin.

"Thanks."

"We all love you, Frank. All of us."

Yes, but do you? He didn't ask. He hung up.

There were voices in the hall. He opened the door, and the woman he had seen earlier, arguing by the elevator, was talking to one of the other mourners.

"I'll get to you later," she said. And she smiled. He didn't understand. She gave him a business card for Dave Dessick, Attorney at Law.

Frank knew that the reporters did not know, did not know that the letter writer was alive, had not heard Mary Sifka's name. It must be the airline, he thought, controlling the story. They'll let Mary's name out, or let out my name, when they want to destroy the lawsuits. He was thinking this, and chewing on a gummy room-service croissant, when the phone rang. It was Mary Sifka.

9. The General Theory of the Letter

In the morning the letter was everywhere. Frank woke up early, and the paper was outside his door with the Continental breakfast he had ordered the night before. The letter he had written for his wife to read was on the front page. It was also the lead item on the morning television news.

THE GENERAL THEORY OF THE LETTER:

The author, as well as his wife, have died in the crash. Reporters are trying to find out who they were. There is a debate about the public's curiosity, and the rights of the couple's mourning relatives to keep this private. Women newscasters are asked by the men beside them if they would forgive an unfaithful husband if he wrote them in this way. Frank is grateful that they all say yes. A few of them add, winking at the camera, that they would easily kill their men, though, if they catted around again.

"It's you, isn't it? That's your letter, isn't it?"

"Yes," said Frank.

"So the name, the one that they're keeping out, it's mine, right?"

"Yes." There was silence. He was trying to be kind, but nothing he intended mattered anymore.

"You stupid asshole, did you say 'Mary,' or did you say 'Mary Sifka'?"

"Mary Sifka."

She screamed out, "No!" And then, through terrible sobs, she said, "They're going to find out, you know that, don't you?"

"Yes. They'll call you," said Frank. He could try to be as direct with his mistress as he had failed at being direct with his wife.

"I know that. I think they already did. The phone rang last night, and my husband answered, but they hung up. They must know who I am, that I'm married. It's not hard to find that kind of thing out. So they're probably waiting until I answer the phone myself."

"What are you going to do?"

"What can I do? I can't deny it. I can't say that's not my name. It's my name. It's not a common name."

"I'm sorry."

"This is going to ruin my life."

"I know that."

"Yours too."

"Probably." I could have said, Mine is already ruined.

"No, definitely. I'm going to see to that. Your life is going to be destroyed in some way that you can't even imagine. I want to see you die without dying."

"I don't think we should talk now."

"I'm telling my husband."

"Maybe you should."

"He hates attention. He's a quiet man."

"Will he leave you?"

"You think that's what I want? If I had wanted him to leave me, I could have arranged for that the first time we fooled around in your office. Do you think that's what I want?"

"I don't know," he said.

"If that's all I wanted, to be without him, if I'd wanted to leave him, I would have already. Do you think I couldn't leave him if I wanted to?"

"Yes, I think you could."

"I can do what I want."

He wondered if this repetitive belligerence of hers came from vodka. "Well, since you love him, maybe you should go somewhere with him. To help him see that it was over with us, that you were back with him. Take him someplace."

"Mexico?" she said, with great bitterness, implying, and Frank thought this cruel of her, that if they got on the plane to Mexico, they would die in a crash.

What if I volunteer to pay for the tickets? thought Frank. Would she try to kill me? "The name might not come out," he said. He was trying to convince himself of this, so he could go to the memorial service and not faint, or start barking. There was the picture in his head, he saw himself growling and yelping, rolling around on the floor, shitting his pants again, because everyone in the world knows his worst secrets.

"You think so?" She also wanted to believe this.

"You might be able to deflect this. You may need a lawyer."

"A lawyer, yes." Frank understood that Mary was desperate, and she was hanging for her life on this raft of hope.

"A lawyer could, you know . . ." He didn't finish the sentence, because then she could say,

"A lawyer could threaten to sue if they print my name without permission. But you'd have to claim the letter from them, wouldn't you?"

"Maybe I could do that." It was a possibility. What had started as something to keep Mary Sifka from going out of her mind had come back to him as a way through this mess. If he asked for the letter back . . . but what would that do? They'd know who he was, they'd know Mary. And the letter had been in his wife's possession, and she was dead. The letter had been discovered in a public place. "No," he said, "that won't work. We can't do anything about this."

"This is my fault," she said. "If I hadn't sucked your dick, you wouldn't have made this trip. If I hadn't let you give me a hand-job in your office—"

"Don't say that." Actually he wanted her to say that; it was giving him an erection.

"We're the most miserable animal in the world," she said. Philosophy. He hated this. "Whatever we touch, it turns to shit. There's really no such thing as love, is there? Deep down?"

"Probably not," said Frank.

"Because if there was, then we really would hold on to each other."

"I held on to you. We held on to each other."

"But we weren't supposed to. We're supposed to hold on to the people we married. There's a Commandment about it."

"I guess we're going to be punished," said Frank.

"Don't you think that *this* is the punishment?"

"I suppose," said Frank. He wished that he had thought of that line, it would have impressed her.

"I wonder if we'll have any friends left."

"Don't worry, Mary." He said her name, trying to find a way out of the conversation. "The roof will fall harder on me than on you."

"They'll see me as the whore who stole the husband."

"They'll see you as the woman who was seduced."

"Or the businesswoman who sold her pussy to get a deal."

"I don't think so."

"No, you just hope they won't tear us apart like that."

"Just think about other scandals. How long do they last when nobody famous is involved? A few days? We're not the news, we're just a human-interest story. And when the whole story comes out, what really looks that bad? We had an affair. We broke it off. I went back to my wife, you went back to your husband. I think it makes us look sort of good. Maybe even noble. We could be heroes."

"Frank, no, the only way you could have come out of this a hero would have been if you had died with them. And the letter was found. And with my name in it, I'd have to be the Jezebel. You know that."

"I guess so."

They were both calm now. Frank knew they needed this moment of peace, because when it ended, they would say good-bye, and it wasn't likely that they would talk to each other soon, or even again, ever.

It was time to say good-bye.

"Don't forget," he said, "that we had some nice times together."

She snapped back at him, "They weren't nice, Frank. What we did was cheap. It was dirty. Death in life for you, Frank, death in life." And then she hung up.

And then the phone rang again. It was Lowell, calling from the lobby.

"How are you feeling today?" asked his brother.

"Much better."

"We have to decide on a lawyer now. Everyone involved is choosing now, and there are two guys people are gravitating to. I have to check them out. They both sound good. But there happen to be differences of opinions. Has anyone talked to you about Dessick or Berberian?"

"Who?" asked Frank. He didn't want to say anything about the lawyer's card.

"The two lawyers. Different styles, but similar results. And they're experts at this sort of thing."

"No one has talked to me, but I thought you wanted to hire an independent lawyer. I thought you were going to hire Aaron Waramus."

Lowell made a sound of discouragement. "These guys are good. I think it's better to join the fold."

"But I want to make the final decision."

"Of course, of course," said Lowell. "And maybe also a publicist."

"Good," said Frank.

"I thought you said it was a bad idea."

"It might be good for the family." Meaning: Once the world knows the letter is mine, we'll need a press officer to keep the reporters and the cameras away from us. Could anyone buy this as a movie? Or is it too internal?

"She'll call you later. Anyway, I'm coming up. I brought you a jacket and tie."

He put the receiver down, and the phone rang again. This time it was Bettina Welch. She told him that the buses would be leaving in half an hour.

"Buses?" Frank said. "I thought you said we were going to get limousines."

"I'm sorry, Frank," said Bettina. "I tried."

Frank made a face, but he didn't know what it looked like. He supposed the airline knew that anyone's protest over the switch from limousines to buses would look awfully bratty, and this was a day for everyone to appear so occupied with grief that the material world was momentarily dissolved.

"We'd really appreciate it if no one talks to the press today," she said.

"Why is that?"

"We just think that with everything that's going on, people are losing sight of the tragedy, of the lives that were lost, of the respect that we should be paying to the victims of this terrible tragedy."

He knew that she was really saying that the airline was trying to keep the families of the dead from taking center stage.

Lowell was at the door. Frank let him in while he was on the phone.

"What's going to happen at the memorial?"

"The governor will be there, and the mayor of San Diego."

"Why isn't this happening in Los Angeles?" he asked.

"We'll have a memorial in Los Angeles too, maybe even a funeral if I can say that, but this is where the tragedy occurred. And if we have a memorial service in Los Angeles, we'll be missing the op-

portunity to complete our bereavement for the innocent victims who
died on the ground."

Lowell made a face: Who are you talking to? And Frank said,
"Good-bye," and hung up.

"Who was that?" asked Lowell.

"The front desk." Frank didn't want to talk about anything.

"What did they want?"

"Do I have everything I need? Is there anything they can get
for me?"

Lowell handed Frank a garment bag. Frank took it to the bathroom and put on the shirt and tie and the jacket. While he was in
the bathroom, the phone rang, and he let Lowell answer. Frank
heard him say, "Hello, Mother," in a loud voice meant for Frank,
and then his voice dropped.

Lowell knocked on the bathroom door to tell him that it was
time to go.

They met their parents in the hallway, by the elevators. There
were others there, new faces, and some Frank recognized from Los
Angeles, late arrivals who had missed the morgue.

Someone said that they really shouldn't be going to this without
first checking with a lawyer, someone else said, with tears, that this
was no time to worry about the suit, that the suit would follow its
own course whether or not the airline was managing this memorial.
Someone added that there were already a few groups of lawyers
circling the event. Yes, someone said, there's Dessick and Berberian. The Barbarian, someone else said, that's his nickname. And
who was going with them? The people in the elevator called out
their choices: Dessick Berberian Berberian Dessick Dessick Berberian. Frank had not made his choice yet. Someone told him that
he should. Then another person said that he knew that the airline
had been warned about this nigger, and someone said that wasn't
nice, and the person who said "nigger" then said he didn't have to
protect the niggers when a nigger killed his daughter and son-in-
law on their honeymoon. Someone else said there were black people
on the plane too, and the man who said "nigger" said, So what?

They took the elevator to the mezzanine floor, where they met
Bettina Welch and Ed Dockery, and others, and were introduced
to the president of the airline, Dennis Donoghue. Frank had seen
the man's picture in the paper a few times. He lived somewhere
else, maybe Texas—Frank vaguely remembered that he had worked
at a few other airlines and had rescued this one during difficult
times. His confidence was so practiced that he wasn't really there
in the room, he projected an image of himself; this was a hologram
Dennis, not the real thing. When Bettina introduced him to Frank,
Donoghue's smile changed. Something that looked like satisfaction
replaced his relaxed concern.

"Yes, Mr. Gale. You've been through a lot, haven't you?"

"I guess."

"No false humility here, Mr. Gale." And then he said, quietly,
with a threat, "We know what happened."

"I just meant that I'm still alive."

"You don't really wish you had died, do you?"

"It's very difficult."

"But you're not going to kill yourself over this, are you?" Where
were these questions coming from?

"It doesn't seem fair, does it?" asked Frank, drawn into Donoghue's orbit.

"If you don't believe in God, these things have no meaning."

"Do you believe in God?" asked Frank.

"Of course," said Donoghue. "And I know that He's not fair."

Frank turned to Lowell, panicked by this conversation. Why
were they talking this way? Donoghue had dropped all pretense of
grief, or interest, and the impatience with which he talked to Frank
was personal, was directed at Frank as though he knew who he
really was, as though Frank deserved a harsh judgment.

Lowell wasn't listening to him, any more than in the big room
when that unhappy couple pressed Frank on his relationship with
the insurance agent, and Frank had added to his lies.

"What about you, Frank," said Donoghue, "do you believe in
God?"

"I guess if you really believe in God, then you have to pray."

"And you don't pray?"

"I don't think so."

"Not even when you're alone? You don't hear yourself begging the Creator of the universe for mercy?"

"I don't have an answer for that," said Frank. Again the picture came to him, of getting sick like a dog. What did this mean, this urge to roll around the floor, shitting and pissing?

"Start thinking of one," said Donoghue, leaving Frank for someone else as Bettina came over and took his arm. She looked back at Frank, and Frank knew, without doubt, that she knew the letter was his.

What grace this knowledge gave her! And Donoghue, nothing else could explain how miserably he treated Frank than the power he obtained from knowing Mary Sifka's name. He will turn this against me, thought Frank. Somehow this will be used to help the airline. He gave the letter to the press. He will give away Mary's name when he needs to.

Donoghue shook hands with Frank's parents. His mother showed him a picture of Madeleine, at a year old, lying on a Mexican blanket on the beach. Anna's foot was in the corner of the picture. He thought of her foot severed from her leg, sitting in a bin of feet in that cold warehouse by the bay.

Bettina asked everyone to start on their way down to the buses. Donoghue shook hands with Frank's father. Whatever secret feelings he held for Frank, they were not extended to his parents. Frank thought this was odd, but could not explain it to himself.

How did Frank feel? This is how he felt: Tie a man's wrists to two posts. Nail his feet to the floor. Take a razor blade or a scalpel, and cut the skin in a circle around his neck. Then, from his neck down to his waist, cut a series of strips, an inch apart. Then pull each strip away from the body, and let them fall, making a loose skirt of flesh. Then throw boiling ammonia on this swamp of blood. Wait three minutes for the blisters to rise. Rub them with hard salt. This should overload the myelin sheaths that protect the nerves from agony. Better yet, don't find a surrogate, do this to yourself, or ask a friend to help.

Bettina Welch and Dennis Donoghue led the mourners out a back door of the hotel to three buses parked by the kitchen loading dock. Piet Bernays was there to hand out black armbands, each with a strip of elastic sewed inside, and Frank welcomed the slight pressure of this mild tourniquet.

"Buses," said Lowell. "They promised us limousines." But he was too tired to complain anymore, or Dennis Donoghue had worked his corporate magic on him and taken out the fight.

When Bernays held Frank's hand to slip the band up his arm, he winked at him. "Have a nice day," he said, in the manner of someone whose mastery of sarcasm was complete.

On the bus Frank sat next to Lowell, across the aisle from their parents. Had the family ever been on a bus together except when the brothers were young, and they were in Europe, taking guided trips through famous cities? Their father leaned across the aisle. "How do you get the seat to go back?" Their mother found the button on her armrest, and the back went back, just far enough to fulfill the promise of whatever advertisement promised reclining seats, so no one could sue, even though the reclination was insufficiently advanced to offer compensation for the uncomfortably short seat. She tried the button on their father's seat, but it was broken. He looked around the bus for someone from the airline. "Do you think anyone can help me with this?" he asked Lowell. Lowell tried the button, and this time the seat went back.

"I guess I'm not very strong," said their mother.

The bus left the hotel and followed the road along Mission Bay for a while before turning toward the city and Balboa Park.

There were two conversations on the bus. One was about the lawsuits, and the other was about Lonnie Walter.

Someone knew someone who knew someone. The last someone worked for the airline, and was best friends with one of the girls who died. That phrase again. And this person, a woman—What division of the airline? Ground crew—knew Lonnie Walter. And Lonnie Walter had been fired. Someone asked why. Because he drank. No, someone else knew part of the story. Because of layoffs. Or did he think it was because he was black? That may have been a part of the problem. But did you know his supervisor, the one he went on the plane to kill, was also black? I heard a Mexican. No, a black. There were some blacks on the bus. Frank watched them, nervous and embarrassed for them. A stupid resurgence of pity for the race whose collective failure to help themselves had driven their cousin, this one indignant lush, to murder hundreds. Fuck them all, thought Frank, another group to see fucked. Fuck them all for killing my family.

Someone asked if they had identified the letter writer. Someone else said no, someone else said yes. Someone said what difference did it make, and someone said, Well, the letter gave me comfort, and then others agreed, even Lowell and Frank's father. Someone asked if the women on the bus would have forgiven their husbands, and then the women were polled. One woman said she didn't want to talk about it, and then she cried, and Lowell whispered to Frank, "I think her husband was on the plane with his mistress."

Frank said, "Really?"

Lowell said, "No, but that would be great, wouldn't it?"

Frank wanted to ask Lowell how he could make jokes at a time like this, he wanted to take the black armband and strangle Lowell with the elastic, but he knew that he would have made the same joke, that something like it had occurred to him at the same time. The process by which the gruesome, through time, becomes a joke.

Piet Bernays left his seat in the front of the bus to hold the crying woman's hands. He stood in the aisle and then bent one knee to the floor. The woman rested her head against his chest, and he stroked the back of her neck. It seemed to Frank that the others on the bus tried not to watch, but Frank couldn't help himself. He wanted to look into Bernays's eyes, to see what else Bernays knew about him. Bernays looked everywhere, with his placid eyes, except at Frank. Frank studied him: Was he homosexual or not?

After a few minutes, while everyone on the bus was quiet, the woman looked around and, without words, begged to be loved. More of the same: sad-clown-eyes-tear-filled-streaking-mascara-grief-as-excuse-to-justify-indulgence-for-all-the-other-shit-in-her-life. A wave of repulsion washed over Frank, with such force that he almost screamed out to the woman, "You're ugly! We hate you! All of us hate you! We know what you were like in high school! You were unloved then! Why should we love you now? So what if your alcoholic mother vomited on the rug every night, and you had to clean it up! So what if you had three younger brothers to feed and dress and send off to school while your alcoholic mother exposed herself to the mailman! So your father died of pancreatic cancer when you were ten! So what! You're alive!"

Someone said that the governor was going to read the letter at the ceremony, and someone asked, What letter? Frank's father said, The letter, the husband's letter. Someone wondered if they'd found the name of the lover yet. Lowell said, I bet she knows about it already, and his mother said, She must want to kill herself. Someone else wondered if she had a husband. Piet Bernays finally looked toward Frank, and a little energy ran across his lips, bringing them together, in the tiniest piece of a gesture that would, if completed, be named a kiss. Or else it wasn't a kiss, and Bernays was just breathing with his mouth closed.

Someone else said that security would be tighter than ever at airports now, and Lowell said, You can always get through if you want. Everyone agreed with him; there was a quiet lowing of assent to this.

The bus moved up the hill to Balboa Park, where an escort of police on motorcycles pulled in front of them and then behind them. Frank wondered why they had not started with the buses at the hotel. Of course, there was a simple answer. There were no cameras there, no need to attract attention, but now the show begins. As the motorcycles rode in file with the two buses, the mourners stopped talking. Piet Bernays walked to the front of the bus and took the microphone from the hook beside the driver. "We're at Balboa Park now," he said. "The service will last about an hour. The governor is here; so is the mayor of San Diego, of course, and the city council. We've reserved the first three rows in front of the podium. The cardinal of San Diego, a Protestant minister, and a Conservative rabbi will be giving benedictions. They drew lots, to choose the order of the prayers. This way there's no implied opinion expressed, on behalf of the airline, either respecting or disrespecting the superior or inferior importance of any one of the religions by the order of the appearance of their ordained representative."

The bus drove up to the back of the band shell. Frank's father cut in front of a woman who was in the row before them, and she looked at him with some disgust and said something to him, but quietly, so Frank couldn't hear her. He tapped her on the arm. "What did you say?" he said.

"Nothing." Frank saw that for a moment she forgot where she was and why, because this stranger had just discovered her muttering, and she was too embarrassed, even though she was right to be angry.

"I thought you said something to my father."

The woman shook her head no.

"It's not important," said Frank, and then they were off the bus.

Lowell asked him, "What did you say to her?"

"I think she swore at Dad."

"Why?"

"He cut ahead of her in line."

Lowell didn't know what to say, he just shrugged, but it was more in surprise that Frank would bother himself with this, and at the same time accepting that Frank had every reason to be sensitive to everything around him.

Bernays and then Bettina Welch, who was on the other bus, led the mourners around the band shell to their seats, in rows that had been saved for them.

The sun was high and strong, and the air smelled of eucalyptus and freshly watered lawns. There was something else in the air too, the smell of hay and animals, from the zoo, which was just beyond a stand of eucalyptus trees. And then there was a bit of the ocean on the breeze too. So there was something to San Diego after all, thought Frank, to make people want to live here, something pleasant and forgiving.

Until he saw the two or three hundred strangers waiting in the sun for the ceremony to begin, Frank didn't know he had expected a large crowd, thousands and thousands. He thought of the crowds that used to gather for public funerals, in black and white, before television, when all the men wore hats. Now everyone waited to see these things on television. Not even wait, not expect anything, just see it when it comes. He supposed these people, Mexicans and blacks, in T-shirts, carrying paper bags with beer, smoking, had not even come to the park for whatever was going to happen, but had been there already, had slept there during the night, as they must have now for as long as they had been able to stay away from the police. Most of them sat beside bedrolls, a few had backpacks, and parked along the fringes of the scene there were shopping carts filled with plastic garbage bags stuffed with old crap. Then in the rows just behind him, Frank recognized a few people from Dana Street. There was the man whose house he had passed through to get beyond the police line, and a few others too, the neighbors of the dead. And in the front row men and women in suits, officials. The man who let him through nodded his head with tight lips, his face a quick mask of compassion, eyebrows drawn together, eyes to the side and down, but then everything emptied, and Frank saw the man's shame for his inability to offer more than a nod.

Frank wanted to say, But what can you give me? And then Frank felt shame and turned away.

His mother nudged him. "There's the governor, and the mayor."

His father said, about the governor, "I met him at a fund-raiser years ago, when he was running for the state assembly."

"He looks well," said his mother.

The rabbi made an invocation.

The governor, who was sitting next to Dennis Donoghue, walked to the podium. He took a piece of paper from his jacket pocket. He scanned the crowd, and his eyes met Frank's. They held them as he began to talk. He knows, thought Frank. Donoghue told him that the letter is mine. And he's going to read the letter now.

"There are times when it is impossible to say anything," he began. "And those are the times when we have to speak."

"Very good," said Frank's father. "That's very true."

Lowell touched his father's hands, to be quiet.

The governor had not stopped talking. "What do we gain from

this? We know what we lose. We lose a bit of our heart when God throws us this kind of test. So we have to face the test. We have to draw strength from wherever we find it. And in the middle of this catastrophe, we find a miracle. We find the miracle of love. I'd like to read something to you."

He picked up the piece of paper. "I suppose by now most of you have read the letter that was found in the wreckage. We don't know who wrote it, or to whom it was sent, but the letter asks for something that all of us need to give, and that's forgiveness. I'd like to read it to you. It begins, 'I love you.' And it continues, 'You asked me a few weeks ago why I was so desperate to take this vacation and I said that I needed to get away from the office for a while, and that's true, but there's more. For six months you've noticed that I've been distant, and I have been. You asked me if there was another woman, and I said no, but I was lying. I had an affair.' " Frank saw the governor skip past the line that named Mary Sifka, but he hesitated, and looked at Frank again. " 'It's over now. I wanted to take this trip so that we could find a way to heal ourselves. I don't know how you'll take this, and all I can say is that I beg you to forgive me, but if you don't want to, I will understand. I love you.' " He stopped. He began again. "I think that's one of the most beautiful letters ever written, because it tells the truth and asks for nothing in return except the truth. And forgiveness. And so we have to begin now. To forgive."

Reading the letter in the newspaper, Frank only saw the viciously clever adjustments he had made toward bludgeoning Anna with the example of his self-sacrifice.

"What about the fucking lawsuit?" Lowell asked under his breath. "It's a little too soon to forgive. No mercy without justice. And look who he's sitting next to, the president of the fucking airline."

This time it was Frank who touched Lowell's hands, and Lowell shut up. Frank needed to think; he was filled with a big idea, an inspiration bright enough to illuminate the meaning and consequence of his life. Listening to the governor, Frank heard something new in the letter, something pure, and he liked it. Look at how I have touched so many people. Something in this letter means something to them, something I wrote comforts them. Do all writers struggle with their lies when they tell the truth, and regret the failure to tell the complete truth, which sits there, just beyond the reach of language, and mocks them as they smudge the truth, as they favor themselves? Of course they do! The balance that I wanted, between begging for Anna's mercy by telling the truth and not giving her too much ammunition to use against me, didn't that emotional design also give to the letter the grace of something that, if pursued further, might lead to art? What I did, in my own way (and I could have said "little" way, but why qualify?) is what all creative people do. I wrestled my demons to the mat. If I didn't win, it was at least a draw. Maybe that old dream of music is a mistake, maybe I should become a writer. I could take a course! I could write a novel composed of letters. I could write one letter a day, and in a year I'd have a book! If the letters are long enough! Or plays! The way the governor read the letter, there was so much emotion in the language, and everyone listened. I could write a series of dramatic monologues, they could be autobiographical. I could write a series of confessions, just like the letter, a confession cycle! And then someone, a composer, a real artist, might set them to music! And opera! In New York City! And I would have everything.

Lowell whispered in Frank's ear. "The governor is working for the airline. Watch the news tonight, you'll see, it'll look like a commerical for the airline. Airline spokesmen everywhere."

Someone behind them said, "There's Dessick." A few turned. There he was, the man who would represent the families. He stood to the side. He was just a white man, late forties, normal height, a suit of no distinction or flair, and a neat haircut. Someone else muttered, "Ambulance chaser," and someone else said, "So who are you with, Berberian?" And someone else said, "And it's not an ambulance, it's a hearse."

The Dessickite persisted. "He happens to be one of the greatest lawyers in the country."

"What difference does it make?" asked the Barbarian.

"Because we all have to have the same lawyer represent us."

"Why?"

"Because divide and conquer!"

"So join our suit, then."

"I don't trust Berberian."

"What is that supposed to mean? How do you know him?"

"I know."

"He has an incredible reputation."

"He's overrated."

"According to whose standards? You've been talking to the Dessick people, that's all, you're using their standards."

"I trust them. They feel right. Berberian's people feel wrong."

"I'm one of Berberian's people. Are you saying I feel wrong? In my hour of grief are you saying there's something wrong with me?"

"I don't want to say that."

"But you mean it."

"Most of us are going with Dessick. I'm sorry you're not with us, but this isn't the place to fight."

"I'm not fighting. I mean, the only fight I have is with the airline, and I've got the best man working for me. Berberian."

"Fine. You go with Berberian, I'll go with Dessick. Don't get in our way."

"You'll back down. You'll be afraid to let a jury decide the case, because you'll be hearing a little voice in your head that says your lawyer didn't do a good enough job. You'll settle out of court before we do."

The governor introduced the mayor. The hissing of accusation and counteraccusation, this gauntlet of rage in which Frank felt beaten and trapped, continued anyway.

"If we do settle out of court, it'll only be because the airline knew it would cost too much to go all the way."

"So if Dessick is so sure of winning, why not go all the way to a jury? Or is he scared that a jury might go against him?"

"He's not scared of anything or anyone."

"Then he doesn't have to settle out of court."

"Berberian will settle before Dessick does, I promise you."

"You don't have to promise me anything."

"Berberian will have to settle because he knows that juries think he's sleazy. Do you know his percentage of wins before juries after settlements have been rejected? I have those figures!"

"Yeah yeah yeah. You know what they say: 'There's lies, there's damned lies, and there's statistics.' "

"That's one of the stupidest quotes in the history of the English language. Berberian likes to come on like the full-court-press kind of guy he wants you to think he is, but in the last three years he's lost forty percent of those cases that could have been settled out of court. He's an egomaniac."

"And Dessick was threatened with a jury-tampering indictment last year, did you know that?"

"So? Was he ever charged? No. And tell me you don't know who engineered that threat. The lawyers working for the company he was suing. And do you know who the chief lawyer was?"

"You can't scare me or surprise me. I know who it was. It was Berberian."

"And you'll still stay with him?"

"These guys all play hardball, and I like Berberian's style. And this case is open-and-shut. It's not that complicated."

The mayor of San Diego stood at the lectern, but Frank couldn't hear him. He couldn't hear anybody now, not the mourners debating their lawyers, not the plane flying overhead, not the helicopter circling the park, not birds in the nearby trees, not police motorcycles cruising the roads near the band shell. Nothing. Mouths moved, and Frank saw how fiercely rigid we keep our faces, except for our lips. Frank's mother whispered something to the man she had married so many years before, but what she said Frank thought he would never know. His father patted her hand, in silence.

After the mayor spoke, the marine band lifted their instruments. The moment of expectation. The inhalation. Lips to horns. Their conductor brought his baton down, to start the music. Frank strained to hear the brass. Nothing. And yet . . . his frustration, his panic, were released, as though the music had actually touched him. It seemed to him as though this was what they had come to do, that their memorial to the dead would be just this, a respectful silence played on loud instruments. To be moved by silence, reminded of the silence of death by the silent breath of twenty men with horns. What better way to compel true grief than a pantomime of music? Reserve sound for joy! For the battle cry on the way to the fight. And nothing for the field when the combat has been settled.

Then the cardinal, and with a gesture that was understood to mean "Rise," everyone stood. People lowered their heads as he spoke. There were tears. A baby in a mother's arms opened his or her mouth . . . blue blanket . . . his . . . the baby opened his mouth, the agony was understood even without the sound.

I could say something to my brother, thought Frank, or my mother. I could say I can't hear. But would I hear myself saying this? What if I can't hear myself speaking?

He was afraid even to clear his throat. He swallowed hard. There was no sound, no liquid in his mouth trickling down. How did it normally sound? Did it make a sound? Maybe the body is silent to itself? No.

He wanted to hum, but what if the sound was loud, what if he screamed just to hear a sound pierce the silence, and heard nothing himself, but was heard by everyone else? He would make a small sound first. He coughed.

Nothing.

He hummed, and felt the vibration between his lips and his teeth.

The hell with it, with everything he could, he forced the air from his chest and his gut through a constricted throat, epiglottis engaged, and tried to make, without hearing it, the loudest scream he could.

Before they were on him, holding him, trying to shut him up but at the same time trying not to strangle him, or rather, to strangle but not to hurt, only to silence, because the cardinal was praying, Frank saw Lowell's expression, the look to his mother that said this is hopeless, this is worse than we thought (which meant they talked about his condition, and the shitting in his pants had not been moderately excused or forgotten by them, as if it could!), and then Lowell took him by the hand and hugged him, but the hug was without love, without equality, there was a sense of family in it, but only as a collection of memories, not as something still alive. Frank knew that he was dead to his family.

10. Lonnie Walter

They had taken him to the hospital, where he was quickly tested. Bettina Welch came by his bed in the emergency room, and Dennis Donoghue sent him flowers, with a card. His mother read the note aloud to everyone in the room, and then, since Frank could hear nothing, she gave it to him. The note was simple: *We're thinking of you.* Frank couldn't imagine the mayor of any city, even the mayor of the smallest, stupidest town, reading this aloud to anyone. But his father seemed to be impressed with this, and took the card and studied it. Lowell didn't seem to care about it one way or another. Frank hated the note, because it wasn't the right thing to say to a person in the hospital, even if everyone thinks he's a psychotic. The note should have said, "Get well soon," or something like that, to encourage his recovery, without, at the same time, and this makes the job tricky, losing the need to show respect to the necessity for condolence. But what did "We're thinking of you" really mean, except to tell him that his existence entered into their strategies? Instead of comforting Frank, they were threatening him.

And then the doctor handed him another note, on a prescription pad. The note read, *How are you doing?*

Frank took the doctor's pencil and wrote below the question, *Not very well. This is all so embarrassing.*

The doctor wrote, *I suppose it is.* His name tag: Ben Nelson, M.D. He was young, perhaps thirty. He looked as though he enjoyed San Diego, he had a suntanned face and the sort of happy age lines a man might get squinting at the luff in a spinnaker.

How long will this last? wrote Frank.

I think you just need some sleep. You're going back to the hotel. That's my recommendation.

I want to stay here, wrote Frank.

His mother and father and brother crowded behind the doctor to look over his shoulder. At this last note they shook their heads, almost in unison.

The doctor wrote, *No.*

Why not? wrote Frank.

Because there's nothing wrong with you. Frank wanted to cry, but he couldn't force any tears, and without hearing his voice, he worried that any sound he made would drive everyone away from him. He thought there was something monumentally cruel about the doctor, for releasing him without at least one night in the hospital, but perhaps the doctor, having consulted the hospital's chief of staff, regarded this expulsion as the most efficient means to a cure. And Frank knew, regretfully, that the doctor was right, that there really wasn't anything wrong with him. Still, it seemed shocking that everyone would cooperate in this refusal to care for him. What kind of Jewish family would let a thirty-year-old Christian doctor release their son from the emergency room without a second opinion? He suspected a conspiracy. Where were the teams of psychiatrists in all of this? Or even one chubby social worker?

The doctor took the pad away and walked out of the room. Lowell showed Frank his clothes and indicated that Frank should get dressed. Everyone left the room.

They all must know, he thought, and if they don't know for sure, they can guess. He put on the clothing, and went with them back to the hotel.

By ten o'clock he was back in his room. Lowell wrote him a note. *We'll be down the hall. Dial Mom and Dad's room if you need us. Let it ring twice and hang up. We'll be here.*

What's next? wrote Frank. He wanted to write a long essay, complaining about the danger in this plan. What if he fell and hurt himself, and couldn't dial the phone? What if there was a fire in his room, and he couldn't scream for help?

We're going back to Los Angeles in the morning.

Frank wrote, *How?*

Lowell wrote back, *Driving.*

Frank wrote, *Thanx.* He wanted Lowell to smile, and Lowell did, but the little grin betrayed the weight of the days since the crash. And Frank was sure that Lowell didn't like him anymore.

Frank grabbed the paper and wrote this: *Publicist? Lawyer?*

Lowell drew a circle around each word, and a line from the circle to a dependent note. For Publicist he wrote *Handle this in L.A.* Attached to Lawyer was this: *Berberian, probably.*

Lowell turned, and again Frank needed to say something. He wrote, *I think I should have stayed at the hospital.*

Don't be silly, his brother wrote. Then he took the pen and paper, and he too left the room.

Frank had a dream. In the dream he could hear things. The dream, the images, were unimportant, and even in the dream he could feel their insignificance; the dreaming part of his brain threw them up only for show. Trees, sky, faces, rain, a factory, dogs, scary monsters. And for each image, a different sound. The wind in the trees. A jet across the sky, distant, trailing a sound that summons regret for all the lost opportunities for something real to regret, for loves that were never there to be lost. The rain on a tin roof. A bottling plant, something like a factory he had visited on a school trip, glass bottles rattling down an assembly line. Three black dogs fighting with each other. He woke up from the scary monsters, shrimp-eared Africans begging on the sidewalks of London, and he heard himself shout.

He rubbed his head against the pillow and wanted to write a poem about the sound of skin on cotton—or was the pillowcase a blend of cotton and polyester? Well, that should be in the poem too. What a miracle he would make of the absolutely ordinary. Now that I'm a writer, he thought, I can exploit all of my perceptions. This is so liberating. A poem about the sound of the sheet against the ear, and not some fruity ode to cotton, no! Fuck the natural, I'll include the synthetic in the experience, I won't revile the polyester! I'll be a poet of sounds! And so my interest in music will not be wasted.

He got out of the bed and looked through his bag for the brown notebook. He reached into the place where he kept his pen, but it wasn't there. He searched the room, but there was nothing to write with. He could call Lowell, or his mother, but they were asleep. He would speak to them in the morning, to tell them he was fine. Of course, they think I'm already fine, that nothing is wrong with me. If they thought something was wrong with me, they would have left me in a hospital, or my mother would have stayed in the room with me, or Lowell would have. If they loved me, I would be in the hospital. But I'm not sick. So he was angry with them, even while he knew they were right.

A pen. To find one.

He got dressed and went into the hall, and to the elevator, and took it downstairs.

In the lobby he asked the clerk at the front desk for a pen. He thought she might have been a man whose sex had been changed. There was something about the size of her hands, a little too large for a woman, too wide, and there was an added pleasure she took in the humiliation of the job, a delight in how busy it kept her, that suggested to Frank that she might have once been a man whose fantasy was just this, to wear a woman's uniform, and serve. Or not, and she was just a woman with large hands, and Frank was a ridiculous man.

She gave him a cheap ballpoint imprinted with the hotel's name, the kind of pen that drags on paper, that forces the writer to use a strong hand, leaving a deep groove, a trace of the hand more definite than the faint color of the ink. He asked if the bar was still open, and it was. He wanted a beer. Then he thought that if he drank, he would forget his poem, and then he thought about all the poets who drank and for a moment considered something to loosen himself up, but he decided not to drink, that he had to follow his own muse, this proudly sober muse. After all, he had been sober when he wrote the letter to Anna, the letter, that first entry in his collected works.

Bettina Welch was in the far corner of the dining room, her back to the door. She was standing at a table, and the others with her, Piet Bernays and the two women who were always in the crisis center, were laughing. He had already forgotten their names. Frank saw that he could sneak close to their table without being recognized if he stayed on the other side of a divider between the dining room and the bar.

He felt silly crouching low to avoid being seen, but it worked. When he was about ten feet from them, he could hear them clearly. They were making fun of the families. Why am I here? he asked himself. I should be in my room, writing a poem about a pillow.

They were making fun of red-haired Brenda. "My baby, you killed my baby!"

And then Piet Bernays said, "Frank, let me take care of this." And then he did the next voice, "Whatever you say, Lowell, whatever you say!"

"Whatever you say, Lowell, whatever you say!" said Bettina, imitating the imitation.

"Who's this?" said one of the women, and she closed her mouth and made the sounds of someone without a tongue trying to speak through lips sewn together. "Nnnngggg. Mnnnnggg."

"Frank Gale this afternoon," said Piet. "Give me someone harder to do. Give me someone else."

"Give me anyone else," said Bettina.

"And his brother," said one of the women.

"At least you can talk to him," said Bernays.

"There's this guy on the phone, yesterday, and today," said one of the women, finding a new target. "It's like, 'I want to speak to the man in the charge, I want to speak to the man in the charge.' And I'm like, 'Sir, we understand how you must feel now, and we'll do everything we can to help you, in any way that we can.' "

"So what did you do?" asked Bernays.

"I gave him to Dockery."

"And Dockery pretended to be Donoghue?"

"Dockery tried to let him think that he was the man in charge, and the guy spilled out his whole story, and then he found out that Dockery didn't have the power to hear his story and do anything about it, that he'd have to get to Donoghue and tell the story all over again, so he said he'd sue Dockery for something or other."

Bettina said she'd heard that the survivors were split pretty evenly between Berberian and Dessick.

Bernays lit a cigarette and said, "This is a real mess. It's going to take a long time. If I were one of the survivors, I don't know who I'd go with. They're both good."

One of the women said she favored Berberian; the other said she trusted Dessick. Bettina said she was glad she didn't have to have an opinion. She asked Bernays whom he would go with if he had to make a choice.

He thought for a moment. "I don't know." He said this with deep awe for his confusion, and his ignorance gained such a degree of power that the choices the women at the table made seemed immediately stupid, that having made a choice, having seen a distinction, far from granting the choosers a degree of authority, made them look immeasurably dumb.

The table was quiet. Frank hoped that some backwash of guilt had swept over them, that the sewers of their emotions could not contain all of their cruelty. They sat in silence and sipped their drinks in reveries of a nostalgia stolen from a cultural idea of boozy meditation.

This is how the silence was broken: "Nnnngggg. Mnnnnggg." It was Bettina Welch this time, and her version of Frank's paralysis was better than the other woman's. They all laughed, each in turn, and made the sound, cracking each other up.

"What can you do?" she said. "You have to laugh."

Frank thought, Why won't they let me hate them? Why am I so weak that I can't hate them?

He crawled back along the wall, in the shadows of the room. He stood up and turned around, and when Piet Bernays saw him, Frank was sure that it looked as though he had just come into the room. He stood there, watching the table. No one said anything. Bettina and Bernays looked at each other, that secret exchange, but this time Frank would not let their knowledge of what he had done get in the way. He would confound them now.

"Hello," said Frank.

Of course they couldn't talk; he was the ghost, he was Christ risen.

"Yes, my voice. It came back to me. The doctor said I just needed some rest. He was right."

"Well, that's wonderful," said Bernays. "We were all thinking about you."

"Thinking what?" asked Frank.

"Hoping that you would get better, of course."

"Thinking or hoping?"

"Thinking hoping," said Bernays. He wouldn't be trapped, even with a few drinks inside him.

"May I join you?" asked Frank.

"Of course," said Bettina. Her training battled whatever she'd been drinking, but she betrayed impatience with him, and she knew it and tried to fight it, she tried to be nicer to him, which only made her that much more false.

"We were just . . ." said Bernays, unable to complete the sentence, lost, guilty, because he suspected that Frank had listened to all their impersonations.

"We were just having a drink," said Bettina. "But if you need anything, anything at all, I'm here for you." She was back on track.

"Do you want a drink?" asked one of the women. What were their names? It was making him desperate, that he had forgotten their names. Well, they had only been introduced once. Why weren't they wearing name tags? But Frank had to answer her, name or not.

Frank, very quietly, to sound ruminative and deferential, said, "Nnnngggg. Mnnnnggg." He hoped it was the kind of "no" that comes under the breath, full of exhaustion and shame.

"Are you sure?" asked one of the women.

No one acknowledged his parody of their parody. But if they had, what would have been the appropriate reaction? A sudden shower of blood from every pore? Or a ghastly release of crap in their pants? Frank imagined the four of them sitting there, and then, in shame and fear, discovering how little control they really have over their intestines clogged with rotten meat, their fetid colons.

"I think so," he said. "It's been a hard day."

"A drink might be good for you," said Bernays, and Frank was sure he wanted to slit his own throat for having given him the chance to accept, that his good breeding, his manners, had for a second overcome his cunning. Frank considered accepting the drink, just to sit at the table with them. If he did, he would say nothing, he would answer their questions as briefly as possible, or not answer at all, no, answer briefly, and let them try to talk to each other without including him in the conversation. If Bernays had any hope of fucking any one of them tonight, or all three, Frank's ghoulish silence at the table would have dampened the possibility of an orgasm for any of them.

"Don't you drink beer?" asked Bettina, surprising Frank with her memory. Yes, he'd had a beer in Los Angeles. So she'd been watching him. He fought against feeling a little respect for her.

"Why don't we see what's on tap?" said Bernays.

"Oh, that's okay," said Frank, which didn't really mean anything. It could go on like this forever he thought, I can stand here, and we can talk like this, about nothing, yet aware of everything, not just for another three minutes, but until time is finished, until everyone knows everything about everything. I can keep us alive for eternity if I stand here, all of us forever afloat on frustration. Death from boredom? Never.

This is how to torture them, thought Frank, and then he wanted to say to them, You see, after all, I can hate! I am capable of reflecting back all the hate that is beamed to me. I can stand here, ten feet away from you, so that you have to raise your voices just a little, which must irritate you, and I like that, I like to see the strain of forcing this geniality when the last thing you want to do is work, since being nice to me is what you've been paid to do. And yet you do not fully comprehend the source of this irritation. You think you are uncomfortable because the social traffic among people always hurts. You do not know that were I standing next to you, the power you have as a group would override my weak force, so I stand here, just this far away, and it gives me great pleasure. You may think that I am some pathetic loser of a brother, some kid brother to my younger brother, some kind of desperate loser—*loser at work, loser at airplane lottery*—but I am the king of these few seconds of your lives, the moment belongs to me, I am the master, I am in control.

He came close to saying to Bernays, God, I can't believe it, I thought you were gay. And what would Bernays say: Maybe I am, maybe I'm not, what's it to you? And Frank would say, Well, what are you doing with these women? And Bernays would say, Whatever they'll let me get away with. And Frank would say, So you're gay or you're not? And Bernays would say, Would you pursue this if your brother were here? And Frank would collapse with shame. Frank felt himself wavering, and he needed to regain his balance.

"Are you going back to Los Angeles tomorrow?" asked Bettina.

"I don't know," said Frank.

One of the women said there was going to be another memorial in Los Angeles, and the other woman said it would also be a funeral.

"A funeral," said Frank, knowing that if he said nothing else, the four of them would imagine that he was imagining the GRIM SCENE of all those caskets, some of them flag-draped, baking in the sun, dry-roasting the body parts inside.

"We'll be there," said Bettina. She played with her drink. The secret she carried, the truth about Frank Gale, was not, at this moment, the most important thing in her. She wanted to fuck Bernays, it was obvious, and she didn't want to be reminded of her duties. Frank nodded to the bartender, and made a circle with his finger, toward the table, meaning: another round. Everyone at the table protested.

"No," said Frank. "Please, you've all been so good to me." He reached into his wallet and took out a twenty-dollar bill. Would it be enough? He added another ten and walked to the table, knowing that if he stayed, he would lose the game he had invented.

"That's too much," said Bettina.

"We'll give you the change when we see you," said Bernays.

This was such a ridiculous self-imposed mission that for a quick moment Frank wanted to say, Fine, I'll see you at the funeral, just to put Bernays through the trouble of holding on to the change, of keeping it in a separate envelope, but he had a better idea. "Don't give it back to me," said Frank. "I don't need it. But if there's a charity, you know, for any of the children on the ground, or if the pilot had kids and someone sets up a trust fund for them, give them the money." And then the most diabolical sentence bubbled up, and he heard himself say, "Unless you want another round."

Frank thought the last suggestion was so hilarious, such an insult, that he had to turn quickly and run from the room. Let them think he wanted to cry, but when he got to the elevator, and the door closed, he leaned against the wall and shrieked with laughter, cackling like the madman he had become. But it isn't just insanity, he told himself. This is really very funny. What can they do now? They'll buy themselves another round, with the change that remains, and if there's not enough left over, they'll add to the money with a little extra from their own pockets, and they will, each of them, have to forgive themselves for stealing a few dollars from charity, while they'll promise themselves, each of them, privately, to give, what, five dollars to the next bum they pass in a doorway, or maybe stuff five dollars into one of those collection cans with the coin slot, next to the cash register and the red strips of licorice. And maybe a little extra to a collection plate the next time one is passed, if they ever go to church, but they'll also know that when they next see that plate, they won't put in any special supplement while thinking of Frank. Perfect, perfect, perfect.

Back in his room the message light flashed on his phone. He called the hotel operator, who told him that his brother had called, also someone from the National Transportation Safety Board, Guy Ingle. He left a number, but added that he would call in the morning. Frank supposed this was about the identification of the bodies, although the name was new, and wouldn't that call come from the coroner? There was nothing he could do now except to worry about it, and he would try not to. And his brother: Did Lowell think that he was asleep, or still deaf? What had he wanted? Don't call him now, thought Frank. Write that poem about the pillow.

He picked up the notebook, to write the truth, and with the bad pen scraped into the page, *I woke up and I was happy to hear the pillow.* This was true, but he hated the way it looked on the page. He crossed it out and held the pen over the paper for a long time, and then closed the book. He opened it again and wrote, *I do not have to do this.* He liked that sentence more than the first one, and thought it might be a good first line for something, but he had nothing that wanted to follow.

He turned the television on, to the news channel, and a picture of Lonnie Walter. This is the man who murdered my family, thought Frank. A letter had been discovered in the wreckage of the plane, the reporter said. Walter had written a message on an air-sickness bag to the boss who had fired him. It said, simply, "Hi Nick. I think it's sort of ironical that we end up like this. I asked for some leniency, remember? Well, I got none, and you'll get none."

Frank turned the television off, and reconstructed the story. Walter must have passed the note to the boss just as he was getting his gun out. He shot the boss, shot a flight attendant, and then went to the cockpit and shot the pilots, and shot out the controls. How long had it taken from the time he pulled the gun out of, what, a briefcase? . . . until the plane started to go down. Had he shot himself, or did he stand in the cockpit, over the bodies of the crew, to watch the ground come up? It was daylight. He had time to think about things. He would have heard the passengers screaming. And how did he feel as the plane went down? Had a bullet exploded the windows of the cockpit? He would have been sucked out of the plane and killed in the air. But if the windows had held, and the pilots were dead, and the flight attendants were crying, and the passengers were wailing, might Lonnie Walter, for an instant, in his exhaustion, regret what he had done? Might he have turned to the passengers and said he was sorry? The last time Frank had fucked Mary Sifka, how much had he hated her after he had come?

Frank had an idea. The day's papers were on an end table. He looked for the article about Lonnie Walter.

Lonnie Walter was a forty-five-year-old native of Los Angeles. His parents had come to the city from Louisiana. His father, a plumber, died when Lonnie was fifteen. Lonnie had joined the marines and had served in Vietnam. He was divorced, with a son and a daughter who lived with their mother in Phoenix. He had two sisters. His older sister (forty-seven), Teresa, lived in Los Angeles. His younger sister (thirty-one), Lovie, lived in Seattle. Frank thought of black children on a hike in the Cascade Mountains, their freedom, black faces, red parkas, green trees. And their uncle, who had destroyed an airplane, a Boeing, made in Seattle.

After leaving the marines, Lonnie Walter's first job was with the airline, and he'd stayed with them until he was fired two weeks ago.

Frank picked up the phone and called Information in Los Angeles, and asked for Lonnie Walter's phone number. It was listed! There he was! He could call and see if anyone was there.

He dialed. Someone answered! A woman!

"Hello," said Frank.

"Yes?" asked the woman.

"Is Lonnie there?" asked Frank.

"Who is this?"

"It's Larry Levy," said Frank, taking the name of one of the dead from the list in the paper.

"Do you know what time it is?"

"I'm calling from New York, it's six in the morning here. Lonnie and I used to talk at this time, all the time."

"And you're in New York, and you haven't read the news."

"No, ma'am," said Frank. "And you must be . . ." Frank wanted her to complete the sentence.

"If you know Lonnie so well, you should know who I am."

"You must be his sister, Terry."

"Yes. Terry." Could she imagine that out in the world someone so diabolical would take her name from the *Los Angeles Times* and use it so coldly?

"Where's Lonnie?"

"Lonnie's dead."

"What?" asked Frank, sounding bewildered. "No."

"You don't know?" she asked.

Frank pretended to not understand that she was asking him if he knew about everything, and limited himself to acting as though she just meant that his not knowing about the death surprised her not because the whole world knew, but because no one had called him yet to tell him of the passing of a friend in such an awful way. He could let her think that he thought the death was ordinary, something at work, or a car crash. "Oh, my God," said Frank. "I can't believe it. That's awful, what happened?"

"I can't talk about it," she said, and she hung up the phone. Frank waited a second and called her back.

"It's me again, it's Larry."

"I can't talk now."

"Wait!" he shouted. There was all the command he had ever had in his life in that one shout. No one could have refused him. Finally he was stronger than his brother. "I have a terrible feeling about this right now. After he was fired, he was really upset."

"Yes," said his sister.

"Oh, my dear sweet Lord," said Frank. "He used to joke about it, but did he kill himself?"

"Yes," said the sister. She was crying again.

"Oh God, oh God, oh God," said Frank. He was smiling now. Fuck the writing, thought Frank, I should be an actor!

"I don't know who to talk to," said Walter's sister. The part of her accent that was black, or the South, also had a brittle quality, and if she weren't tired, and her brother hadn't done what he had done, and she were just talking to Frank under whatever circumstances were normal in her life, she would have sounded arrogant.

"You can talk to me. I spoke to him last week. I was away on vacation until last night. We'd talked about him coming with me. I went to Jamaica."

"He said something about that," said the sister. "About a vacation with a friend."

"That was me," said Frank. And if it was someone else, let them call her. He was sure no one else in the entire world had his wacko courage.

"So you haven't read the papers, or seen the news."

"The news is not my strong suit," said Frank. "I used to have Lonnie tell me who to vote for, even in New York elections, you know, the mayor and stuff. He was always up on that." This was such a specific lie that if she had never seen her brother read the paper, now she would add this to the collection of THINGS SHE NEVER KNEW ABOUT HIM, that he had a friend in New York, that they talked politics, that Lonnie had someone in the world who looked up to him, a white man, a Jew.

"Did you hear about the plane crash?"

"The one in Argentina?" He didn't know if there really had been a crash in Argentina, but it seemed like the thing to say, to keep the flow of credibility going. And don't the planes in Argentina always crash?

"The one in San Diego."

"What are you saying?" asked Frank.

"They say Lonnie shot up the plane."

"With the Colt?"

"You knew about the gun?"

"Goddamn it. I told him not to get that gun."

"He got it."

"My God."

"The plane was full. A 737."

"A 737, standard configuration, eight rows first class, thirty-two in coach?" He made a crazy face, this was the most fun he had ever had in his life.

"A 737, a lot of people. And it went into a crowded neighborhood."

"Oh my God. And they think Lonnie shot down a plane from the ground, with his gun?"

"They say he got on the plane and shot the pilot."

"No! Lonnie? No! But you don't believe that. I don't believe that. Lonnie? No! Not Lonnie."

He let her stop his rant. "That's what they say."

"No."

"Mr. Levy, I think it's true."

"But you can't get a gun past security. The girls who run those machines may not look it, but they're awfully sharp. And call me Larry."

"They say he did. They say he used his old pass to get into the airport, where they didn't have a metal detector."

"And you believe this."

"I'm afraid it's impossible not to. How long did you know him?"

"I've known him," said Frank, not wanting to speak of Lonnie in the past tense, "for about five years. I lived in L.A. for a while. I worked with him."

"How well did you know him?"

"Well, he did have his demons," Frank said, shaking his head and remembering, as did his sister, the man described in the papers, a man who could drink all night, a man who started fights for no reason, a man whose wife left him because of his pathological jealousy.

"That's no comfort to the families of all the dead."

"Terry, I can't know how you feel, but I'm not talking to the families of the dead. I'm talking to you. And you need to remember the man we both knew as someone who was troubled, but also capable of love. You need to remember the love he had for you. I know I will. And you didn't pull the trigger, he wasn't you, he was your brother. Someone has to remember him, you know, as he was, most of the time, when he wasn't, you know . . . I mean, he never killed anyone before."

"It's a terrible burden."

"He was a good friend, that's what I want to say."

"No one else has called."

"Bastards."

"You can't blame them," said Terry.

"But he was a friend. I haven't read anything, so I don't know. And maybe he did this just as they say he did, maybe it was even worse, but he was a friend. And whatever happened to him, whatever happened to his mind, he was in a lot of pain. Maybe we could have given him more help, more love, maybe he wouldn't have done this. So he was lonely. He needed me and damn it, I failed him. I don't know about his other friends, but I know about me, and I can blame myself."

"No," said Walter's sister.

"Yes. I knew how upset he was. He told me about the gun. He had fantasies. I heard him, but I didn't listen. I didn't listen with my third eye." What? thought Frank. Hear with my eye? Is his sister listening to me? He went on, "I just don't know if I ever told him. Told him that I really liked him. Damn it."

She started to cry again. The sobs built to something too painful for Frank to hear, and he was ashamed of his joke.

"Maybe you could call another time. I need someone to talk to. I need a friend."

"Good-bye," he said. He didn't know if she could hear him, but he hung up.

What wrong did I do? he asked himself. I gave her comfort just now. Has anyone else been nice to her in the last week? Maybe she can sleep now. Maybe I can finally sleep.

He turned off the light. It was quiet in the hotel room. It wouldn't have been quiet like this in Mexico. If there really is a heaven, he thought, and if my wife and daughter are angels now, and belong to God, can they see me? Did they watch me call Terry Walter? Are they watching her now? Do they forgive me?

It was three in the morning, and he wanted to let his family know that his voice was back. He called his mother's room. The phone rang five times, and then she answered, with sleep in her voice.

"Hi," said Frank.

"Lowell?" she asked.

"No, Frank."

"Frank," she said. He thought she was trying to remember if she knew any Franks. "Frank," she said again, after a frightening pause, and then again, "Frank," and this time her voice indicated the surprise he expected.

"Yep, it's back," he said, pleased with the creepiness of his "Yep," which was too full of excitement, as though his voice were a puppy returned from a day's exploration. If his family was turning on him, he would make them pay for it, with an unpleasant friendliness that would make them worry that this ugly, forward part of his character was something so deeply a part of his structure that he was revealing to them something they all shared, something fundamental in the Gale genetic design; the thing that marked them, and now was revealed by their son, would be the thing they would all, against their will, express to the world, this oily, insistent blindness to the privacy of others, to their hatred of the Gales and their Gale-ness. He was sure that his mother was scared that in the morning she would call Bettina Welch and ask her what she really thought of her.

"Well, I just wanted to say that I was okay."

"The doctor said you were."

"Yes, but doctors are wrong sometimes. I mean, I could have really been deaf."

"But they said there was no physical reason for that, nothing caused it."

"But maybe it could have been something unrelated to everything that's happened this week. Maybe it could have been some kind of virus, or microbe, that had been growing for a long time, and had cut the optic nerve."

"That's to the eyes."

"Maybe that could have been next. To the ear canal, you know. Something inside the ear. It could have been that."

"But it wasn't. Because you're fine now."

"For now, yes. But how much longer? Maybe it'll come back."

"The doctor was certain."

"Are you taking his side or mine?"

"Frank, he's a doctor, he ran the tests."

"Oh, and was he the world's expert on S-H-L-S?"

"What?"

"Sudden hearing-loss syndrome? S-H-L-S?" He spelled it out for her again.

"S-H-L-S? Is that something real?"

"I don't know," said Frank, "but maybe I have it."

"I don't think so."

"Just admit that it's possible."

"Of course it's possible," she said.

"Good night, Mom," said Frank, as though nothing had happened, not the hearing loss, not the plane crash, not his marriage, not this ridiculous phone call, nothing.

He hung up the phone and turned off the light. He studied the darkness, the pulses of light inside of it, and he thought that it was getting dark; he was sure it was getting darker.

He turned on the light to make sure he still had his vision. Everything was there, in color. He let his eyes take in the details of the room, and for the second time in a week, since looking at the blue plate in his parents' condominium, he felt the pure gift of sight. Everything had the aura of the greatest luxury. The brown imitation-wood-grain veneer on the television cabinet had never been so rich, and not only that, but the right angle around the doorjamb had a precision that made his teeth ache, it was so beautiful, so appropriate, and it was white! He studied the far corner of the bed, with the rotten avocado-green blanket hovering above a canyon of shadows at the bottom of which lay the carpet, its brown nubs alive with vibrations that were as pure as any in the universe. Nothing is ugly if you really get to know it, thought Frank. He needed to call Lowell and tell him this thing he had finally learned. That might be the title for the poem about the pillow: "Nothing Is Ugly If You Really Get to Know It."

He picked up the phone, and after four rings the machine answered. He heard the message, but after the tone he hung up. Would he really tell his brother something he no longer believed?

11. Headlines

In the morning Frank found two letters on the carpet next to the door. One was from Berberian, the other was from Dessick. Each letter urged Frank to make a decision. The letters were personally addressed to him, and at first he assumed that they had been composed on a computer, merging his name from a list of addressees. The text of each letter was directed at no one but Frank. Both identified him as the only holdout among all of the relatives of those who'd died in the crash, and while those who had survived the destruction on Cohassett Street had not yet signed up, most had, and anyway, as both letters averred, the lawsuit for those who lived on the ground would be filed separately, in a different jurisdiction, and would be more complicated. Berberian said, and Dessick echoed this, that associated attorneys in San Diego would handle the Cohassett Street suits.

Berberian's letter, in its first paragraph, urged Frank to sign.

> *We do not need to remind you of the im-*
> *portance of a fully pressed lawsuit. Worse*
> *than a lawsuit split between two firms is a*
> *lawsuit not fully pressed by all of those*
> *eligible to sue.*

Dessick said:

> *Of course I want you to join our lawsuit,*
> *but I understand that each of us has to*
> *make a choice. Not making a choice, in*
> *this case, would be a terrible mistake, one*
> *that would reflect badly, I think, on*
> *everyone else who has already decided*
> *which of the two teams to join. It is sim-*
> *ply unfair to the rest of us, for you to*
> *hold out like this.*

Frank heard himself talking to the room: "But I need more information." No, he thought, not quite sure of the idea, I need less. Berberian added a postscript to his letter.

> *I have to inform you, Mr. Gale, that your*
> *reluctance to press the suit against those*
> *individuals or institutions responsible for*
> *the deaths of so many people may put you*
> *in the position of impeding an effort to*

*which everyone else has committed. If you
are used by the airline or its representatives as a figure of compromise, if you
make a separate settlement with the airline that forces all of those grief-stricken
survivors into settling the case themselves
prematurely, then in our considered opinion this could be cause for action and we
might be forced to find a remedy for our
complaint against you. While it may have
been sentimentally appropriate for the airline's president to read, at a memorial
service, that letter from the husband to
his wife, I warn you not to succumb to
those impulses to forgive and reconcile
which everyone else connected to this inci-
dent, all of those who have so far joined
one of the lawsuits, have admirably and
with great difficulty, resisted.*

Dessick's letter, in its second paragraph, had a similar thought:

*We have heard and read a lot in the last
two days about forgiveness. Now this is
certainly a genuinely admirable goal for
all of us, and perhaps someday, when
this is all over, we will, each of us, according to our consciences, which must
always be private, forgive. But, Mr. Gale,
don't be swayed by appeals to mercy until
we know who it is we ought to forgive. In
other words, we need to know just who is*

guilty before we can forgive them, and the guilty will still have to accept their expensive punishment, not because we want to get rich, but because if we can scare the airline industry into cleaning up its shamefully lax practices, then the next time this happens, it won't happen. Your current refusal to participate in this process will be held against you by the future. Do not give us cause for action.

Frank held the letters next to each other. A pleasant smell came from them, and he sniffed Berberian's. The letter smelled nicely of horses, blended with pine, or incense, or smoke, something of a forest above a desert. The smell was exciting, comforting, American, a pungent cowboy smell, the wide and wild West. He brought Dessick's letter to his nose. There it was, that same remarkable spice! Someday I will have to ask these lawyers if any of their workers stuff envelopes next to a fire made from the logs of piñon trees. The smell was too strong on both letters to have transferred osmotically from one to the other while he had been holding them. No, he was sure, each letter's smell was independent. And the same! And these were delivered by hand, presumably by two different hands. Again he missed his wife, who might have shown the two letters to their daughter and asked her to smell them.

If I had not written the letter, thought Frank, but I had still missed the airplane, what would have happened? I would have called Anna at the airport, she would have wished me a good flight, she would have let me talk to Madeleine, and then she would have died. Then I would have probably done everything as I did, except I wouldn't have crapped in my pants, and I wouldn't have collapsed at the memorial service, and there would have been no letter to publish. Or was I going crazy from the beginning because the ex-

istence of the thing weighed on me, because I felt the pressure of
the letter, even before its discovery in print? No . . . as soon as
Anna discovered the letter, I was in trouble. And if I had never
written the letter at all, and they had not died, what would Mexico
have been like?

We're in Mexico. I get to the room, she's happy to see me. Well,
if not thrilled to see me, because there has been a strain in the
marriage lately, at least she's trying to be polite, because she wants
a pleasant vacation, but she has not accused me of bad behavior.
She believes that I was late to the airport because business held me
back, because I was working. She suspects something, but, for the
good of the marriage, and for her daughter, asleep in the next room,
she waits for me to confess, and she knows I will, because she
knows I love her, or want to love her. She understands the reason
for the trip.

And then on the beach the next day, while I'm walking with
Madeleine. No . . . there is no walk with Madeleine designed to
give Anna the time to read the letter and decide if the marriage will
continue or stop. No . . . I give her the time just to be by herself,
so she can read, or shop. I tell her to go to town and buy something
for a lot of money. She tells me nothing in Mexico is worth a lot of
money. I tell her to buy a silver necklace, and she does, and she
spends two hundred dollars. The necklace, a yoke of sterling, has
an Aztec motif, a spiral made of right angles with a turquoise chip
in the center. It is something she would never wear at home, and
she tells me not to think of the necklace as something she'll never
wear again, something she'll come to regret, something that will
embarrass her when she sees it in her jewelry box. No, she says,
think of it as something I bought only to wear here, as a kind of
costume. She tells me we would not begrudge each other a dinner
that cost two hundred dollars if we had a bottle of expensive wine
or champagne, and that the necklace, by virtue of the way it screams
RICH TOURIST IN A RESORT, celebrates our vacation, that it is
true costume jewelry, because in the costume she can just be the
woman who came to Acapulco to be different from the woman she

is at home. In the necklace she is no longer Anna Klauber from Los Angeles, but someone from another city, someone who would actually wear the necklace at home.

And I will find this powerfully seductive, my wife's tactics, because the new character arrives with the promise of a sexual challenge to me. She is telling me to be scared of the necklace. I will learn from this woman how to make love to my wife. She will teach me that the best technique is surrender, that I should let my weakness provoke her strength. Somehow it will all work out, the necklace says, there is no need to confess, if you let me punish you, and if you accept your punishment, you will see, so clearly, that after all, I truly really love you.

But I wrote that letter, thought Frank. And she read it. And she died. My wife is dead. My daughter is dead.

What if she had never read the letter, but it had still been discovered in the wreckage? Did I go to Cohassett Street looking for the letter? Would I have gone there if Anna had not found the letter? Yes, no, yes, no. I can't say. I would have forgotten it, probably. But then if it had been discovered? That is, if the letter had been discovered, though Anna had never read it. I would not have been quite so crazy, my grief would not have this current of panic running through it. I would have chosen a lawyer by now. I would have just been one of them, one of the indignant survivors.

And if I had not written the letter and I had not missed the plane, and the plane had not crashed?

Everything has happened as it has happened, thought Frank, and there is nothing to be done except to continue as I have, out of control, shredded by fear.

He called his parents' room.

Lowell answered the phone.

"We were going to call you," said Lowell. "It's time to go."

"I can talk," said Frank.

"Mom told me."

"It's all better now."

"We figured it would be okay."

"Now what?"

"We go back to Los Angeles today."

"What about identifying the bodies?"

"Why don't you let the coroners do that?"

"I want to know."

"Frank, please, not now, I don't have time for this now."

"Time for what?"

"Time for you to be crazy all the time."

"But I need to know."

"And we need to have some peace. You're not the only one in this family who was related to Anna and Madeleine."

"I'm the only one who seems to be upset about it at all. I'm the only one really grieving."

"You can't say that."

"I just did."

"Frank, what do you want me to do?"

"I want you to call the coroner and find out if we can identify the bodies. I want to get it over with. This really means a lot to me."

"Let's have breakfast," said Lowell.

"I can order room service," said Frank. "We can meet in my room."

"Downstairs in the coffee shop in twenty minutes," said Lowell. "I have to help them pack."

Frank showered quickly, and as he dressed, he turned on the television. The crash was still in the news, because another thirty bodies had been found. Police dogs searching through the wasted zone had found them in burned cars and flattened houses. The work crews now wore gas masks to protect themselves from the smell of death. A few neighborhood dogs and cats that had wandered into the zone had been shot by police, and their owners had filed complaints. The mayor, who Frank, with an annoying shiver of unnecessary excitement, recognized from the memorial, defended the police, saying they were protecting the bodies of the dead, and protecting the city from the spread of disease by contaminated animals. The owner of one of the dead cats was interviewed. He said that cats were free animals, that it was hard to keep them inside if they wanted to go out.

He heard something drop outside his door. He opened it. The San Diego paper was on the carpet. Frank opened it. The headline was simple: HER NAME IS MARY SIFKA.

Someone had given Mary's name to the local television station that had first revealed the letter. Once the station broadcast her name, the night before, the paper felt that it no longer needed to keep the name hidden. No one had answered at Mary Sifka's phone number in Los Angeles. She was missing from work. The identities of the letter writer and his wife were a secret.

At the same time, on television, Frank heard the newswoman say, "Mary Sifka." And a shot of her house, which Frank had once driven past, just to see it, a blandly modern wall in the Hollywood Hills.

He called Mary Sifka. The line was busy. He called the front desk, to see if she had called him, but there were no messages from her. Another five reporters had called, also Julia Abarbanel, to say she was in Los Angeles, and Frank's secretary had called. Karen would know everything, wouldn't she? She knew who Mary Sifka was, and wouldn't she make the connection between Mary and the plane crash, and the letter?

He called her at the office.

"I've been thinking about you," said Karen. Had she been talking to someone from the airline, or was that the appropriate thing to say?

"We're coming back up today. I just have to identify the bodies." He said those last words quickly.

"Have you seen the paper today?" she asked, without acknowledging the grotesque formality he had just described to her.

"What?"

"Mary Sifka, that's who the letter is about."

"Really." So Karen didn't think it was Frank. Because she accepted what the papers all said, that the writer of the letter was dead.

"That's what they say."

"Poor Mary."

"She's married. So her husband knows all about it now."

"He must feel awful."

"I hope he doesn't have any guns around the house."

"Maybe he already knew about it."

"It doesn't matter, that marriage is finished."

"Do they know who wrote the letter yet?"

"That'll come out. What's really sick is that the guy who wrote the letter gets made into a saint, and poor Mary Sifka gets the shaft for all of this. This is so sexist."

They'll know my name by the evening news, thought Frank. My life is finished.

"What did you need?" asked Karen.

"Nothing," said Frank.

"You were just checking in?"

"Something like that," said Frank. There was a knock on the door. He excused himself to Karen. "Someone's at the door. I have to go."

"Check in any time, Frank. You need the continuity with your work, I understand that. It helps you get over the pain."

"That's right," said Frank. "What are you telling people who call?"

"I'm telling them that you'll be out for at least a month. Is that okay?"

"That's fine. Thank you." The conversation was over. He opened the door. It was his family, with their bags.

"Lowell called," said his father. "The Coroner's Office says they think they have the bodies ready for identification."

"What does that mean?"

"It means they have bodies which they think are Anna and the baby. And they're ready for you to come down. Are you ready?"

"Yes," said Frank. He took a few dollars out of his wallet and tucked them beneath an ashtray, for the maid.

In the coffee shop, after they ordered breakfast, Frank's mother asked if he really needed to go to the mortuary.

"Yes," he said. "It's important."

"Why not let the doctors make the identification? It isn't natural for you to see."

"I need the closure," said Frank.

"Closure," said his mother, with disdain for the grief counselors. "I can't think about you seeing them like that."

"You don't have to."

"I'm not in control of the things that trouble me, not all the time."

Lowell said, "That's quite a confession, Mom."

They were quiet, until their father said, "Mary Sifka. That's an amazing story. I can't believe they released her name."

Lowell turned a suspicious face to Frank. He looked ready to punish him. "Yesterday, when you were talking about lunch with Mark Sifka, the name rang a small bell, because Sifka is sort of a familiar name. Mary Sifka works for Jack Ney, doesn't she?"

"If it's the same one," said Frank.

"You think there's two Mary Sifkas in Los Angeles?" said Lowell, cutting Frank with his scorn.

"Maybe one of them lives in the Valley," said Frank.

"So you had lunch with an insurance agent named Mark Sifka, and then there's a Mary Sifka who also works in insurance, who you know."

"It's a strange world," said their father, and Frank wanted to kiss him for distracting Lowell from the truth. "Touched by tragedy and coincidence. What would the Talmudists say about that?"

"I don't know," said Frank.

"What's Mary Sifka like?" asked Leon.

"I only know one of them," said Frank. "And I don't really know her."

"The one you do know," said Leon.

"She's nice," said Frank.

"Nice," said their mother. "What does that mean?"

"It means," said Lowell, "that she may have been having an affair with a married man, but that doesn't mean she couldn't also be nice. She's not a vampire. And it was over, remember. The affair was over."

"How do you know that?" asked their mother.

"It says so in the letter."

"So that's what he was telling his wife. Maybe he knew that someone was about to tell her about it, or else he suspected that she knew, so he was making a preemptive strike against her accusing him."

So this is where my mind comes from, thought Frank. From my mother, from the way her brain works and thinks about things.

"I think he was being sincere," said his father.

"Why is that?" asked Frank.

"It's just a feeling. He wouldn't have named her if it was still going on."

"Good point!" shouted Lowell, in triumph. "He's right, isn't he, Mom?" Lowell was glad to see his father outwit his mother.

"Probably," she said.

"Probably," his father said, repeating the word to show his frustration with her, for refusing to accept that he was right, that he had to be right.

"He's right, Mom," said Frank.

"It's not important," she said. "Let's not talk about it anymore. The whole thing is very depressing."

Frank wanted to ask her to divide the depression pie into sections, the size of each piece corresponding to the percentage she would assign to the different causes of the depression, so many degrees of depression for the general misery generated by the loss of daughter-in-law and granddaughter, so many degrees of depression generated by the son's remarkably bizarre grief, so many degrees of depression generated by the continuous humiliation of living in a condominium instead of a mansion. He imagined the graphic rendering of this pie, each section shaded to give the impression of three dimensions. The *Los Angeles Times* could print this pie chart every day, allowing the world to record the changes in the marketplace of his mother's emotions. Would there be a small wedge under the heading of "Miscellaneous Annoyances," to cover such daily sources of pain as the publication of a mistress's name? And would there be a futures market in which speculators could bet on the likelihood of certain minute problems becoming major issues deserving of their own pieces? The letter today means nothing more than the usual events of the unmerciful world (arson, rape, death squads, political scandals, serial murders, child molestations, the embezzlement of pension funds), but tomorrow, or even later today, when Frank's name has been broadcast into the ether, the letter's slice might swing past 180 degrees, might go as high as three quarters of the whole pie, could even become, for a day, the entire pie, in which any other causes for unhappiness will have been so occluded as to be left statistically insignificant, or converted to crust, for statistical accuracy.

And what of his mother's rage when she recognizes the extent of the shock to her life from the letter? Nothing would ever be the same for her. Nothing would ever be the same for the family. Would anyone blame her if she killed herself? Would anyone be surprised if the whole event ended when the Gales laced their pudding with poison and died together, dying of shame?

As they left the coffee shop, they were approached by two men, one black, one white.

"Mr. Gale?" said the black man.

"Yes, Frank."

"Dave Armitage, and Bill Brewer, NTSB." He showed a badge. "May we talk to you privately?"

Frank looked to Lowell for help.

"You better go with them," said Lowell.

"I'd like my brother with me," said Frank.

"That's okay," said Lowell, "you can go without me."

"But what if I need you?" asked Frank.

"The days of rubber hoses are over," said Brewer. "We're not going to hurt you."

"So if those days were still here, you'd be working me over?" asked Frank. "Lowell, we really do need a public-relations person now."

"Too late for that," said Lowell.

"The hotel's manager has given us his office," said Brewer. "We can go there."

Lowell told Frank he would get the car, and Frank could meet him outside when the interview was finished.

They led him to a room behind the front desk.

"So how can I help you?" asked Frank.

"Why did you visit the crash site?" asked Armitage.

"I wanted to see it."

"You're the only one who went," said Brewer.

"There were a lot of people there," said Frank.

"None of the survivors went. You were the only one of the survivors who went."

"I can't speak for anyone else."

"You haven't joined the lawsuit either. That's a form of speaking for someone, isn't it? It's a form of criticism, isn't it?"

"Is my lawsuit your business?" asked Frank.

"What were you looking for when you were arrested?"

"Nothing," said Frank.

"But you found something."

"Yes, I found my wife's suitcase."

"You had no business looking for it."

"I wasn't really thinking about what was right or wrong at the time."

"When did that start?"

"What?"

"Not thinking about what was right or wrong."

"I don't know how to answer that question."

"Try."

"Can I have a lawyer?" asked Frank.

"Berberian or Dessick?" said Brewer. It might have been a joke, but he wasn't smiling.

"You were looking for the letter, weren't you, Frank?" asked Armitage.

"What letter?"

"Do you want to take that back? Do you want us to pretend that you don't know what we're talking about?"

Brewer answered a knock on the door. He opened it only a crack, but Frank could see into the hall, where a few photographers were there, with reporters. Armitage said, "Soon," and closed the door.

Frank said no.

Armitage asked again, "Were you looking for the letter, Frank?"

"No," he said. Then he added, with an attitude of what he hoped was reckless defiance, "I don't think so."

"But you knew it was in the suitcase."

"I packed it in my own."

"That's not where we found it."

"She must have moved it."

"Anything is possible," said Armitage.

Everyone was quiet for about a minute.

"What are you really trying to get me to say?" asked Frank.

"Are you going back to Los Angeles today?" asked Brewer.

Frank said he was.

"See you there," said Armitage, and then everyone left the room.

Frank left the office. There were photographers in the lobby, taking his picture.

Someone asked if he had spoken yet to Mary Sifka. Someone else asked, "Where is she?"

A reporter called out, "Did your wife read the letter?"

Lowell's Explorer was at the curb. Frank ran to it as his father held the door open for him. Copper-haired Brenda and sad Geoffrey were putting their bags into a taxi, and Brenda cursed him as he ran past. "I hope you haven't fucked this up for all of us!"

Frank pulled his door shut, and as Lowell drove away, with the press taking pictures of them, Frank looked back at the hotel, trying to fix it so he would remember the place forever. Was there such a thing as the mind's eye, he wondered, something the vaguely mystical often talked about, the thing inside that is the true eternal self that controls destiny, that turns wishes into reality? Of course, the hotel was like eight hundred others just like it around the country, but he could fix the shapes of the clouds behind it, the usual zoo shapes, of course, a few big puffs, a few small ones, animals, a castle, and a profile of Sherlock Holmes. He closed his eyes and saw the tan building, the two wings visible from this side with their slight angle embracing the thin strip of garden between the parking lot and the hotel. The cobbled pavement of the driveway underneath the archway to the lobby. The photographers and reporters hurrying away, on to deliver their videotapes or process their film. Frank wanted to remember them, and also the palm trees in the circular islands at the end of each row in the parking lot, and the twenty-passenger hotel bus that ferried businessmen to and from the airport, with the hotel's name on both sides and the back. It was a stupid place, but Frank had felt deep emotions here, and so it was important to him. He opened and closed his eyes three times, taking in more space around the hotel, until the camera in his brain told him that the subject of the shot was too far away and would not register clearly on the emulsion of his memory. I will not forget this moment, thought Frank, I do not want to forget it.

"There was never anyone named Mark Sifka, was there?" asked Lowell.

"No," said Frank.

"You have made fools of us," said his mother.

Frank didn't say anything. He shut his eyes. He tried to re-member what Anna and Madeleine looked like. He could picture their faces, but without emotions, like passport photographs. He tried to conjure an image of them smiling at him, but their smiles looked forced. Well, they are forced, he thought. I'm forcing them.

They drove through the gates of the naval yards, and then to the cold warehouse. Lowell turned to Frank and stared at him. The look meant: Do you really want to go through with this? Frank replied by opening the car door and stepping out, wordlessly.

"Okay," said Lowell, matching him in this fabrication of man-liness. As they walked away from the car, Lowell said, "I can't believe what you've done to the family. I can't imagine a way to make all of this better. In the old days if they didn't kill you for bringing on shame, you would have been banished from the kingdom."

They gave their names at the door. A medical corpsman from the National Guard took them into the main room.

Everything inside was different. A cadre of robots was lined up by the wall, like golf carts in winter. The buckets of flesh were gone, and all that remained were a few hundred stainless-steel caskets, some of them draped with American flags, lined up in five rows. There were other corpsmen leading the bereft through the rows. A casket in the middle of the room was opened for a woman Frank did not recognize: She was fat, in her thirties, and she must have lived on Cohassett Street. She looked inside and nodded her head, and the casket was closed.

Frank and Lowell were led to two caskets in the second row. "They're all the same size," said Frank.

"Yes," said the corpsman. "It's the only size we have. You know, the military."

"Not much call for child size in the navy," said Frank.

"No sir," said the corpsman.

Frank stood by the first casket and put his hands behind his back, imitating something he thought was appropriately stoic, something that suited the room, the occasion, the rigid dignity of the silent robots.

"Sir," said the corpsman, "your wife and daughter were in a plane that crashed. You know there were no survivors. We have done the best we could to maintain the physical integrity of the dead, as we found them, and to deliver the dead to these caskets with as much respect for their integrity as possible."

"Yes," said Frank.

"He's trying to tell you that it's an ugly sight," said Lowell, with contempt.

"Thank you, sir," said the corpsman.

"I need to know."

"Sir, the bodies were hurt."

"I know that."

"There was fire."

"I know that."

"They were thrown against the ground from a great height."

"I'd like to see."

"They were identifiable only through tissue typing and medical and dental records."

"And you've done a remarkable job."

"Try to remember them as they were, sir."

"I do that."

"This is your wife, sir," said the corpsman, as he opened the first casket. Lowell grabbed Frank's arm. A barrel of meat, with an arm and hand attached, lay on the bed of black plastic lining.

"What happened to her head?" asked Frank.

"We have allocated to the proper casket, sir, every part that could be identified. Obviously with her fingerprints we were able to identify her. There were so many loose body parts, sir, you understand."

"Yes," said Frank, who understood the enormous difficulty of putting every last scrap of a person into one box.

"But the hand, sir, the fingerprints match."

"Close it," said Lowell. "This is ridiculous. This is sick. This is more of your sickness, Frank."

"Sir?" asked the corpsman, looking to Frank for the final word.

"So what happened to her?" asked Frank.

"By the looks of it she was cut by debris."

"In the air or on the ground?"

"When the plane hit, it rolled a few times. That's when it blew up. She could have been thrown out of the cabin and into the air, and then been cut down by whatever it was that hit her, before she came to rest. Or she could have been bounced on the ground a few times. She could have hit a chimney, or gone through a window."

"But you don't know for sure," said Frank, not meaning to accuse, only to satisfy an assumption.

"We'll know soon. They can make a pretty close guess. They start with a computer model of the plane at impact, knowing where everyone was, and then a computer model of the plane and the bodies when all movement had stopped. When people sitting next to each other are scattered, we get a sense of the forces within the crash, the different directions of those forces."

"My daughter was sitting next to my wife. Is it the same with her? Is she this badly cut up?"

"I don't know, sir. I haven't seen everybody."

Lowell grabbed Frank's hand and held it in both of his. "If you ask to have that casket opened up, Frank, I can't be responsible for what happens to you. It would be like trying to stop history."

"No one is forcing you to look," said Frank.

"I don't even want to know about it."

"I do."

"No, I don't even want to know about you knowing about it. Once I know what you have in your mind, then I have it in my mind, and I don't want it there."

"I can handle it," said Frank.

"You're thinking only of yourself," said Lowell. "And if that's how you want it . . ."

"What?" asked Frank.

"Nothing," said Lowell.

Frank turned to the corpsman and told him to open the other casket. "I want to see my daughter."

When the casket was opened, Lowell hit Frank on the shoulder, hard. "That's the end, Frank. That's the end of you. You're fired."

Her face was gone, from the jaw to the top of her head. A brain pan, scraped clean, with her dark hair still fixed to the neck. Her left arm below the elbow was missing, and her right hand was smashed flat, and her knees were almost gone. A little mole on her shoulder. That's her.

The corpsman studied her. "She must have been found in her seat. Some seats blew out of the plane as it broke up, and most of the people in them came out of the seat belts, but I don't think your daughter was one of them."

"How can you tell?"

"The seat rolled on the ground, and that's how she lost her face and knees, and I guess her hands were outside the seat, or something caught them. I think that's what happened."

Frank touched his dead daughter's hair. Hair is made of dead cells, he thought, and that's why, dead, her hair feels no different than when she was alive. Do the worms feed on hair?

"You can close it," he told the corpsman.

The corpsman thanked him, and he asked Frank to sign a release form, which attested to Frank's identification of the two bodies.

They were told that the caskets would be delivered to a location to be determined, in Los Angeles, tomorrow or the next day. After that the caskets could be picked up by a mortuary and buried.

Lowell asked about the funeral in Los Angeles.

"What funeral, sir?"

"I heard there was supposed to be a big funeral, in L.A., for everyone."

"I'm just based here, Mr. Gale. I wouldn't know about Los Angeles."

"Mom and Dad," said Lowell, meaning: Mom and Dad are waiting for us, and we've taken too long on a bad mission.

And so they went outside, and back to the car, and drove home to Los Angeles. They listened to the radio a few times, looking for news of the crash. The lead story was the search for Mary Sifka. By now everyone knew she was married, and where she worked. Reporters were camped outside her door, but no one was home. They went to her husband's office, but he was gone, and no one knew where to find him. The police worried that he might have murdered her and then killed himself, out of shame. On the radio stations where people call and let their opinions be heard on the air, everyone had an opinion about Mary Sifka and the letter.

One caller said that the crash was God's punishment against the adulterers. Another caller defended Mary Sifka. "The man who wrote the letter lied to his wife, and he was probably lying to Mary Sifka. Maybe she didn't even know if he was married. I think it was wrong of the press to publish her name."

"Finally," said Frank, meaning: Here's an intelligent person who has perfectly defined the real scandal of this sordid episode in all our lives, that none of this was anyone else's business but mine.

"Frank, I want to listen," said Lowell.

"And besides," said Frank, ignoring his brother, feeling rather giddy about plowing ahead against everyone's hatred of him, "I never lied to Mary Sifka."

"But you lied to your wife, didn't you?" asked his mother.

Lowell grunted in approval.

Frank felt a surge of blood in his cheeks. Was this the final embarrassment? No. Now anything could happen. His mother had caught him. She was right. He should have kept his mouth shut. And then, as though the blood in his flushed cheeks was at a boil, and the steam melted all of his good sense, a petulance which he knew was wrong, which he knew would make him look even worse, incompetent and stupid, but which he could not resist, forced him to say, "Well, I'm not joining the lawsuit."

After that, he was silent for the rest of the trip home, although no one asked him any questions.

The End

Julia Abarbanel was waiting for them on the front porch at Frank's house. As he walked up the steps with his family, his brother said, "They don't know yet. They don't know what you've done."

Julia was older than he had remembered, and more tired. He looked for something in her face that could excite him the way her voice had on the phone. He thought she looked disappointed in him, too, but he didn't know, and knew that he couldn't know, if she was disappointed because he had aged poorly over the last year, or if the past week's miseries had corroded his face, or if she knew how weirdly he had behaved and now looked upon him as a stranger.

"Your mother gave me the key so I could clean up."

"Thank you," said Frank.

"I picked up some things at the dry cleaner. And I also bought some storage boxes, for when you want to pack things away."

"Madeleine's toys, Anna's dresses?"

"We could give the toys to charity. I'd like a doll."

"Take whatever you want."

"Oh, no, that's not what I meant. I don't mean I want to talk about taking things, I just meant, it was something I wanted to remember the baby by. To have a doll. You know, to hold it, so I could think about her."

In the house Lowell made a few calls, and soon fifty people were there, cousins, friends, with trays of food and bottles of scotch. Potato salads and raw vegetables, and sliced meats from a delicatessen, and bottles of mineral water and juice-flavored sodas. Someone came with a fifty-cup coffee percolator and a carton of Styrofoam cups.

Anna's parents arrived from Philadelphia with her sisters. When they came through the front door, the house, after so much activity and conversation, and the noises of children too young to understand that this was not a normal party, and the chatter of children old enough to understand that this was about death but too young to know better than to rehash the issue of the plane crash with Frank, became quiet. Someone said, "The Klaubers are here."

Peter and Margot came in with Andrea and Barbara. This is another one of those moments, thought Frank, that everyone here will use as coin for a long time, an anecdote that their friends will hear more than once, the entrance of the other side of the family. The crowd had been in the house for an hour before the Klaubers arrived and had made of the wake something festive. Now the handshakes between the men, and then the deep hugs, and the tears, reminded everyone that this was better than a party, because this was about something real.

"I want to see the baby's room," said Margot.

Ethel took her hand and they walked up the stairs. Frank
followed.

"I can't," said Peter.

Leon offered him a drink, and they went to the bar. On the way,
others extended hands, hugs.

In the baby's room the grandmothers picked up the dolls, opened
the drawers, took out the clothing, and wept. "There is no God,"
said Margot, "there is no God."

Frank wanted to tell her that he had heard this before, but what
would that have proven?

"My baby, my baby," said Ethel, holding a black-and-white
teddy bear in her arms. She kissed it.

"Her name is Panda," said Frank.

"Panda," said Margot. "I'd like to hold Panda."

Frank saw that Ethel was afraid that Margot, once she held
Panda, would never let go. Both women wanted the doll, wanted to
keep it. Well, it's mine to give away, he thought.

Julia knocked on the inside of the door. "There's a phone call
for you, Frank."

"Who is it?"

"A woman, a friend."

"Did you ask her name?"

"Yes."

"What did she say?"

"Just answer the phone."

He went to his bedroom and told Julia to hang up once he was
on the line. He said, "Hello," and Mary said hello back. The line
clicked, and they were alone, or at least their voices were.

"We're in the car. We've been driving around. It's the only way
to stay ahead of the press. How come your name isn't in this yet?"
she asked.

"I don't know."

"They have to know."

"I think they're just waiting."

"My husband wants to talk to you."

Then he came on the line. "Frank?"

"Yes?" Frank had forgotten his name. He felt stupid, but didn't want to ask. It's normal, isn't it? he thought. I'm under terrible stress.

"You fucked my wife, Frank."

"I didn't force her."

"What do you want me to say?"

"You can't say anything. It's over. It's all over. Everything has been revealed."

Frank said, "What does that mean?"

"It means what you think it means. Everything has been revealed."

He hung up. Frank left the bedroom and went to Madeleine's door, but the room was empty. Panda was on the bed.

He walked down the stairs. The television was on in the kitchen, with the sound off. There was a picture of the crash, and then a picture of Mary Sifka, and then a picture of Frank. The photographer had used a long lens, and you couldn't tell from the picture where Frank had been, but he knew, by what he was wearing and his look of dismay, that this was the picture taken in the hotel lobby after his run from the crisis center. He turned off the television, because he didn't want to know anything else.

His mother told him to turn it back on.

"I can't look at this anymore," said Frank.

"That's not your decision to make, is it?" asked Margot Klauber.

"It's my house," said Frank.

"You can't expect to go on living here," said his father. "You have no one to take care of you."

"I can take care of myself," said Frank. He said this to everyone in the room and, turning to them in supplication, he wanted to make of them an audience, or a jury, but he felt the weakness of his performance, or was it his argument?

"And my brother says he doesn't even want to work with me anymore," said Frank. "And what did I do? I didn't do anything."

The front door opened, and Mary Sifka came in with her husband. He had black hair and a black close-trimmed beard. The beard surprised Frank, and then he wondered if part of his allure, when Mary had found him alluring, was his smooth skin. He looked at Stewart Sifka's beard and touched his own cheek, trying to remember what Stewart's wife's hand felt like when she was tender to him.

"You fucked my wife!" cried her husband.

"I'm sorry, I didn't get your name," said Frank, trying to be terribly polite, hoping that if he maintained his grace, his friends and family in the room would vote for him in the contest for sympathy.

"You don't need it."

"I remember," said Frank. "It's Stewart." And then he remembered the names of the women from San Diego, those names he'd forgotten in the bar. "Kelly and Chris."

"What?" asked Stewart.

"Nothing," said Frank. "I was just remembering some names."

"I'm sorry about everything that's happened," said Lowell. "I don't know what we can do now."

"Do you know what you've done to me? I'm famous now," said Mary Sifka. "I never wanted to be famous, I never asked to be famous. I made a mistake. You know that all I ever wanted in life was to live my life quietly. I don't want this. I love my husband. He understands. He could have forgiven me, but how can we go on now? We've been branded."

As Mary spoke, Frank remembered why he loved her. He thought that everyone watching her, as they compared her to Anna, to his dead wife, could see what was so spectacular about this woman who compelled Frank to break a commandment. She was a little younger than Anna, but not so much prettier, maybe a bit taller, although her haircut seemed cheap, a permanent that was growing out, and his wife's hair had been famous in the family for its thickness and luster. But here was Mary, standing in his living room without taking the obligatory and understandable glance around the room to see the house she could never have visited during the affair, unless THE WIFE was out of town.

"I'll still forgive you, you know that," said Stewart.

"You say that now, but everywhere we go people are going to recognize me now. And all of our friends, and our families, they know all about this. My life is ruined."

"Don't say that," said Frank's mother. "It's only over if you want it to be over."

"That's right," someone said. Frank didn't recognize the voice, and he looked behind him. It could have been any one of four men, but none of them looked to him, they were waiting for Stewart or Mary to speak. They didn't care about Frank anymore. Frank's attention withdrew from the room as a new reverie pulled him into its spell. If he took Mary's side, perhaps he could prove that logically the only person in the world with whom she could share a life was him.

"Maybe this will bring you together," said Frank's father.

"That's an awful lot of death to heal a marriage," said Stewart. "I don't know that the price of anyone's happiness, let alone ours, should be so high. How can we repay that kind of sacrifice?"

The startling nobility of this little speech illuminated the room. Frank knew what everyone in the room was thinking: that this woman, Mary Sifka, for whatever reasons she had been drawn to Frank, was lucky to have such a fine, fine husband. Somehow Stewart Sifka's automatically gracious words, spoken so quietly, without hesitation, and delivered for the precious benefit of everyone in the room, although his eyes calmly shifted their focus from Leon to Ethel to Lowell, so none would feel favored or excluded, restored to all the Gales, the Klaubers, the Abarbanels, the cousins, the friends, the old and the young, a sense of the possibility that the terrible sacrifice of all those lives would indeed have a meaning. Could anyone not deny their souls' recuperation as Stewart's simple truths gave them the blazing torch of courage, whose hot beam they could now bravely point at the mistakes to which we are all entitled and which we have all committed, errors of judgment clouded by the murkiness of damaged character? Everyone is forgiven, thought Frank. Everyone but me.

"Maybe you should stay here," said Lowell, "until all this blows over."

"That's a gracious offer," said Stewart, "but I don't think we can really accept it."

"You must," said Lowell. "After all, the press only knows what Mary looks like, they don't know you. And it's better to hide out here than in a room at an Embassy Suites. You must be our guests."

"Frank will stay with us," said Ethel. "When the press knows he's not here, they'll have no reason to watch the door. No one will bother you. And you can have time, together. And that's what you need."

Frank looked to Julia Abarbanel to find something in her eyes, some hint of disapproval for the coup that had robbed him of his palace.

"I think it's a good idea," said Julia. "Everyone needs to cool off."

Leon offered Stewart a drink, and then Mary. Frank was sure that Stewart would ask for water, but he wanted vodka on the rocks, and he asked for it with some relief. Mary followed her husband's choice. Perhaps this was a signal she shared with him—the call for hard liquor was the beginning of sex, rough sex. He thought they must be ready for some hard lovemaking, because they seemed so secure with each other, and in spite of their agony, wasn't Mary glowing?

Mary sat down. "This is a beautiful house," she said. There was a photograph in a silver frame on the mantel, Anna and Madeleine in the snow. Frank had taken it in Aspen. The week had been a disaster. Anna had hired a baby-sitter through an agency, but she was too young, and Anna did not trust her. After the second day, Anna let her go, and then demanded of Frank that they take turns coming down from the mountain and playing with the baby, who was one and a half. It would be impossible for the two of them to ski together. Frank told Anna that he had seen little to complain about in the baby-sitter, but he knew that he was only trying to get her on the slopes with him, so they could ride the chair lifts together and ski together. He would not admit to her what he knew, which was that Anna was right about the sitter, who had been cold and nervous with the child, and that Madeleine had had good reason to nervous with the child, and that Madeleine had had good reason to cry in her arms. So every time it was Frank's turn to get off the mountain and take Madeleine for a few hours, he pouted, he refused to smile, or he came down half an hour after the agreed time. Looking at the happy woman and happy child in the picture, Frank remembered how Anna had struggled to put aside her rage at him for his resentment at the hobbled day.

Julia volunteered to help the Sifkas make their bed and to show them around the kitchen. "And there'll be plenty of leftovers from all of this," she said, sweeping her hands over the trays of cheese and meat and salad and bread and cake that all of Anna's friends had brought to share with each other.

"This doesn't feel right," said Frank.

"That's not really your decision," said Lowell.

"It's really more of an opinion," said Frank. He heard Julia say something under her breath. "What?" he asked, although he knew that if she answered, he would only feel worse.

"I said, 'I can't believe it.'"

"We should go," said Leon, and he put his hand on Frank's shoulder. The touch, so frighteningly unfamiliar, so old, so full of authority, brought Frank to tears.

He followed his parents to the door. No one looked at him. Already his cousins and friends were collecting dishes, glasses, napkins, and cups from around the room. Anna's father was in the kitchen, putting plastic wrap on the fruit salad.

Stewart stood up and offered his hand to Leon. The contact between them, the look that passed, was martial, full of an unspoken knowledge that only men can share. Frank recognized pieces of the code, but could not break it. Behind them, Mary's head was turned away, she was talking to Julia, who nodded her head a few times, and glanced over at Frank in a way that told Frank that Mary was telling her side of the story of the affair.

Frank's mother opened the door and let him go through first. He turned to look inside, just as Stewart asked Lowell a question.

"Lowell, have you settled on a lawyer?"

"Yes, we have, and I'm sure we made the right decision," said Lowell.

"So who will it be, Dessick or Berberian?"

Before Frank could hear what his brother said, their mother closed the door, and the sound of the lock clicking into place destroyed the answer. And then he heard Stewart say, "An excellent choice, Lowell. That's what I would have done. He's a good man."

Frank hovered at the door, hoping to hear more, but his father called to him. He fell in step behind him, and they walked to their car, parked on the street.

"How did your car get here?" asked Frank.

"What difference does it make?" said his father.

Frank couldn't say. He tried something else. "Julia looks good, doesn't she? Well, maybe she looks a little tired, but don't we all?"

Neither of them answered. They drove to Wilshire Boulevard, and to the condominium.

Frank coughed a few times in the elevator, just to be heard.

"You should have some herbal tea," said his mother.

"I think I'd like a drink," he said, happy, finally, for a conversation.

"No," said Ethel, "herbal tea."

As the elevator rose, Frank wanted to yell at them, he wanted to curse his mother and his father for being born, he wanted to soak the curtains of their bedroom in lighter fluid and then burn the fucking place, he wanted to push his mother and his father into the rooftop swimming pool and hold their heads under water with a steel garden rake, he wanted to pull the doors of the refrigerator off its hinges and smear the food over the living room walls, and wait a few days for the mayonnaise to rot, so that the manager of the building, when he responded to the neighbors' complaints about odd smells, would vomit from the stench when he used his pass key to open the door, he wanted to skillfully crack each of the apartment's windows with a brass candlestick and force big sheets of glass to the street, to decapitate mailmen and Guatemalan nannies pushing downstairs, he wanted to stab his feet with cuticle scissors and then turn the burners on the stove to high and stand on a stepladder and push his feet into the flames, he wanted to do all of this, but he asked himself, Yes, so, where will the profit be?

And so he said good night to his mother and his father. "I have some shopping for you to do in the morning," she said. "The list is by the phone in the kitchen."

Frank said nothing. He went down the hall to the guest room. There was a single bed against one wall, a desk, and bookcase. Everything came from his old bedroom at the mansion in Bel Air. There were the books he'd read in high school, photographs of Frank and Lowell at summer camp. There was his old baseball glove, and the first reading lamp he'd had as a child, part of a set of cowboy furniture. The lamp was a covered wagon with a bulb inside. There was a little carved man holding the reins of a team of carved horses. Frank undressed and got into bed, thinking that he should go to the bathroom because he needed to pee, but he decided he could ignore the pain in his bladder, and hold it in until morning.

He turned off the cowboy light, and looked at the darkness, saw nothing, and fell asleep listening to the muffled sound of the television in his parents' room, as they watched the news.

That night he had this dream:

He is standing in the middle of a dirt road, in the mountains. There are two lines of people on either side of the road. Dessick is at the head of one line, Berberian is at the head of the other.

"What is this?" asks Frank.

"We gave you a chance," says Berberian. "I'm sorry you didn't take it."

"Why are you all here?"

"It's too late to ask questions."

As Frank walks between the two rows, he is struck on the face, the back, the chest, and he is kicked. When he is hit, the hands are always open, and the slapping, from a distance, might even look like a celebration, but by the end of the line, he is in pain.

And these are the names of those who beat him: Dessick, Berberian, Dennis Donoghue, Bettina Welch, Ed Dockery, Lowell Gale, are always open, and the slapping, from a distance, might even look like a celebration, but by the end of the line, he is in pain.

And these are the names of those who beat him: Dessick, Berberian, Dennis Donoghue, Bettina Welch, Ed Dockery, Lowell Gale, Leon Gale, Ethel Gale, Peter Klauber, Margot Klauber, Barbara Klauber, Teresa Walter, Dale Beltran, Chris, Kelly. And others, too, are also there, to beat him.

At the end of the line, after passing the last of the people in the two rows, he sees clearly to the top of the road, and a little cabin in the woods. He turns to say something to the crowd, but they are already leaving. His father and mother and brother go with him up the hill.

"I'm sorry," says Frank. "The letter was never supposed to be published. She was supposed to have read it in Mexico. It was private. I think it's against the law to open someone's mail. I think we can sue."

No one says anything, and he is ashamed of himself for suggesting a lawsuit now, when he has been so diffident about joining the other suit. But he can explain that, he wants to say, he isn't so much against a lawsuit, he only wants to know whose suit to join.

"Someone will bring you food," says Lowell.

"You have been a disgrace to us," says his father.

His back and shoulders hurt, but he thinks, with some pride in himself, that he really wasn't so badly damaged by the gauntlet. The hell with them, he thinks, and would have turned to say this, but then the word *prudence* comes to him. So he goes into the cabin without saying good-bye to anyone.

It would be a good place to bring a child, when the child is ready for camping. There is a simple metal frame bed with a gray blanket. Next to the door is a small stove, and a refrigerator. The room smells vaguely of horses.

He lies down on the bed and looks up at the ceiling. Someone has nailed a piece of wood to the beam over his head, perhaps the same person who has carved, "This is more than you deserve."